NICOLE A OLIVER

DEDICATION

To Paul who helps me tame the chaos.

To Ian and Olivia
who inspire me to live my dreams.

CHAPTER 1
Sophia

I'm soaring and the room comes into sharp focus as adrenaline surges through me. My gaze sweeps over the small group watching the debates. I make direct eye contact with several of the onlookers as I stand tall at the handmade wooden lectern before flashing a wide smile at my debate partner. We've been paired up with students from our host school, Sherwood High. I've never met Garrett, the sandy-haired boy who did a fantastic job of keeping up with me at the Hallowe'en debate today. The organizers chose a paranormal theme for the practice event. We usually debate serious topics at our competitive events and partner up with teammates from our own school.

The regular adrenaline high of a debate win is eclipsed by an electrical buzz that shoots up my arm. The room plunges into darkness and a few shrieks sound from the crowd. The power must have gone out. I glance out the window. It's not storming. Must be some sort of equipment failure. As I'm shaking out my arm, the lights pop back on.

Garrett's eyes meet mine. "Are you okay?"

"Yeah, I'm fine. That was weird. I wonder what happened there?"

His sandy hair flops over his forehead as he shakes his head. The confidence I always feel in front of a crowd wilts at his intense eye contact. Public speaking has never been a fear of mine, but meeting new people is squirm-inducing. The cuteness of the boy next to me only intensifies the squirm factor. Bright hazel eyes sparkle and a dimple in his left cheek pops out with his victory smile. Who actually has a dimple like that in real life? I scurry toward the safety of my bestie, Xavier. I give him a quick hug and shake the hand of the cute, freckled girl he's paired with. The mass of wild curls framing her round face causes a brief moment of envy. My hair wouldn't hold a curl under threat of death.

"You guys definitely got the raw end of the deal on this one," I say to Xavier and Emily. No way would I want to debate on the yes side for the existence of spirits or vampires or the other nonsense they picked as topics. I mean, it's always fun to debate a topic from the side I don't believe in. Gives me a chance to really stretch my brain and my debate skills to see things from the other side, but no way could I have stretched my brain around that lack of evidence.

Emily's curls bounce as she nods her agreement. "Right? Luckily, this was just for fun. You guys should totally join us for the afterhash. We always head over to Arabica Nights after debate club to relive our glories and failures. It usually devolves into chaos and ridiculousness. Their mochas and scones are the bomb."

She arches a pale brow at Garrett with a long look I can't decipher. I prefer textbooks and journals full of facts any day to trying to figure out the meaning behind a mysterious look.

"Yes, please come, it'll be fun, and we can get to know each other better." Garrett's gaze shifts to Xavier. "All of us."

"Definitely, I'm always up for a dose of that sweet nectar of life also known as espresso, and some new frenemies." Xavier goes for an intense stare, but the crinkle of humor around his eyes gives him away.

Well, I guess I'm not getting out of this one. Not that Garrett and Emily don't seem like our kind of people—smart and nerdy—but I'm the absolute worst at making small talk with strangers. My heartbeat picks up at the thought of it. At least I'll have Xavier to back me up. One of his best features is his ability to befriend anyone.

"Should we share a car? I can drive." Garrett offers politely.

"No, we should take our own car, and then we can head straight home afterward. I have an English essay to work on." That gives me a reasonable excuse to flee if it gets weird.

"Really, Soph? That's not due for another week. You are such a nerd. But yes, we can take my car. Hit us up with the addy my friend."

"Says the boy who helps run the Science Fair." I shoot a long look at X calling him out on the nerd comment. He knows I embrace my inner nerd.

"Boy? What am I, five?"

"Wellll…sometimes I do wonder."

Garrett shares the info with Xavier. I smile when I spot Emily and Garrett climbing into a shiny silver Eco-friendly hybrid before hopping into Xavier's Volvo, which is an indeterminate shade of rust. It's seen better days, but my chest tightens up with memories of my dad whenever I sit behind the wheel, so I have no problem allowing Xavier driving privileges. I usually walk to school when the weather is cooperative, unfortunately around here it can be pretty temperamental, so I often hitch a ride with a friend.

"Looks like you've got a not-so-secret admirer, Soph." Xavier's eyebrows dart up a few times and I give him a friendly whack on the shoulder.

"Cut it out with the creeper brows. What are you talking about?"

"Ummm duh, Garrett totally has the hots for you. And he's got those dreamy eyes." He releases a sigh worthy of a teenage girl pining after her boy band crush.

"He does not! I thought he was into his friend Emily. She kept giving him weird looks." It dawns on me that he could be right. I'm used to the boys at school passing me over at this point. High school boys have fragile egos and when you turn down a few of them, they eventually leave you alone. This has been a great strategy for keeping them at a distance. Leaves me free to focus on my goals. Garrett doesn't go to my school though. My lack of interest in dating is not on his radar.

"You are so oblivious to the charms of the opposite sex. She was playing wingman by orchestrating the get-together so he could spend some time with your lovely self."

"Oh. You think I'm lovely? Well thank you." I smirk at him. Two can play his game. My brain gets all twisty though at the thought of it. Do I want him to be interested in me or not? I'm not sure.

I've never been great with guys, Xavier and Brendan being the exceptions. But they're both super smart and I've known them since we learned our letters together in kindergarten. Not to mention that the thought of kissing either of them is unappealing at best. Dating, on the other hand, I don't have time for that. Boys and romance will only get in the way of my life plan. Graduate top of my class, undergrad, med school, and become a surgeon like my dad. Usual high school girl goals.

The road meanders past a series of quaint shops lining the adorable downtown section of Ridgewood. It's a small town about a 20-minute drive from the bigger and busier suburb where we live. The lack of Starbucks and other fast-food chains adds to the small-town vibe. I forgot how cute their downtown is. My mom used to drag us here when I was a kid for window shopping and ice cream. She's too busy at work now though, and my friends and I have everything we need at home, so we rarely visit. I'm definitely going to drag Xavier back here to try some restaurants though.

Xavier pulls off a smooth parallel parking job in a spot he snags right in front of 1001 Arabica Nights. That boy always has all the luck. Meanwhile, the closer we get, the tighter my skin feels at the thought of hanging with strangers, one of whom might be into me.

"That's a good one. I love a clever name. Hope the food lives up to the hype," he says. Of course the food is his greatest concern, not embarrassing himself in front of strangers.

"Me too. I just wish you hadn't told me that about Garrett. Now I'm going to be all awkward around him."

"You'll be fine, just pretend he's a person with no interest in ravishing you in the backseat of his Prius." His lips quirk up in a smirk the devil wouldn't be ashamed of. "Seriously, Sophia, you have to know how amazing you are. Plus, I'll be there for backup. Do you need a safe word? How about…unicorn. If you work unicorn into the conversation, I'll whisk you out of there."

"Xavier. You are too much." I clamber out of the car and run straight into a hard-muscled chest. "I'm so sorry." I whip my head up and meet the intense stare of a stranger. For some reason, I can't pull my eyes away from this guy despite my usual complete and total lack of awareness of the male species. There's something about him. There's a tug at the back of my brain that finds him familiar, but there's no way I've met him before. I would definitely remember that face. He appears to be a couple of years older than me, but then again, I've never been an expert judge of age. Xavier hasn't stopped teasing me for the one time I described a child's age by holding my hand up to demonstrate his height. His skin is the perfect shade of Instagrammer gold as if he spends his life artfully arranged on the deck of a yacht. It contrasts with the tousled spikes of midnight hair and a body that is all long, lean muscles. All of this fades away when I stare into his eyes, which are such a stunning shade of turquoise they look unnatural. I can't stop staring with my mouth gaping open in what I'm sure is a most unattractive manner until he catches me at it and gives me a raised eyebrow and a smirk.

"Feel free to take a picture. I'll show you my good side." Random hot guy has the nerve to tilt his chin in a douchey pose. His arrogant words immediately douse the flames crackling under my skin during my moment of temporary insanity.

"Seriously? Get over yourself. Come on Xavier."

I grab X's arm and march indignantly through the cheerful red door that tinkles with a string of bells as we enter. I scan the room until I spot Garrett and Emily settled into some poufy armchairs in a prime corner of the cafe by a gas fireplace. My palms start to sweat as we stroll across the rustic pine floor and weave through the eclectic mix of seating areas.

I like the chaotic vibe of the place with its comfy chairs and couches scattered haphazardly around random coffee tables, and elegant wingbacks with satin upholstery, all intermingling with a mixed bag of retro diner chairs and Formica tables. My eyes skate over the well-dressed professional types talking too loudly on their phones and the denim-clad students scribbling away in notebooks or binders. I don't understand the desire to study among the noise and chaos of a public place. I'd rather hide in a cubicle in the quiet section of the library. I smile at the group of older ladies chattering in one corner as they take small sips from assorted colorful China mugs and wince at the raucous laughter coming from a group of muscular guys in their mid-twenties checking out girls. I choose a path that avoids their unpleasant leers.

I wave at Garrett and Emily as we get close to their table, but then drop my eyes and shuffle through my purse when I realize how awkward my weird half wave was. I perch on the edge of an oddly formal cranberry wingback with gold stripes and give them a small smile. It could be more of a pained grimace though. My encounter with the handsome, rude boy outside, as well as Xavier's revelation in the car shook me. My heartbeat picks up, and the room dims around me as my introverted soul balks at the unfamiliar faces.

"Hi! So glad you could make it." Garrett's mouth spreads in a wide smile. "This spot was free when we walked in, so we snagged it. I can go up and order while you two get yourselves settled. Let me know what you'd like."

"I can come up with you to order. Man's work, right?" Xavier winks at me, knowing he'll get a rise out of me for that comment.

I give him an affectionate roll of my eyes. "You are such a Neanderthal, Xavier, but I'll let you do the work if you so desire. I'll take a mocha and….," I glance at the chalk menu board behind the baristas. "…a Cheddar Thyme Scone as per your recommendation, Emily."

"Smart! I have excellent taste. I'll have my usual, Garrett," says Emily.

I pull my pink wallet with a gold Pi symbol on it out of my purse and start handing a twenty to Xavier. Garrett waves away the offer.

"I've got this one. Consider yourselves our guests," Garrett says.

Xavier shrugs and raises a barely perceptible eyebrow at me before the two guys thread their way through the tightly packed tables to place our order.

"Well, that was nice of him. I thought you said some of the other debaters would be joining us," I say to Emily.

"Oh yeah Jake and Maddie usually like to come with, but they begged off tonight. I'm pretty sure they had a hot date planned. Maddie's parents are away in Jamaica for the week. Lucky them."

"Who's lucky? Maddie's parents or her and Jake?"

"All of them will probably get pretty lucky tonight." Emily bursts out laughing.

"Oh." My cheeks grow warm.

"Don't mind my big mouth."

"Don't worry about it. Just wasn't expecting that to come out of you." I glance at her round cherubic face.

"What? Were you fooled by my adorable looks? It's not the first time." She bats her long pale eyelashes, then gives me a shrewd sizing up. "I imagine you are frequently underestimated, as well. It must be fun to whap people over the head with your brains after they've dismissed you as a dumb blonde."

I shift in my seat. It was pretty stupid of me to judge her based on her looks. I was doing the same thing to her that people have done to me a million times. At least she was nice about it. I'm pretty convinced now that Emily and I could be friends and I don't make new friends easily. It's strange that I've never spoken to them before this year. I know a lot of the kids on the debate circuit. We all see each other at the competitions and have something of a family. I guess if he just transferred to Sherwood, he could have been competing in a different region.

"Welll...I won't say I enjoy being dismissed or underestimated, but it certainly can make the victory that much more delicious when I debate them under the table." My mouth pulls up at the corners in a small smile.

A different warm tingle starts to flow through me, and I feel my gaze pulled as if by an invisible string to the right. My smile widens when I catch sight of Xavier and Garrett heading back to our comfy corner. The smoky scent of coffee mingles with the sweetness of chocolate. As they sit back down, I catch a glimpse over Garrett's shoulder that throws me off track.

It's the intense, handsome guy I bumped into out front and he's staring at me. He doesn't even have the good grace to pretend like he wasn't staring. Instead, he gives me an insolent wink and waves. This guy is too much. I don't know why I keep looking at him. There's something about him that's familiar, even though I'm a hundred percent sure I've never met him before. I turn back to X and my new friends resolving to pay no more attention to this guy who I will probably never have the misfortune of encountering again anyway.

Garrett's hand brushes mine as he passes me a bright-red mug with a heart-eyes emoji. I drop my eyes and take a deliberate sip of my mocha which is basically heaven in a cup. The rich milk chocolate complements the roasty sweet espresso perfectly.

"Mmmm, this is fantastic, real whipped cream just the way I like it. I can't stand that oily fake stuff." The thought of it squinches up my face. "Thanks so much for the suggestion, Emily. This place is def worthy of a repeat visit." I glance up at her from under my lashes.

"Really? That would be awesome!" Garrett's eyes shine with sincerity. "I'd love for you to come back with me sometime. If you want to, that is." A faint blush creeps up his neck.

I can't quite catch my breath as my stomach drops to my toes. Did he just ask me out? Like on a date? I'm mesmerized by the pattern of chocolate sprinkles topping my mocha. I should have probably expected that after what Xavier said, but maybe not so soon? Do I want to go on a date with him?

"Hey Sophia, do you know that guy sitting behind Garrett? He's glaring at you like you stole his lunch money or something," Emily asks.

"I don't know him. I literally crashed into him out front before we came in, but I've never met him before. I have no idea what his problem is. It's not like I broke his phone or anything." This is all getting to be a bit much. Garrett asking me out and this other guy's stares are making my skin itch. I glance at Xavier. Maybe I should cry unicorn.

"I wish I bumped into him. Maybe he'd have grabbed me with those sexy arms to keep me from falling. I definitely would have slipped him my number." Emily's giggle bubbles out.

"Ugh, he was so arrogant. He reminds me of a character in those sappy Rom-com movies. The ones where the guy is a secret prince of some tiny country imagining he's so much better than us peasants."

"Wow, he really made an impression on you, Sophia. I still think I'd take him home for at least one night." Emily has such an easy air about her. I bet she never brings a book to a party so she can hide in the corner if the socializing gets to be too much. She reminds me of Xavier in that respect. Maybe that's why I like her so much already.

"Seriously, Em?" Garrett rolls his eyes.

"What do you guys like to do for fun around here?" Xavier is pretty deft at bringing the conversation back when he senses it getting too girl-centric, as he hangs out with all women most of the time.

"The usual. Science club, debate team, there's a great little comic book store just down the road here. The owner Max is great. He holds lots of events, game nights, and role-playing games. It's like you're one of the family, you know?" Garrett's eyes light up with enthusiasm.

I mean, I'm all about the science nerdery and it's pretty cool Garrett included his extracurricular as a fun thing to do, but I'm not big into comic books. I prefer to get my nerd fix from a good sci-fi/fantasy novel or a superhero movie. I can tell he's going to get along great with Xavier, though.

"Awesome! Have you read the latest Black Panther? Definitely my favorite series of the year." Xavier jumps in headfirst.

"Yes! It is so good, Acuna's use of color really sets the mood, love his visuals. What about Saga? Still amazing, this latest arc really sucker punches you when you're least expecting it," Garrett replies.

I let their voices fade into the background as I do anytime Xavier gets onto the comic book topic with one of our other friends. These conversations have a tendency to barrel on like a train with failing brakes, eventually ending in a fiery crash when they strongly disagree on some ridiculous nonsense like which superhero could survive longer in space. My eyes are drawn back to the unfortunately handsome guy behind Garrett. Those sculpted cheekbones and eyes you could go for a swim in are definitely wasted on someone so deficient in basic human manners and modesty. As if he can sense my stare, his eyes lock on mine and I quickly shift my gaze, pretending to find the colorful chalkboard menu endlessly interesting.

Emily leans in and whispers, "I saw that. You aren't as oblivious to angry-dreamy-guy's looks as you pretend."

"I never said he wasn't good looking, just that his personality detracts from his face. There's something about him, though. I can't quite place it, but almost feel as if I've met him before. Like déjà vu if I believed in that sort of thing."

"Agreed. We're women of logic, right? No room for pseudoscience. Thank god you're not into the comic book scene like those two. Sometimes, when I'm hanging with Garrett and our other friend Jake, I start reading a textbook to keep myself entertained."

"Yes, I would just leave them here to enjoy their date, but…Xavier is my ride home. And since my mocha's all gone," I make sad puppy eyes at my empty cup, "I think we need to head home so I can finish up my schoolwork. What type of force do you think we'll have to use to drag the boys apart?"

"Well, let me see. If Garrett weighs 165 pounds and Xavier, what maybe 150? We'd have to determine our own acceleration rates...."

We have our private joke at the guys' expense before I snag the last bite of Xavier's brownie. The only thing he likes more than comic books is food, so this is a sure-fire way to get his attention.

"Sophia, foul! You know I don't share my food," Xavier says, snapping out of his animated world to slap my hand away.

"Well, that's what you get for ignoring me. In case you hadn't noticed, it's getting late, and some of us have GPAs to maintain. I've got work to do. You guys can continue your bromance another time, I'm sure."

"Fine." He lets out a pained sigh. "It was great meeting you two. We'll have to see each other again soon. I'm just going to run to the restroom before we head out. Meet you at the front entrance, Sophia?" I give him a brief nod before gathering my things together.

Emily shoots a quick glance at Garrett and gives him a shove. "Me too!" She sings, then leans over to give me some air kisses. "See you again, Sophia!"

Now that we're alone, I am very aware of Garrett's presence. I start to stand up in an attempt to avoid the awkwardness when Garrett reaches across the table and puts his hand on my arm.

"It was really fun debating with you this afternoon and I had fun here, too. I was wondering...if we could maybe do this again, just the two of us?" His sandy hair flops over his eyes as he ducks his head.

His hesitation is kind of cute. I like that he's not full of himself like some guys. I'm still not sure if I'm into him in a romantic way, but I figure one date can't hurt, right? It certainly won't throw my life plan off. Especially not with a guy as smart as Garrett.

"That would be...nice." Nice! Omg, that was the worst reply. I couldn't have come up with anything better than that? Great, fantastic, wonderful, fabulous, or any of its numerous synonyms. It doesn't seem to deter him, though.

"Really? Great. Here's my phone, add yourself to my contacts and I'll...call you. If that's ok."

I add myself before handing his phone back. He has a Guardians of the Galaxy case on it, which is pretty cool. "I'll talk to you soon. Bye."

"Bye, Sophia." His voice deepens and he leans in a little as he says my name.

How into me is he? Given my indecision, should I even be considering going out with him? He seems like a really nice guy. I wouldn't want to hurt him. My brain is fried at this point. Maybe I just need to get home and sleep on it. Or better yet, I could make a pros and cons list. I internally roll my eyes at that thought. This is not a teen movie and even if it were that never ends well, does it? With one last glance back at him, I head toward the door to wait for Xavier.

I stare out the window at the old-fashioned lampposts and signs proclaiming, Pumpkin Fest! Saturday October 27th, to avoid the smug look on Xavier's face. I should have known better than to think that he could keep his opinions to himself for longer than it takes to pull out of the parking spot. The tension from socializing with strangers eases up now that it's just the two of us.

"What did I tell you? You guys make a date or what? I mean, I'm not one to say I told you so," he totally is, "but…I told you so. He's hella into you, my friend! You didn't even have to use the safe word."

"Not that it's any of your business, but I gave him my number. It's not a big deal." My cheeks heat again. This is starting to become a bad habit. Even as the words come out of my mouth, we both know I'm lying. I've been avoiding the attention of the male half of the species throughout high school. I'm not even sure why I'm considering it. Garrett is cute and nice and smart. He checks all the right boxes. But I've seen what love can do to a person.

"Uh huh, don't suppose you mentioned that one when you slipped him your digits, did you?"

"Slipped him my digits? What am I, a gangster? You're too much, X." I sigh in exasperation. I love Xavier to pieces, but he's certainly perfected the art of driving me crazy.

"You know you love it, baby! And BTW it's totally my business who you date. I'm your best friend and also a guy. Two points for me in the boyfriend confessions department."

"He is *not* my boyfriend. I just met the guy. I'm not the type to fall in love at first sight. I don't get how people even believe in it. With 7.6 billion people on this planet, you can hardly expect that there is only one person out there for you."

"Trust you to get all technical when threatened with a hint of possible emotion. Just give him a chance, Sophy Girl, that's all I ask. You deserve a little bit of romance and fun in between all the studying, planning, and more studying."

"Let it go. I said I'd meet up with him. What about you? What'd you think of Emily?" Maybe I can foist the focus onto Xavier. Use his own tricks against him.

"Oh, she's super cute. I'm definitely going to ask her out. We can double date, awwww." He bats his eyes at me.

"Ok enough, I'm taking a nap." I drop my head on the seatback and close my eyes.

I feign sleep for the rest of the ride home and hop out of the car as soon as it skids to a halt in my driveway.

"See you tomorrow, Xavier!"

"Nighty night, sleep tight, don't let dreams of cute guys get in the way of your sleep!" He teases.

I slam the door with purpose and walk up the neat brick walkway into my house. Thankfully, Mom does not appear to be home. I can lose myself in Hamlet, physics problems, and a skeptical review of celebrity endorsed natural health remedies for my extra credit critical thinking class.

I finish the day with my evening ritual. Staring up at the velvety ink of the night sky. A multitude of stars pierce through the darkness as if they're beacons guiding the way to new worlds far beyond our lonely planet. As a kid, I dreamed of exploring the universe and discovering these worlds. I always thought I would be an astronomer. My plans may have changed, but I've never stopped staring at the sky and wondering what else might be out there. Out of the reach of our current knowledge.

CHAPTER 2
Sophia

I shiver as the icy water hits my face. It's the only way to shake off the grogginess after an unusually restless sleep. Vivid dreams full of bright colors and intense feels interrupted my REM. If I believed in curses, I might have blamed Xavier, but maybe I can pin it on him anyway courtesy of the power of suggestion. The brain is highly suggestible after all.

The boy who interrupted my sleep hadn't even been the cute one with the messy crop of dirty blonde hair, hazel eyes, and large brain that I should be lusting after. Instead, I had uncomfortably familiar dreams about a certain turquoise eyed, dark-haired jerk I'd randomly bumped into yesterday. My unconscious mind clearly doesn't have a clue what's good for me.

The strangest thing about the dreams was both how real and surreal they seemed at the same time. I've never been the sort of person who remembers my dreams with clarity, but these are seared into my brain for whatever reason. I could feel the summer heat warming my skin, the touch of his calloused hand in mine, smell that fishy, murky scent of lake water, and feel the cool water caressing my skin as we'd splashed each other. The dream world has never activated my senses that intensely before now.

There's got to be some sort of scientific explanation for the experience. I'll have to do some research on the phenomenon after school. The thought of solving the mystery of the strange dreams via a research project is enough to cheer me up and finally shake off the sleepiness dragging me down.

The heavenly aroma of roasted coffee beans invades my nose before I even hit the kitchen. Mom drops a quick kiss on my cheek and hands me my favorite mug with the molecular structure of caffeine on it. "Good morning! Sleep well?" she asks.

"I slept fine." Lying to my mom doesn't sit well with me, but no way am I telling her about those crazy dreams. My cheeks heat just thinking about it.

"Good to hear. You know how important sleep is."

"Yes, Mom." I roll my eyes at her and smear some herb and garlic cream cheese on a toasted bagel.

We chat during breakfast, but the house hasn't been the same since Scott went away to school last year. I never thought I would miss tripping over the backpack he left in the doorway or yelling at him to find his own keys, but here I am.

"I've really gotta head out now. Don't want to be late! Bye Mom, love you!" I give her a quick hug, but she pulls me in for a longer one.

"I'm working late this evening, so you'll have to make your own dinner. Love you so much. Are you sure you don't want a ride to school? You are my favorite daughter, after all." As her only daughter, it's kind of a given, but she thinks it's funny or something. Mom jokes.

"I'm fine. You know I like walking, gives me time to contemplate all the mysteries of the universe. May as well enjoy it before it gets too much colder. Love you too."

"Well, be safe." The creases between her eyes deepen with her frown. I hate seeing those signs of worry. Ever since we lost dad, she's clung extra tight to my brother and me. And now that he's away at university, she directs all of that focus on me.

"What are you afraid of? I'll get abducted by aliens?" My mom has never had to worry about me getting into trouble and our town full of soccer moms and commuters is hardly a den of criminal activity.

She laughs along, but the hint of concern that never leaves her eyes is still present. "Of course not, you know there's never been any conclusive proof of the existence of aliens." Ah, there's my practical mom coming through. She taught me well, that's for sure.

With one last wave, I crunch out the front door onto the colorful leaves littering the front walk as a soft breeze rustles my loose hair. I swipe it behind my ears already regretting I didn't pull it back into my usual tight ponytail. The air smells crisp and woodsy and my mind drifts off.

I'm reviewing for my upcoming bio test when a loud crack startles me from my thoughts. A massive black dog leaps out from the bushes growling at me. A curled lip vibrating with aggression exposes its huge fangs. Panic shakes me and I throw up my arm as it comes at me. As if I'm going to ward off the dog with my nonexistent martial arts training or something. A buzz of energy flares up my arm. There's a small flash of light and the angry canine falls back whimpering as if it hit a wall. The neighbors must have one of those invisible fences to keep their vicious hell beast from running amok. Right? I shake my arm out. Those things aren't supposed to affect people, are they? I'll have to look into that.

I push my shaky legs into action, not wanting to tempt fate, and take a few deep breaths to ease my racing heart.

A vehicle pulls up beside me and a guy leaps out, leaving the door hanging open behind him. My mouth matches his truck door when recognition knocks me back a step. I squirm when I recognize the subject of my awkward dreams last night. What is he doing here?

"Are you okay?" he asks, running his gaze over me as if checking for injury.

"What? Yeah, I'm fine. Are you following me?" I back away a few steps as a different kind of fear sends fingers of ice through my body.

"I was driving to school, and I saw that dog jump at you. You shouldn't have done that." His sharp eyes scan our surroundings.

"Done what?" I'm confused. He didn't really answer my question and now he's accusing me of doing something? My insides clench up with anger as my hackles rise.

"Stopped the dog. You're going to attract attention and make my job harder."

"What are you talking about? I didn't stop the dog. It must have been an invisible fence or something."

He snorts. "Don't those invisible fences need some special collar or something?" He nods toward the dog which is on its feet again but leaning back in a fearful posture with its head and tail dropped down. I spot a worn leather collar around the animal's neck, but there's no receiver pack on it or anything. He's right. I should have spotted that. Maybe it's some sort of newer technology. Super small. That doesn't sit right with me, though.

"What exactly are you suggesting stopped the dog?"

"You," he says. No further elaboration. Helpful and not at all crazy.

"How do you figure that? Was I using the Force or something?"

"Something like that."

I burst out laughing. All the built-up nervous energy from the almost-dog-attack and the appearance of the stranger who haunted my dreams last night, escapes in hysterical laughter. When I finally pull myself together, I swipe the back of my hand across my eyes to clear away the tears.

"Okay then. Thanks for the laugh. I needed that. I have to get to school now though." I start walking. My jaw aches from clenching it and I glance over my shoulder to make sure he's not following.

"We'll talk about this later. Try not to use any more magic, though. Need a ride?"

"Uh no thanks. I don't even know you." Like I'm going to take a ride from a random stranger who might be stalking me and is definitely hallucinating. Magic? Is he messing with me? It sets my nerves on edge when he says we'll talk later. He must be following me. I pull my phone out and hover my thumb over the emergency call button.

"Suit yourself. It's Logan, by the way." He tosses this over his shoulder as he lopes back to his truck. My nerves settle as he climbs back in and drives off. If kidnapping is his end goal, he could have easily snatched me. I've got a few moves from the self-defense classes my mom made me take with her, but I doubt they'd hold him off for long.

I stretch my stride out, trying to speed walk away from the thoughts that are now preying on my mind. I glance around but don't spot his truck again. It is a pretty weird coincidence that this is the second time I've seen this guy in two days. Of course, he could live around here, and I could have passed him hundreds of times without noticing him. He's only on my radar now because I ran into him last night.

A black blur catches my peripheral vision, but there's nothing there when I whip my head around. I take a few deep breaths and focus on the facts. I've gotten myself all worked up and now I'm the one hallucinating. Fact one: The dog attacked. Fact two: Something stopped it. Fact Three: There was no visible barrier or technology holding it back. Fact four: Hot guy from the café yesterday made a random appearance and claimed it was me who stopped the dog. This last fact just doesn't fit in. Where did he come from? If he was following me, why did he just drive off? There's something else scratching away at the back of my brain. That tingle in my arm when the dog stopped. What caused that? It has to be related to some sort of electrical current or something, right? There's always an explanation. Sometimes you just need to dig deeper to find the answers. Because magic is clearly not the answer.

I ease up my pace as the school looms into view faster than I expect. The red bricks are a tired, rusty color, as if the years of students flowing through have worn out the building itself, but its familiarity is comforting. The weight of fear on my shoulders lightens up and the knots in them untangle. I've never been afraid of dogs before having never had a bad experience with them, so my brain is telling me I shouldn't let this isolated incident shake me, but sometimes you can't overcome that primitive part that's let man evolve and survive on instinct alone.

The fear dissipates further as a head of wild, curly black hair approaches. The black hair tops off a tall girl with stunning dark-chocolate eyes and perfect mocha skin. She's wearing a Galactic Battles shirt and a comfortable pair of jeans torn through years of use rather than for fashionable purposes. Charlotte is gorgeous and her parents are well off, but she'd much rather indulge in a marathon gaming weekend than wear the latest fashion trends or waste time on her makeup.

"Charlotte!" I give her a huge smile. "How was your weekend? I didn't hear from you for a few days so I'm assuming you picked up Galactic Battles: Star Crossed at the midnight release on Thursday."

"Of course, you wouldn't expect less of me, would you? I'm calling Friday a mental health day, as in I would have lost my mind if I had to spend all day having my soul mindlessly sucked from my body rather than fighting off Arcturian fighters." Her laughter bubbles out as she tosses her curls and names the prime enemy from her fave video game.

"Well, I wouldn't know anything about that, but I do know that you missed Ms. Sasakis' Functions quiz and you're never going to get into a game design program if you flunk out of math." I roll my eyes at her.

She's been kicking my butt at video games since we could barely hold the controllers, but we're super-tight despite our differences. I can count on two fingers the number of times I've been absent from high school and my mother basically had to tie me to my bed to keep me home on those occasions, even with a fever so high it incited delirious dreams. My skin starts to feel uncomfortably tight again as my dreams from last night resurface.

"Oh, don't worry about me, I'll sweet talk Sasaki, and you know I'm second only to Brendan in all our math classes and he's like in Mensa. I can't be expected to compete with that."

"I know, me either." I sigh. I try not to be jealous of Charlotte, but I could never blow off a day and maintain her GPA. I need a scholarship and I work hard for it. Brains will only take you so far. "I have to head to class now. Don't want to be late for my bio exam first period. I'm pumped." My skin is itching with the need to get inside before the bell rings.

"Are you actually excited about a quiz? I've got a quick mission before first period, but I'll catch you at lunch. You can totally leave the exhilarating details of your quiz behind, though. Luv ya." Charlotte heads off in the opposite direction.

"See you later! Love you too slacker."

I hurry through the crowded hall to get to room 236. I need to sit down, get settled, and organize my thoughts before class starts. As usual, I'm the first one there, including the teacher. My favorite teacher, Mr. Andrews, will get here soon though. He lets us watch Spacex rocket launches and live broadcasts from the International Space Station when they're on. Most of the other kids prefer our Econ teacher because he lets us watch movies. Not me.

The rest of the class trickles in to steadily fill the uncomfortable metal chairs. As usual, the only vacant seat is in the front row right beside me. I'm the only one eager to get up close to all that learning, exposing myself as a target for questioning.

Mr. Andrews proceeds with instructions for our scheduled quiz on metabolic processes after the announcements finish on the tinny PA system. Someone saunters in late as he's handing them out. All eyes zero in on the newcomer. No way. It's him, café guy, Logan. He can't possibly be a student here. Right? He has a maturity to him that's lacking in the rest of the student body. He scans the room with a sharp gaze as if searching for someone until finally his piercing blue-green eyes settle directly on me. An uncomfortable heat rises up my neck when I'm caught staring, regardless of the fact that the entire class is participating in the voyeurism. He doesn't seem the least bit bothered by the staring or his disruption of the class.

"Hello, can I help you with something? We were just about to start a quiz." Mr. Andrews is unflappable as always.

"I'm Logan Armstrong, apparently this is my first class." His deep voice slides out in a bored drawl.

"Ah Mr. Armstrong, yes indeed, well we weren't expecting you until next week, but please have a seat next to Miss Tennant there." He graciously gestures to the only available seat right next to yours truly. Of course. "As I was saying, we were just about to start our quiz on Molecular Processes. You're welcome to participate if this is something you're up to date on from your previous school. If not, you can have a seat and peruse the course syllabus." The stack of papers on his desk threatens to topple over as he rifles through it.

"I'll pass on the quiz," the boy says, settling back in his chair with his arms linked behind his head and his denim-clad legs stretching out for miles in front of him.

I look down in mortification only to find a quiz on my desk. How did I miss that being delivered? There's no way I'm letting this insolent newcomer mess with my plan. Not that he'd give me the time of day, anyway. He definitely looks like he'll shoot to the top of the school's social ranking in like an hour. I can already hear the illegal phones being slipped from pockets to send stealthy pics of the newest hot guy in school.

I wrestle my attention back to the task at hand to finish my quiz and muddle through the rest of class. I tear out the door and off to second period English the minute the bell sounds, only to have Logan magically appear and take a seat directly behind me. A constant wave of heat burns me from behind through the entire class, almost as if he's emanating energy at me. I know this is completely illogical, which means my reaction to him is purely psychological. That is way worse. I'd almost prefer him shooting actual lasers at my back.

At least I'll be free of him at lunch. I relax a little at the thought of a chill lunch with my posse.

As predicted, the entire student body of 636 students is buzzing with Logan's name as I weave through the long rows of cafeteria tables. The school is not so large that you get totally lost in the population, not so small as to be up in everyone's business constantly. Apparently, someone as good looking as Logan can't just slip unnoticed into the flock of geese flying south for the winter. They're all honking about him as if a genuine celeb has joined them, not just someone who looks like he should be one.

"Soph!" My shoulders loosen at my friends' cheerful greeting. I hadn't even realized how tense I was. When I spot them at our usual table, there's an unfamiliar face with them. If you're into boxing people up, the jealous teens would classify ours as the nerd table, while the more enlightened teens would refer to it as the smart table. The new girl's dark bob looks as if it has been dipped in teal paint and her eyes are the same startling teal shade that has been disturbing me all morning. This girl must be related to Logan. I've never seen eyes quite that color until yesterday. She flashes a huge smile that brightens up the room. It's the magnetic opposite of the glares I've been suffering through all morning. I sigh and settle down across from the newcomer.

"Hi guys!" My lips spread in an easy smile for my friends. "Hi, I'm Sophia." I extend my arm across the table toward the new girl. The comfortable warmth of my close friends surrounds me, so I don't mind reaching out to the new girl.

"Nice to meet you, I'm Liz." The girl introduces herself and her tiny hand grasps mine with a grip that almost has me wincing. A warm tingle travels up my arm. I think she might have cut off my circulation for a minute there. I shake it back to life as Liz looks at me with a curious gleam in her pretty eyes.

"Liz was in my history class this morning. I forgot my pencil case, so she was kind enough to lend me a pen. I thought I'd return the favor and invite her to eat lunch with us." Anne fills me in. That means Liz is in the eleventh grade. The rest of us are in twelfth but Anne's in a few classes with us, so she hangs out with our crowd sometimes along with a couple of her friends who float in and out on the fringes of our crew.

"Nice to meet you." My mother taught me to be polite. Besides, it's not Liz's fault who she's related to. "You must be Logan's sister?"

"You met my brother! That's great. He'll probably be along soon. You don't mind if he joins us, do you?"

"Talking about me, were you?" The subject of our discussion swaggers up, swinging his lean, muscled leg over the bench and settling down next to his sister. Right across from me, of course. He gives me a confident smirk. My skin prickles at the memory of my stupid dreams last night and I shift in my seat.

"We weren't…." I start and then trail off at his laughter.

"Really Logan? Ugh, your head is so big I'm surprised you can find a hat to fit. Obv Sophia can't help but notice the resemblance." She points at her eyes then his with a disparaging look. "You must be in one of her classes? That's nice!" Nice definitely isn't the word I'd go with. After our encounter this morning, he spent our first two periods acting like nothing happened. I tried to focus on my schoolwork rather than think about the incident with the dog or his strange words after. There's no point in dwelling on it until I can do some research. That conclusion did not stop my mind from wandering. I missed Mr. Andrews asking me a question for the first time in ever.

"Both of them actually." His bored drawl is a sharp contrast to his sister's exclamation mark infused words. "We seem to be stuck together."

He's the one who seems to appear wherever I am.

"Well, I'm sure we'll have a different schedule this afternoon," I say. There's no way he can possibly be in any more of my classes.

He replies with a noncommittal grunt.

The general chatter picks up again, with Liz joining in the conversation and fitting right in as if she's always been part of our squad. Logan, on the other hand, just leans back with his arms crossed looking unimpressed with the world in general and us in particular. I'm not actually sure why he's still sitting here. I'm sure any one of the other tables in the room would be happy to welcome him. In fact, there's a table of girls to our left that are just barely keeping their drool contained.

"Are we still on for our Monday study sesh at your house this afternoon, Soph?" Xavier runs his hand through his untidy mop of brown hair.

"Of course. Gotta keep those grades up. Who's in?" My eyes flit over my friend's faces. "You're welcome as well if you'd like to come, Liz. We get together every Monday to keep each other motivated. You can bring whatever homework you want." I'm happy to invite our newest friend.

It's Logan who pipes up with his first sentence since he sat down. "We'll be there."

"Wha...of course." I stumble over the words in my confusion. Did this boy who has seemingly no interest in us invite himself to my house? "You know we're just studying, right?" I slap my hand over my mouth after this slips out. Just because he's being a bit of a jerk doesn't mean I have to.

"Of course. I loove studying." His velvety tone slides over my skin.

Our Monday hangout and study sessions are sacred. Irritation wells up inside and threatens to spill out at his attitude. It's not like I even invited him.

"Seriously, Logan, you don't have to be so rude. What's with the attitude?" Liz shoots her brother the kind of glare that would send an MMA fighter scurrying for cover.

"Well, it's not like I was asked my opinion about coming here. Babysit..." He mutters that last word under his breath before shoving off from the table and storming away without another word.

"I'm so sorry. He's not usually such a jerk, I swear. Our parents made him come here. I know that's not an excuse." Liz winces and pleads with us as if the request has more weight than just adding him to our friend circle. Then she chases him out the door with a backwards wave and a "See you later."

"Well, what do you make of that?" asks Anne.

"I think he's seriously hot. I wonder if he's a gamer. Probably not. With those muscles, he's likely some breed of jock." A fleeting look of disappointment passes over Charlotte's face.

"Really? You're into that sullen, don't give a crap attitude? I mean, I admit when I first met him the temperature definitely rose a few degrees, but now that he's shown disdain for pretty much everyone and everything, he's lost his charm." I sink back into that first moment when I ran into him outside the coffee shop and got lost in his eyes. I figure maybe if I express my indifference out loud, it might come true cause he seems to have crept under my skin against my better judgment.

"Whoa, you actually noticed how good looking he is Soph?" It's kind of embarrassing how incredulous Charlotte's tone is. "I was pretty sure a former member of One Direction could stroll in here and you wouldn't pull your nose out of a textbook long enough to give him a glance."

"I notice good-looking guys. I just don't have time for dating. Life plan, remember?"

"What are you talking about, Sophia? Don't you have a date with Garrett?" Xavier has to butt in.

"What? Sophia has a date? What did I miss? Tell me everything." Charlotte leans in.

I shoot death lasers at Xavier. "It's nothing. We just made some new friends at the debate yesterday."

Xavier snorts. "Is that what you call friends? I should get more of your kind of friends."

"Spill. Did you get a picture? What does he look like? I need details."

I shift the death lasers to Charlotte. "Of course I didn't take a picture. I'm not a creeper."

"Well, good thing I am." Xavier brandishes his phone and passes it over to Charlotte with an evil gleam in his eyes.

She glances down and her eyes widen in shock. "Oh."

"What is it?" I ask.

Charlotte mutters. "Oh, it's nothing. He looks familiar, but he probably just has one of those faces. He's cute though." She tosses the phone back to Xavier. "Time for class. Don't want to miss anything! See ya later." She jumps up so fast I double check to make sure there's not a tarantula lurking on the bench.

Charlotte is never in a hurry to get to class. Now if she were leaving it, then I'd understand her rush. I place my matching containers neatly back in my lunch bag, which unashamedly displays a picture of the Mars Rover on it. I narrow my eyes at her disappearing back. "I don't know what you're up to, Charlotte, but I'm keeping my eye on you."

She just laughs and swivels her head around. "I'm not coming tonight, even to ogle Logan. I've got some aliens to battle. I'll def come next week, though."

"Seriously Char. Do we need to host a gaming intervention? Anne and I will swing by later. We're staying at school to help Mrs. Granger set up for the science fair," Xavier says.

"Of course, well I'll see you all later." I give them a wave before heading to my next class.

The first thing I see when I get to Calculus is Logan already there sitting right up front next to my usual seat. I'm tempted to take a different one but don't want to draw unnecessary attention to myself and mess with the classroom politics.

"Are you following me or something?" I narrow my eyes at him.

"Looks to me like you're the one doing the following. Believe me, I'd rather be anywhere but here."

"Oh, you've made that fact abundantly clear. Why did you decide to invite yourself to my study session if you dislike me so much?"

"Gotta get my study time in." Logan's tone is laden with sarcasm.

Cool. Well, I'm done with this sad attempt at a conversation, so I bury my nose in my calculus text. Stupid me, I'm actually a little hurt. It's not like I want to be friends with this guy, but I never did anything to him unless he really hates getting bumped into by clumsy strangers. He's nothing but a distraction anyway, so I guess he's doing me a favor. Flashes from my dream last night keep popping into my head at inappropriate times though, and I can't stop comparing the surly guy beside me to the sweet one my brain made up while under the influence of sleep.

The minute hand on the old-school caged clock at the rear ticks down the minutes like a sloth looking for the perfect branch to nap on. The bell finally sounds its triumphant buzz, and I dart for the door, dodging the crowds of students eager to escape the confines of school. The fresh autumn air should clear my head on the walk home.

CHAPTER 3
Sophia

Icy needles of rain bombard me the moment I step outside. My weather app was clearly lying about the sunny day. Of course. A soft sigh escapes me as I duck back under the awning that graces the front of Westbrook Secondary School, and the driving rain hits the metallic overhang with an overwhelming roar.

I could try calling Mom for a ride, but she usually works late on Mondays, so the chances of that happening are somewhere in the realm of nil. My other option is the city bus. The thought of shivering in the bus shelter is unappealing, but it looks like that's what I'm stuck with. As I'm mentally preparing myself to get soaked through, a black SUV pulls up in front of me (in the no stopping zone of course), and the tinted passenger window rolls down enough to see a set of instantly recognizable eyes peeking out.

"Hop in Sophia! Since we're coming over to your house anyway, we may as well give you a ride."

I probably shouldn't accept a ride from Logan, but it's Liz doing the asking and the thought of standing in the smelly bus shelter like a wet dog is unappealing. The wail of a car horn interrupts my hesitation. A beaten up red Civic belonging to one of the football players has pulled up behind the SUV, and that pushes me into action. Making a scene makes me squirm, so I pull open the back door and climb up onto the tan leather seat.

"Good decision. I'd hate to have had to blast that Civic into the Nether Realm," Logan says from the driver's seat. Maybe he is a gamer. The Nether Realm sounds like something I'd hear Char emoting about. She's going to be in heaven if that's the case.

"Logan! You wouldn't." Liz smacks her brother upside the head. Maybe not the best decision when he's behind the wheel.

He just snickers at his sister. "Wouldn't I? This school and this town and all these mundanes are really starting to chafe my style, sis."

I'm beginning to think maybe it was a bad idea to take a ride from someone who might well be delusional. He could be the very sort of person Mom warned me about when she said don't take rides from strangers.

"Oh sorry, I didn't know that I was in the presence of royalty, and you don't have time for all of us, what was your term, 'mundanes'." My tone is heavy on the sarcasm, light on the patience. Who does this guy think he is anyway?

A snort escapes from Logan before he stifles it under his usual air of ennui and judginess. Did I actually almost crack him? I'm more pleased with myself than I should be.

Liz, on the other hand, doesn't try to control the fit of giggles caused by my dig at her brother. "Oh, I really do like you Sophia! You are going to have no problem keeping this one in line."

"Thanks…I think, although I have no intention of spending enough time around him that I'll have to worry about keeping him in line."

Liz sobers up a bit. "But we are going to be friends, right? I can tell already we're going to get along in spite of my lame-o brother." Logan gives her a dirty look.

I don't really know what to say. It's pretty weird for me to be here in a car with two people who are essentially strangers. It's like they've crashed into my well-ordered house and moved everything. Between them and Emily and Garrett yesterday, I'm struggling to maintain control of my life. I already have a good group of friends. I'm not against making new ones, but this is all happening a little too fast for my brain to keep up. If it weren't for Liz, there's no way I'd let Logan come over to my house. Especially not after all his strange comments this morning. I've been doing my best not to think about it, but it's been preying on my mind. That weird current of electricity that shot up my arm during the dog attack has been gnawing at the back of my mind like a moth slowly eating away at my wardrobe. Logan's presence is an uncomfortable reminder.

"I'm sure we will. Turn right onto Winchester here. My house is number 79, the third one on the left. You can park in the driveway. My mom won't be home until late this evening. She always works late on Mondays, hence the study sessions here." I mentally smack my forehead at the questionable decision to reveal the lack of parental supervision to Logan. There's something I'm just not sure about him. It's not that I'm afraid, although I probably should be. He throws me off balance.

Logan slides into our curving driveway and parks in one of the spots that branch off the side. We clamber out, well I clamber out all awkward limbs and angles. Liz and Logan hop out with a little more grace. Logan moves with the smooth, efficient stride of an athlete as he pulls ahead of me, and I absently check out his denim clad rear before catching myself and shaking it off. This guy is a class A jerk, and I would do well to remind myself of that.

The crisp fall breeze kisses my cheeks. It's a relief after that seemingly endless day at school. That thought annoys me to no end. I love school, but now Logan has made it an uncomfortable place to be. I shoot him a glare from under my lashes.

A mosaic of rust, gold, and red leaves drift aimlessly in the light breeze and crunch underfoot. Contentment settles over me despite the presence of my new friend and my somewhat unwelcome hanger on. The weather hasn't entered the endless winter stage, and my life is on track: good grades, spotless record, extracurriculars. Everything is falling into place to get my scholarship. I'm even on track to graduate early. I'll have enough credits to finish by the end of fall semester, but I plan on sticking around to take some extra courses and graduate with my friends. These thoughts help me shake off the feeling of uneasy anticipation that creeps in when Logan's around. It's as if I'm waiting for something to happen.

"Welcome to my house." I give a flourish Vanna White would approve of. God, that was kind of lame. I eye the black shutters hanging a little askew and the peeling paint. They frame each symmetrically balanced window of the Colonial, but it looks tired. The covered front porch protecting a set of white wicker furniture with red cushions is my favorite part. I'm just now realizing that the cushions are threadbare and the wicker is splitting. The house has grown worn and sad since my dad's death. I'm a little uncomfortable bringing strangers over. Guilt balls up in my stomach at the thought. Mom works so hard. I know she doesn't have the time or money to deal with these issues.

"What a lovely home," Liz says, taking one step closer to friend status.

Logan just saunters in as if he owns the place without comment.

My mom's design aesthetic demonstrates her personality, comfortable and practical, with lots of conveniently hidden storage containers like the chocolate brown leather cube that functions as an extra seat, a footrest, or storage space when you lift off the top. There's also a plethora of bookcases that reflect my family's love of reading and constant drive to learn new things. My brother Scott is smart and driven, just like me. However, he seems to have missed out on the cleanliness gene. He went away to university though last year and I almost miss his sports equipment, piles of papers, and books that he always left lying around when he was here. The house has been a lot quieter since he moved out, with only brief periods of chaos upon his rare visits home.

"We can study in the kitchen. There's a nice big table with enough room for everyone, once they get here, and lots of light."

Logan and Liz share some sort of secret sibling glance at each other as I take them into the kitchen, where I lay my bag on the table and pour myself a glass of water from the fridge.

"Can I grab something for either of you? We have water, still or sparkling, orange juice, milk, no pop or anything. Sorry my mom is into the healthy lifestyle, and she doesn't keep any sugary snacks or drinks around."

"I'll take a sparkling water, please." Liz is all politeness.

"I'm good," Logan says.

"Okay great." I grab a can of fizzy water from the fridge and head back to the big pine table. There's one small blemish where my brother carved my name in it to get me in trouble. My parents could always see through his antics though, and he was the one who wound up getting grounded. Liz and Logan seem to have the teasing kind of relationship I share with my brother, and being around them reminds me how much I miss him.

Liz and I pull out our books and start working on our different subjects. My eyebrow drifts up when I see Logan leaning back in a chair, playing on his phone. I have no clue why he bothered to come.

I'm just getting into my physics problems when my phone buzzes. I give it a cursory glance and see that it's a text from Anne.

'Sorry girl got held up with science fair prep gonna be a late one. X and I can't make it. We'll catch u tomorrow. Sad face emoji.'

Well that's Anne and X out. Char is furiously battling aliens for the night, probably kicking some ten-year-old prodigy's butt and Brendan is at the Math Elites competition for the next few days. Sooo, I guess I'm stuck with Liz, which is okay, and Logan, not so okay.

"Looks like Anne and Xavier aren't going to make it after all. Do you guys just want to call it a night and we can reschedule our group study session?" I give them a hopeful look.

Fingers crossed the siblings will bail at this point. Without my other friends to back me up, this is promising to be awkward.

"How about we just have a chat since we have the house to ourselves for a while?" Logan says, as if the invite is his to offer.

"Logan, it's too soon! Let's just study." Liz hisses at her brother.

I glance up in confusion. Too soon for what?

"I know I've got a pile of homework to get through, so I'm with Liz, let's get back to our work," I say. If they won't leave, at least I want to be able to do what we're here for.

"Maybe so, Liz, but she needs to know she could be in danger, and since we were forced to come here, I may as well do my job." Logan responds cryptically, as if he hasn't heard a word I said. Of course.

"Nobody forced you to come here. In fact, I didn't even invite you Logan, I invited your sister. If it's such a hardship to be here, then you're welcome to leave!" It takes a lot to rile me up enough to abandon my manners, but Logan has pushed me too far today.

"Tact Logan, learn some. At least let me do the talking. Clearly, you are not going to get through to Sophia."

"Whatever." Logan leans back in his chair, crossing his beautiful arms over his chest back to his usual state of boredom.

"What's going on? What are you guys talking about? Why would I be in danger? Does this have something to do with the nonsense you were spouting this morning, Logan?" I demand, glancing back and forth between the siblings.

"We have something to tell you and it's going to be hard to believe and I wish I didn't have to...but..." Liz babbles nervously and glances at her brother who gives her a hand wave to get on with it. "Where do I start? Well, I guess the beginning is probably the best. Our parents were like best friends back in the day, like total BFFs."

"Wait a minute, you guys know my mom? I thought you just moved here." I'm confused about the direction of this conversation.

"Not your parents here. I mean your biological parents. They were from Port Grand, like us," Liz says.

"How did you know I was adopted?" My guard shoots up and my mind buzzes with agitation. That is definitely not something I talk about with people I've just met, so I'm a hundred percent sure I didn't share this info with them.

"I'm not explaining this right, Logan?"

"Our parents were besties. Your parents feared for your life, bound your magic, gave you up for adoption, then they were killed."

The chair rocks back as I pull away, and a chill seeps into my veins. Why would he say something like that? I rub my hands up and down my arms to warm them up while my mind races trying to make sense of his words.

"LOGAN, so not cool!" yells Liz, whacking her brother so hard on the arm I swear I see sparks.

Wait sparks? I rub my eyes. I'm definitely seeing things. And hearing things, what had Logan said about magic? I start piling my books up, pushing the edges until they're perfectly aligned in a neat tower to calm my mind.

"I don't know what kind of game you two think you're playing, but this is really not funny, and I need to get some work done, so I think it's best if you leave."

"No, we can't leave yet. Let me fix this, as my jerk brother apparently doesn't understand the concept of breaking news gently. Please hear me out, no questions, no brotherly interruptions and then we'll leave, no questions asked. Please?" Liz's tone takes on a pleading note.

"Fine, tell me whatever nonsense you need to, and then you're out of my house and my life." I sit back and cross my arms, my knee bouncing under the table.

"Okay, like I said, our parents were best friends. They grew up together. The ma…umm community they lived in is close. Your parents, Elora and Greyson Bennett, were well liked and well known. They were both powerful and strong."

I uncross my arms and lean in. I've never gotten any details about my biological parents. My adopted parents are the only ones I've ever known, and I know how much they love me, so I've never felt a deep need to search for something more. Curiosity has passed through my mind from time to time, though. Wondering if I look like them, talk like them, if they're into books and science like I am or if I learned that from my family.

"Then they had you and they knew from the minute you were born that you were something more. And others in the community realized it and word spread and they knew you were in danger. They tried to protect you but realized the threat was too big for them to handle, so they made an enormous sacrifice. When you were six months old, they made secret arrangements to give you up and returned home empty-handed. They claimed to everyone that you had gotten pneumonia and died while they were traveling. They held a funeral and everything. The only people they told the truth to were our parents," Liz gestured to herself and Logan. "and one other person. This lady performed a service for you, but she passed away shortly before we came out here. She was murdered and the people who killed her are seeking you out next. We got sent to guard you. Well, they actually gave Logan the assignment. I'm just kinda here for the ride and the moral support, since he is clearly incapable of that." She glares at her brother with some serious steel on her pixie-like face. "I'm so sorry to dump this all on you, but I need you to understand how serious this is."

I'm confused. "None of this is logical. Why would anyone want to hurt a baby? I'm not anyone special. Although reflecting on the current state of world politics, it makes it hard to have faith in the intellect of humanity sometimes." I go off on a tangent, unable to wrap my mind around the story that Liz has just told me.

"I know. It doesn't make much sense with pieces missing. I needed you to hear me out before I filled in the details that are gonna freak you out. The community I'm referring to is the…magic community. Your parents, our parents, and us, we're all Mages. You were born with a rare mutation that makes you more powerful. Most people only have one magical specialty. You can control all four. This is why you were in danger, why your parents made you disappear, and why they were killed protecting your secret."

They're messing with me, right? A bitter laugh slips out. "I get it. This is all a big joke. Ha, very funny, where are the cameras?"

"Told you she wouldn't believe you."

Logan casually holds up his hand in a fist and then opens it up to reveal a ball of fire dancing on his palm.

My mouth falls open as I narrow my eyes at him, running through everything I know about illusions and magicians. There's always a trick. I'm not sure why these two are messing with me. The only thing that makes sense is that they're trying to make a mockery of me online. That has to be it. They must have seen my science blog or something else I've been involved in at the school. My mind drifts back to the dog, freezing in midair, and the tingle of electricity that shot up my arm. But that can't be. If magic were real, then everything I've ever believed would be wrong. I shake my head.

"Well, I'm not sure how you're doing that, but I know it's some sort of illusion, and you're not going to fool me. I really think it was unnecessary for you to add in the lies about my biological parents, though. That was hurtful. I think it's time you leave." I jump up to escort them to the door and out of my life for good.

"You think this is a trick?" Logan asks, closing his fist on the fireball and seemingly extinguishing it. "I guess it is, but it's a pretty good one, if I do say so myself. We should get out of here, Liz. She clearly doesn't want us around, so let's leave her in peace. She'll realize soon enough and will come running to us for help." He pushes off from the table but not before the fat red candle that sits in the middle of the dining room flares to life as he gestures at it.

Another trick that I most certainly will not fall for. I storm off to the living room, not bothering to check if they're following me. In my haste, I knock my mom's crystal vase off the coffee table and lunge at it in a futile attempt to stop the inevitable crash. For a few seconds, the vase seems to freeze in midair, crystal shards reflecting rainbows in the air, but when I gasp, the world seems to come back into focus and the vase crashes to the floor. A pleased looking Liz and smug Logan are behind me watching the show.

"My mom is going to kill me. That's her favorite vase, Dad gave it to her for their first wedding anniversary. Get out of here now. I'm done being polite. I don't want to see you anymore."

I can feel heat spreading to my face, foreshadowing the tears that want to break free. I want them out before they can witness my pain and anger. I don't want them knowing how much their sick joke has affected me. I almost believed them for a minute, not about the magic stuff that can't be true, it can't, but about my birth parents. I really wanted to believe that they loved me so much they'd died to protect me.

"I'm so sorry. We weren't trying to hurt you." Liz looks genuinely sorry, but I can't believe her after what they've told me. I shake my head when she makes a move to approach me.

Once I shut the door on the pair of con artists, I slide to the floor and give in to the onslaught of tears they stirred up.

CHAPTER 4
Logan

"You are such an idiot! I can't believe you messed this up, Logan! I mean, I can believe it, but seriously."

Liz is right. God, I hate it when that happens. I really effed this one up. Dad will be delighted to throw it in my face. After all, he never wanted to give me this assignment, anyway. He never would have either if it weren't for the bond, which I never asked for, by the way. It's not like I wanted to come here. I was doing fine. Enjoying life and traveling around Europe. I'd still be wandering the streets of Paris right now if it weren't for his call and it wouldn't be all the churches and fountains I'd be visiting. One year of freedom is all I asked for. Pain shoots through my fist as I slam it into the steering wheel.

"I know I did. Thanks for pointing out the obvious." I rub at my chest, trying to ease the tightness. The look of shock and pain on Sophia's face flashes in my mind. It was like her entire world was crashing down around her.

"You know I really like her, Logan. Now she thinks we're some kind of psychos or something. How are we going to get her to trust us now?"

"I'll figure it out. It is my job, after all." When it comes down to it, I am pissed at myself and our parents for putting us in this situation. This girl has done nothing to me. She shouldn't have to rely on me for protection. We've all seen what a hot mess that can be. "I'll fix it." How I'm going to fix it is another matter altogether. I'll talk to her at school. I'll be nicer this time. I can't even believe what a royal ass I've been since I met her.

"You better. Mom told me about another missing Mage. Something's going on, Logan. She needs us."

Her words hit me like a punch to the gut and I heave out a shaky breath. If Sophia went missing, it would be all my fault. She's innocent. It was our parents who tied us together. Resentment gnaws at me over that, but she is just as much of a victim as I am. The image of her big brown eyes widened in fear is etched into my brain, and the thought of them glassy with death wrecks me. I'm not going to take it out on her anymore. I will fix this. Whatever it takes.

CHAPTER 5
Sophia

I huddle on the floor until I hear the slam of a car door. Mom must be home. I scrub my face with the back of my hands and scoot back to my homework set up in the kitchen. No way I could explain this problem to Mom, and I haven't been able to let her see me sad since Dad passed away. She fell apart so completely for the first six months after his death that I buried my own sadness to look after her and manage our lives.

After that she pieced herself together and reclaimed her role as the grown up of the house, but by then I had buried my own feelings deep and had no desire to reawaken them. So we go through life pretending that everything is fine. I'm once again the model student, straight As and no high school shenanigans. She works hard and sacrifices everything for Scott and me.

"Hi, Mom." I glance up as she enters the kitchen, pausing to lean on the door frame and give me a long look.

"Hi Sweetie. Working hard, as usual?" she asks with an overly bright smile stretching her mouth.

"Yeeeessss. What's up? You sound weird." I tilt my head and scan her from head to toe, trying to spot the lie.

"Can't get anything past you, can I? I need to talk to you about something." It sounds like she's asking forgiveness for a crime not yet committed.

"Sounds ominous." I'm concerned now. We haven't had a serious talk since, well since Dad, really.

She slowly walks over to the chair on my left and settles into it, facing me. She fiddles with the wedding ring that hangs from a delicate gold chain around her elegant neck. Someone might classify me as pretty or beautiful, but Mom is truly in a class of her own. Sophisticated, polished, and poised are three words that come to mind when I think of her. Not to mention stunningly beautiful. She is always so put together, so in control. That's why it had been such a shock when she completely fell apart for those six months. She had worn sweatpants, no makeup, and constantly pulled her hair into a messy ponytail rather than her usual sleek bob. I shift in my seat, nervous to see her uncomfortable.

"Seriously, the suspense is destroying me. What's wrong?"

"Nothing's wrong, honey. It's actually good. I...I wanted you to know that I've been dating someone, and it's gotten serious enough that I want you to meet him."

"You're dating? And you couldn't find the time to tell me?" I'm incredulous. This is not what I'd been expecting to come out of her mouth.

"I wasn't hiding it. I just didn't want to tell you until I was sure there was something to tell. I've gone on some dates over the past year, but nothing that was real, nothing that made me feel like I might be able to open up to someone again. Until now. His name is David, one of my colleagues at the university introduced us and we've been dating for a few months now. He's sweet and I'm starting to care about him. I really hope you'll like him too."

I just stare at her, blinking. How have I been so blind to this? I guess I've gotten so good at hiding my own feelings from her and keeping things light between us that I haven't been paying attention. Now that I look at her, I can see the creases between her eyes are a little softer and her eyes have a hint of their old sparkle. The grief faded while I wasn't looking.

"Um, ok. I guess. I mean, I want you to be happy. I just can't imagine. How are you able to do that?" My words stumble over each other.

"What do you mean? Do what?"

"Trust someone, open yourself up again. After…you know." I can't mention the dark months outright, but this is about the closest I've gotten to even grazing the subject. The thought of love is terrifying. Getting close to someone only to have them ripped away from you like that. I don't know how she can do that again.

"It's been hard, honey, but I'm working on it. Meeting someone I really connect with has helped. I hope you don't feel that you can't be with someone. Love is so important. You have to be open to it and the way it changes you. I wouldn't give up my time with your father. No matter how much pain I felt after he died."

This is the rawest she's been with me in years and it's totally freaking me out. I definitely need to get off this roller coaster before the ground drops out from beneath me. There have been too many revelations, true or false, dropped on me for one day.

This would be a good time to bring up a sensitive topic, while she's still vulnerable. I wince inside at that thought but can't lose the opportunity.

"Ok, I can meet him. I need some time to process this, though."

"Of course. Thanks so much for understanding. You know I would never try to replace your father." She pulls me into a warm embrace and gives me a big squeeze. I didn't realize how tightly I'm wound until my muscles soften in her arms. She's about to get up when I stall her.

"Wait a sec! Mom, while we're having this heart to heart. Would you mind if I ask you a couple of questions?"

"Of course. You know you can always talk to me."

"I was wondering about my biological parents. I'm doing a project for school about genealogy, and I was wondering if you knew anything about them. Background, where they lived, anything would be helpful. I know I've never really been interested in them, but this is for school." I'm pretty proud of my improvisational skills. Inventing a fake project to do a little digging. The thought of Liz and Logan's faces when I prove them wrong is enough to make me push Mom a little harder than I normally would.

I can almost hear the click as her guard slams back up at the question. "It was a closed adoption. You know that. We never really got any facts about their backgrounds." The words come out in a rush as she fidgets with her necklace again while avoiding eye contact. Interesting. She's hiding something from me. She never hides things. An icy finger of fear trails down my back.

"Really, nothing? Not even where they were from?"

"Well." She looks up at the ceiling as if she's searching for answers there. "There was information on the adoption papers that they were from Port Grand. I looked it up. But that's it. That's all I ever knew."

The town name sends a slither of recognition up my spine as I recall Liz mentioning it. Mom still won't make eye contact, and for the first time in my life, I realize she has information about my birth parents she isn't willing to share. I've never really thought too much about them, so it never occurred to me she might be concealing something. I'm not going to push that right now, though. I still don't believe their magic nonsense, but maybe they really do know my birth parents or have heard of them, and this is all part of their con. I just can't make it work in my head. What exactly do these lies accomplish? Could our families actually be enemies rather than friends? Maybe they're trying to discredit me or make me look unstable to take something that's supposed to be mine. With no further facts though, this is wild speculation. They have to be up to something, though.

"Well thanks, Mom. That's something, at least." I fake yawn and gather up my study materials strewn across our dining table. "I'm pretty tired. It's been a crazy day. Love you." I give her a brief hug and head up to my room.

I breathe a sigh of relief as I settle onto my galaxy themed bedspread. It makes me feel like I'm floating in space, the insignificant speck that we all truly are compared to the vast cosmos. I then flip open my laptop for some research. If there's one thing I'm good at, it's finding the facts necessary to prove or disprove a story. I start on the Port Grand website. It's your typical small town tourism site featuring photographs of their picturesque downtown and shots of the beach and lake to lure tourists in, especially during the summer months. I skip past the local business and events guides before I discover a link to their local newspaper, the Grand Gazette.

This is where things get interesting. It's only a twice-weekly publication, so I skim the latest issues, avoiding the preponderance of ads that make up most of the paper. It's in the third issue back that a murder is splashed over the front page of what I hypothesize is a normally sleepy small-town newspaper.

It states that a Helena Baldwin was found dead in her shop, Elements of Light. It claims there was evidence of foul play and that ritualistic aspects of the murder resembled those of a double homicide from 16 years ago. Being an open investigation, they don't reveal details of the current crime, but I bet I can do some digging into their archives to find out more about the earlier murders.

I sort through the information I currently have. These pieces could fit in with the information Liz and Logan gave me, but obviously their claims can't be true, so what's their game? Why are they trying to fool me like this? What does it accomplish?

I resolve to do some more digging. If I can't access their newspaper archives online, I'll have to take a drive to Port Grand.

CHAPTER 6
Sophia

The temperature shot up since yesterday and we're experiencing a couple of those freaky but fabulous autumn days that feel like summer. The sun is worshiping my face for what will likely be one of the last days before we settle into fall and then the dreaded drab gloom of winter. I don't mind snow in theory, but in practice around here it just gets messy, dirty, and dangerous as people eschew snow tires and forget how to drive. As if winter doesn't happen every year.

My sunny mood vanishes behind the horizon as the con artists Liz and Logan are the first to approach me in the halls lined with light blue and orange lockers.

"Hi Sophia, are you doing okay? Your mom didn't get you in too much trouble for breaking that vase, did she?" Liz asks anxiously.

Logan stands beside her, looking softer than yesterday with his arms hanging loose at his sides. I start at the small sheepish smile that pulls up the corners of his lips.

"I have to get to my locker." I step up my pace, avoiding eye contact. That's about the extent of how rude I can be.

"Wait Sophia, we should really talk!" Liz calls out after me.

"No, I'm done with you guys. I don't want to hear any more of your lies." I escape to the bathroom to compose myself before class.

As expected, Logan is in all of my classes again today, but I manage to get through them without a word to him. They wisely choose to sit at the table behind our group at lunch.

"I guess we're not cool enough for them," Xavier says. "Little do they know I've got connections everywhere. I'm sure I can arrange for them to become the newest Westbrook social pariahs. Whaddya think Sophia?" Xavier fancies himself the next Machiavelli, wielding the strings and manipulating the entire school as he sees fit.

"I'm pretty sure they've done nothing to merit that. Maybe Sophia just scared them off?" Charlotte teases.

"I didn't...what...it's their fault!" I know my friends have no idea what went down yesterday, and I'm not ready to talk to them about it. Maybe once I have the facts, I'll share what I've learned about my birth parents.

"The truth comes out! What did you do to them? Or did they do something to you? Do I need to break out my Tae Kwon Do skills?" Xavier's gaze darts from me to the siblings sitting in the next row.

I appreciate his concern, but I definitely don't want to get him involved. "It's fine. I'm so over those two. Let's just get back to our usual. How's Star Crossed going? Beaten it yet?" I glance at Char knowing that bringing up her new game will get her going for a while, and even though Xavier isn't as hard core of a gamer as Charlotte is, it will definitely distract him, too.

Charlotte launches into an enthusiastic explanation of her latest on-screen conquests, which shifts the focus off my strange new problems. I grab my phone at the buzz in my pocket and glance at the text.

'Hi, it's Garrett.'

I stare at the screen for a few minutes too long, not knowing how to reply. I'd almost forgotten about him after last night's craziness. Probably not a good sign. Should I say hi back, something more? I've avoided this dating stuff for so long I have no idea what I'm doing. Crap, the typing bubble is back up. Did I take too long to reply?

'From Sherwood. Hope you're having a good day. Any chance you might be free for some dinner?'

Next message.

'Or just a coffee if you don't have time for dinner. Let me know if tonight or tomorrow works for you.'

I realize I have to reply to avoid looking like a complete jerk. He's clearly going to see that I've read his messages. I don't know what I should do. Go on a date with a cute, nice guy who seems into me or continue to hide behind my books and studies as I have for the first three years of my high school life. I'm startled out of my thoughts by a loud laugh at the table next to ours, and I see Logan laughing at something his sister said. He looks way less intense than usual, with a wide smile on his face and his gorgeous eyes sparkling with humor. I feel the same twinge I felt the first few times I met his gaze and get caught up in his joy before I remember the pain and confusion he's inflicted on me. He glances up as if he can feel the heat of my gaze, and I quickly look down as his laughter stills.

I grab my phone and recklessly reply to Garrett.

'I'm free tonight, how about 6 o'clock?'

His response is bullet quick.

'You're on. I can pick you up if you'd like.'

'Sounds like a plan. My address is 79 Winchester Dr.'

'Fantastic. Can't wait to see you again.'

Well, at least he uses proper grammar and punctuation in his text messages. Few things bother me as much as people using numbers in place of words or not capitalizing their sentences. My fingers tingle and my stomach pitches. I can't believe I actually agreed to go through with that after everything that has happened since the coffee shop.

I drop my head on my arms and try not to think about what I've just done when the table goes silent, and someone taps me on the shoulder. I jerk up and a warmth climbs my back all the way up to my neck. A feeling of calm washes through me as if a cool breeze just passed over me on a humid day. At least until a velvety smooth voice ruins the feeling.

"Sophia. Can I talk to you for a minute? Please. I'll leave you alone after that if you'd like." My name is soft coming from his lips, and his voice has taken on a soothing tone as if he's trying not to startle a skittish horse.

I don't know what to make of this new tactic. His caution does show some intelligence. It wouldn't take much for him to set me off right now. My lips press together, and I look him over. The remorse in his eyes seems real, but I don't really know him at all. I mean, what if he actually knows something about my birth parents?

"Fine. You get one talk and then you leave me alone. For good. Are we clear?"

"Crystal. Can we go somewhere a little more private? Like, maybe the hall."

The hall is safe. We're still in school. There are teachers everywhere. Plus, I'd rather my friends not overhear this conversation. I give him a slow nod and stand up, gather my bag, and follow him.

"See you later." I call back to my stunned friends.

Xavier whistles and the rest of them call out byes and see you laters as I trail after Logan. When we're halfway down the hall, he grabs my arm lightly and whisks me into a janitorial supply closet. I'm startled, but my brain isn't sending off alarm bells. He shuts the door and a wave of heat hits me as he places his palm on it. I look around to see where the vent is, but there're only mops, brooms, and shelves of cleaning supplies neatly organized.

"Okay look, I know I wasn't the most tactful yesterday. I am sorry about that. It's just I had plans to be somewhere else this year. I know it's not an excuse for my assholery to you. I can't imagine what it must be like for you to find out about our world like that after living a normal life until now." Logan actually sounds sincere and apologetic as he says this. What's with this guy? Hot or cold and definitely crazy with the magic talk.

"That's all well and good, but you can't expect me to believe all that nonsense about magic and Mages. I do research, I uncover facts, I use the scientific method. There have never been any scientific studies that back up ESP, telekinesis, or any other supernatural phenomenon."

"Do you think that any real Mages are out there letting scientists test them? Of course not. We keep to ourselves and keep our powers a secret from the mundanes. The people out there trying to get their powers tested and shilling their psychic services are human fraudsters or Witches."

"Well, at least we can agree on one thing."

"Don't believe me, fine!" Logan temper flares as holds his left hand out palm up.

I feel the same heat radiating as when he touched the door and take another glance around the room for the heat vent. I let out a shriek as a ball of flame ignites on his palm. I instinctively reach out to touch it, confident that it's some sort of trick or illusion. He quickly pulls his hand back and the fire snuffs out.

"What do you think you're doing? Do you want to get hurt?" His voice has gone gravelly and sharp.

"No, I just figured it wasn't real fire, so I was curious what it is." I explain.

"You're impossible." He growls and then glances around the tiny, crowded space.

I start to feel uncomfortably warm at his close proximity. I try to take a step back and bump into the door for my efforts.

Logan spots the mop sink and starts filling up a bucket with water.

"You probably aren't supposed to be touching that. On second thought, we're definitely not supposed to be in here." My eyes shift to the door as if someone might charge in at any moment and bust us. I never get into trouble. The only time I've ever been sent to the principal's office was to plan school events for my extracurricular clubs or to deliver notes from my teachers. Logan definitely looks like the type to have frequented the office for very different reasons.

"Nobody's going to come in and find us, don't worry," he says, as if he has any control over the school staff. His confidence is a little disturbing. My heart thrums a little faster as I glance around the claustrophobic space.

Logan then turns around holding a red bucket half full of water. The air crackles as he holds his hand over it and the water rises out of the bucket before freezing in midair in a graceful arc. I can't help myself. My hand is drawn toward the phenomenon, and a smooth, cold column of ice meets my fingertips. He then makes a slight gesture, and the formerly frozen water splashes back into the bucket, soaking my fingers in the process.

"How…what…that's impossible." I don't have an answer to this. I've been thinking it's all some sort of trick, but now that I've seen it with my own eyes, I don't know what to do. I've seen and felt the frozen water turn back to liquid. If I've learned anything in my critical thinking class, it is to keep an open mind and accept things once I have solid proof of them.

"It's magic. Like I said. I could show you more, but we don't have time for that. You have to believe me. There are people who are going to come looking for you, and I can't protect you if you won't even accept the truth."

"So, could my parents do that? My bio parents, I mean?" That's the first question that comes out of my mind that's racing from thought to thought. My worldview is crumbling around me with the bricks that form the foundation of my scientific beliefs kicking up dust. If this is real, then my biological parents were killed for me, and I really am in danger? Does Mom know about this? Is that why she was acting so shady?

"Your mother could. She was an Elemental Mage like me. Your father was a Psy. There are four main types of Mages.

Elemental, Psychic, Physical, and Biological. There are a lot of unique abilities within each type and Mages have varying degrees of power. Some can utilize all the aspects of their brand of magic, and some can only perform a few activities. Like me, I'm a pretty strong Elemental and can control water, wind, fire, earth and can manipulate most physical objects. Some weaker Elementals might only have control over one or two elements. I can get into more details later. Or Liz can if you'd rather talk to her. I just needed you to believe me. I need you to understand the danger so I can protect you."

I shake my head at him as I take a step back for a little breathing room. My shoulders collide with the door. I can't get more than six inches away from him.

"Why would there be people after me?"

"Like we said yesterday, your parents realized early on that you were an Archimage and could control all types of magic. Historically, Archimages were killed or imprisoned or had their magic stripped out of fear they could get too powerful. It's a rare mutation, though. There hasn't been another documented for over fifty years. You parents were terrified for you, so they had your magic bound. The Mage who performed the binding spell was killed recently so your powers will slowly emerge as the spell fades."

I shake my head. "They killed someone for me? Who, why?"

"Her name was Helena Baldwin." I shiver at the ice-cold spear that stabs my heart. I recognize that name. As if sensing my fear, Logan reaches out to reassure me before quickly pulling his hand back. "She was a close friend to both of our families and a powerful Psychic Mage. My family and Helena were the only people your parents confided in that you were still alive. Your parents declared you dead when they gave you up, but there were always Mages who suspected that you had survived. Targeting Helena is solid evidence that someone knows you're alive and now they're going to be hunting for you. With your powers unbound, you will be much easier to track."

"This is all too much for me to handle right now." I don't even know what to say. I'm drowning in all the new information. Trying to reassemble the pieces of my life I can still salvage, I pull my phone shakily from my pocket and glance at the time. My heart sinks when I realize I've missed almost a whole period. "I've gotta go. I've already missed one class. I don't want to be late for another one." I think I'm going to need some time to process all of this.

"You can never live that normal life again. You're not one of them. You're only going to put yourself and your friends in danger if you try to. Liz and I can help you. That's what we came here to do. Full disclosure: I've already graduated from high school. I'm nineteen. My parents sent me to protect you, so I needed to be nearby. I'm going to protect you. I didn't ask for the job, but I'm not letting you get hurt on my watch." His eyes blaze at me.

My mouth gapes at his revelation. I did think he looked more mature than the other high schoolers, and I guess I was right. Where does he get off thinking I'm some sort of job, though? I certainly didn't hire him. "Well, it's my life and I'll live it as I choose. You don't have a say. I'm going back to class now, and I have a…a date tonight and I'm going to go." I have no idea why I even said that to him, but there it is. Hanging out there in the world. I grab the door handle to storm out, only to find it locked. "Did you lock me in here with you like some sort of creep?"

He gives me a smirk before reaching over my shoulder to place his hand on the door. His arm brushes my shoulder, and I can feel the heat from his body rolling over me. My traitorous heart races, fueling my anger even more. My skin itches at the thought of the dreams I had about him. I feel the familiar warmth and tingle that I'm beginning to think is associated with magical activity, and then the handle turns of its own accord.

Startled, I jump back, only to bump into his hard body and then scramble to bolt from the room. Luckily, no one is in the hall when I burst out hot and flustered. Logan takes his time following me out.

I make it to the next hall before sliding to the ground against the lockers. I put my head on my knees shakily and take some deep breaths to stop the tears from emerging. Eventually, I pull myself together and check the clock on my phone. Only five minutes left of this period. I've missed a whole class thanks to that episode. I pull myself back up, determined to make it to next period. A little normalcy and schoolwork will definitely help restore my sense of equilibrium.

I make it to English on time and wait in the hall while the previous class spills out, chattering about class and what they're doing after school. When they've all filed out, I trudge in and settle into my desk, expecting Logan to show up again and sit next to me. He must have sensed my need for a little space though as he takes a seat in the back corner and I'm able to immerse myself in Shakespeare and the normalcy of school and forget his revelations that have left me wondering if my whole life has been a lie.

The rest of the day flies by in a whirlwind, and Logan keeps his distance in my classes. On the cool walk home, my brain whirls around overloaded with trying to process all the new information I've learned. I keep flashing back to that perfect ball of fire dancing in the palm of his hand and the smooth chill of the ice column before it melted. I've been trying to come up with a logical explanation, but nothing fits. There's no science or technology I can think of that could be responsible. I can't deny what I saw with my own eyes.

I walk in the front door to an empty house and trip over the mat. Smooth Soph. My school bag goes flying and I throw up my arms. An electric current flows through my veins and my mouth drops open as my bag floats in midair for a minute. Then the moment's gone, and it crashes to the ground. I glance at my trembling hand, studying it as if it's an interesting specimen under a microscope. Did I make that happen? What do I even do with that? I want to say there is no way I possess any kind of magic, but the events of the week are weighing on my mind. I let my shaky knees give out on me as I slump to the couch for a moment to pull myself together.

I fixate on the most normal problem of the day. I agreed to go on a date. Date, eek, that word dredges up a different kind of fear. Should I cancel? I have all of this other stuff to deal with now. Maybe I can have one night. One night of normalcy before I face the other stuff. I'm having trouble even thinking the M word. I need to distance myself from the craziness that Liz and Logan have brought into my life. One night. That's all I ask.

I slowly open the closet door and gaze at my wardrobe selection. Everything looks wrong. I totally am not equipped to deal with dressing for a date. I try on a hot pink blouse with a pleated black skirt and let out a huge sigh. Perfect for a job interview, not so great for a first date. My dresser is stuffed with nerd tees, which are fine for school but not exactly date worthy.

Next is a pretty navy-blue chiffon dress with floaty half sleeves. I roll my eyes. It might work for the prom. I'd definitely be setting expectations a little too high there. What message am I even trying to send with these clothes? "Please distract me from magic and murder and who knows, maybe this'll turn into something?" Finally, I settle on over the knee black socks with the aforementioned black skirt and a black-and-white striped sweater with a scoop neck. I sigh and add a bit of rose-pink lipstick before turning away from the mirror and heading downstairs to prowl the house. My mother always seems to think lipstick will fix any problem. Here's hoping she's right.

I have no idea why I'm even so nervous. I could hang out with this guy, we could be friends, it would be fine. I'm not obligated to get romantically involved with him. It's just one date. I'm overthinking this big time like I do everything.

The cheery chime of the doorbell at 6:00 makes me jump, interrupting my prowl of the living room. Punctual, I like that in a person. I pause a little too long before opening the door.

CHAPTER 7
Sophia

Garrett stands there looking almost as nervous as me and shoves a yellow gerbera daisy at me. I fumble as I grab it from him, and our fingers brush together. His smile is all white teeth with a single dimple in his left cheek.

"Hi Sophia, nice to see you again." His greeting is a little stiff and formal. Maybe he's as nervous as I am.

"Hi. Let me just find something to put this in." I wave the daisy at him and scurry off to the kitchen to find a vase. I settle on a beer glass. We don't get many (any) flower deliveries to our house, so vases are apparently as hard to find as evidence of life on other planets. Although now that I've seen actual magic, I may need to rethink the entire existence-of-aliens thing too.

I grab my black pleather jacket and head out the door. A bitter wind whirls my hair around my face and stings my cheeks. I definitely should have snagged my hat and gloves, but my nerves got the better of me and my mind blanked on the way out the door. Garrett is wearing a black, puffy coat that looks warmer than my thin jacket. I don't normally suffer for fashion that's so nineteenth century.

Garrett holds the door open for me in that chivalrous style he seems to have. He smoothly pulls away from the curb, after signaling, of course. He's almost too good to be true. Polite, sweet, intelligent, good grammar, and he even follows the rules of the road which so many people these days seem to forget about. Just one reason I'm not a huge fan of driving.

"How was your day?" Garrett asks just as our silence slips dangerously close to the awkward zone.

I falter. "It was…okay." His completely normal conversation starter throws me off as I think back to my unsettling conversation with Logan.

"Oh, did something happen? Bad test or something? Sorry, not trying to pry or anything. Just want to get to know you better." I notice a glint of gold around his pupils as his eyes flicker over my face. They are lovely eyes and the flop of untidy sandy hair on his head pairs perfectly with them.

"No, there's just these new kids at school. They've thrown off the dynamic a little. Threw me for a loop today. It was a good day otherwise. You know, usual stuff. How about you?" I'm off kilter. Garrett seems so nice, but I can't possibly tell him the truth about my day. It's strange how much more comfortable I am speaking my mind to Logan.

"I had a great day! Especially after you agreed to come out with me." He looks even cuter as his lips curl up into a half smile.

"Thanks. Where are we heading anyway?" I shift in my seat and clasp my hands in my lap.

"I looked up a bunch of restaurants in your neighborhood. There are some cool-looking local spots on Fitzwilliam Street. I thought we could check out this place called Dark Horse. Looks like they have some good stuff. I hate big chain restaurants. Same bland food everywhere you go, you know? You are good for dinner, right?" He's babbling a bit. I've been there before. Maybe he is as uncomfortable as me, but better at hiding it. That gives me some hope.

"I haven't been there, but I've heard Dark Horse is good. They've got some great veggie options too. I totally agree with you. Independent restaurants always have the best food. Fitzwilliam has really changed in the last few years. Used to be kind of a sketchy area of town, now they have lots of great restaurants and some fun shops." Looks like I'm the one babbling now.

"Are you a vegetarian?"

I freeze. Crap, I probably should have mentioned that when he asked me out for dinner. "Umm yeah, I've been doing it for a few years now since…" I trail off, not yet ready to get into the dead dad conversation. It would be a bit of a downer to kick off my first date like ever.

"That's awesome. I've thought about it. I just don't have the strength to give up steak yet. I'm weak. Are your parents cool with the veggie lifestyle?"

"Uh yeah, my mom and I share cooking duties. I actually do a lot of it. She works late often. She's happy to eat a home cooked meal, meat or no meat." I duck away from the dad discussion one more time as we arrive on Fitzwilliam Street, which provides enough of a distraction for Garrett to change the subject.

The traffic crawls along the narrow street. I stare out the window to avoid looking at Garrett. The street is bustling with a surprising number of pedestrians out and about for a weeknight. The little cafes have their front windows shut or pulled down with the cool fall weather. In the summer, they'll all have garage windows pulled up or front windows open to let the warmth and sunshine in. Instead of being decked out with bright flower beds, there are pumpkins, scarecrows, and garlands of crimson and orange leaves draping the lamp posts. The small trees lining the sidewalk are lit up with white twinkle lights, and we can see a colorful array of customers enjoying their meals.

Garrett skillfully maneuvers into a spot quite close to Dark Horse, but I climb out of the car before he makes it around to my side to open the door.

"Do you need any money for the meter?" I dig in my purse.

"Nah, I've got it covered." Ever the gentleman, he pays the meter, then accompanies me past a few storefronts before we reach the restaurant.

I pull a drag of fresh air into my lungs when we reach the hand painted sign with the rearing black horse on it. My attempt to calm the fluttering in my stomach that's been intensifying the closer we get to our destination is a dismal failure.

I glance at the glass-encased menu posted beside the black painted door. I checked it out online when Garrett told me where we were going, so I know I'll be able to get something other than a plate of weird, bitter leaves. Garrett opens the door into the cramped front entrance and I'm thankful for the wave of warmth that chases away the chill. I eye the cozy booths along the side walls. I'd rather sit at those than the big communal table that dominates the middle of the small space. I guess there are some people that might not mind sitting next to a stranger while they're eating, but the thought makes me cringe. It's cool that you can see the chefs with colorful bandanas and white aprons working away beyond the half wall that makes up the back. They're definitely not hiding any health code violations in the immaculate white space.

A hostess with fire engine red hair approaches us. She's wearing a gray fedora, dark glasses, a midriff baring tight black sweater and cut off denim shorts with leopard print suspenders. Glancing around, I can't decide if the restaurant staff are all actual hipsters or if it's an ironic part of the restaurant's vibe, but there's an awful lot of plaid, dark glasses, and fades on the wait staff.

"Table for…?" Is all that we get out of the bored sounding hostess.

"Two please." Garrett's tone is friendly and welcoming, the polar opposite to hers. My eyes slide to her name tag, Harmony.

Harmony grabs some menus and walks away toward the one available booth without another word. I share a smile with Garrett before my gaze darts away.

We settle into the cozy booth with a colorful piece of abstract art on the wall.

"I never understood abstract art. I mean, if anyone can do it, what makes it art?" I squint my eyes at the vibrant splashes of red, yellow, and orange splattered on the large canvas, trying to discover some kind of meaning in the blobs of paint. Maybe also to avoid making eye contact with Garrett.

"I'm with you on that. I've seen pieces hanging in galleries that my younger sister could have painted when she was six and just between you and me, she is not a great artist." Garrett drops his voice to a whisper as if his sister might hear. His face hardens for just a moment. So fast I might have imagined it.

A server slides up to the table. His skinny jeans, bushy beard, and beanie fit right in with my initial impression of the place. At least he's friendlier than Harmony, though.

"Hi, I'm Matt. Can I get you two anything to drink to start?" The wide grin that spreads across the server's face seems incongruent with his hipster look.

"I'd love a coffee, with some milk please," I say.

"Excellent choice. We hand roast our beans here. Today's selection is a blend of beans from Guatemala. And for yourself, sir?" He eyes Garrett with a little more enthusiasm than he did me.

"I'll have some coffee as well please, black." Garrett barely breaks eye contact with me.

My hands are all fluttery and my leg is jumping high speed under the table. I need a minute to pull myself together, so I take my chance and decide to make a break for the washroom.

"I'll be right back." Garrett gives me a smile as I rise from the table.

I weave my way to the inclusive washrooms. The sign has a picture of a person in a dress, one in pants, and a Triceratops. Fine by me, but I seriously doubt that a Triceratops would fit in the tiny cubicle.

A tingle of awareness tickles at the back of my neck, drawing my gaze to the long counter on my right. I freeze, caught in the gaze of a pair of cerulean eyes.

"What are you doing here?!" I hiss at Logan, who is lounging on a red vinyl bar stool, beer in hand.

"Well, I was enjoying this beer until you interrupted me." He drawls with an arch of his brow.

"I can't believe you're still following me. I needed like one day. One day without all the drama."

"Unfortunately for you, that's not going to stop anyone else from tracking you down, and they likely won't share my altruistic intentions. I told you that you need protection, and lucky for me, I got assigned the job. It's not like I asked for it, you know."

"Yes, you've made that abundantly clear. I didn't ask for your protection, either. And I don't need it. I'm on a date and I don't need any of your weird paranormal problems complicating it." The words ring false even to my own ears. I probably do need his protection, but I was hoping to enjoy this one last normal day.

"Go on then, get back to Floppy over there. You're the one talking to me instead of him. That tells me a lot about your interest in your date." He waves his strong, tanned hand at Garrett, whose eyes are locked on us from across the room.

"I will, but his name is Garrett, and this is so not over!"

I march back over to our table.

"Who was that? He looks familiar, wasn't he at the coffee shop yesterday?" Garrett asks. "Is he your ex?"

"Ugh no, he just moved here. He's the one I was talking about making life difficult. It's a weird story, but his family used to know mine. Maybe it's because my brother's away at school, but he's got this stupid idea that he needs to keep an eye out for me. I don't really know him, but he seems to delight in annoying me."

"If you're worried about him, we can leave."

I appreciate the offer, but I'm becoming resigned to the fact that maybe there is something out there I need to be worried about. As long as he doesn't interrupt us, I think I can live with his presence across the room.

"No, it's fine. I don't think he's a threat, just an annoyance. Ignore him. I intend to." I focus on the menu and try to follow my own advice despite the fact that Logan's gaze is burning into the back of my neck, leaving a constant tingle of awareness.

Matt comes back with our coffees, and we place our orders. I settle on the butternut squash risotto with caramelized apples. It sounds like the perfect fall dish for this crisp day, and I don't think it will leave my breath too stinky for date night in case of… Oh my god am I even considering the option of kissing Garrett? Do I want that to happen? My eyes stray behind me to find Logan's beautiful eyes challenging me.

I try to focus on Garrett. He's nice, funny, and we share lots of interests. I can definitely see him as a great friend. As for something more, who knows. My logical brain has never been able to get behind the concept of true love and soul mates. In a world of 7.6 billion people, I just cannot embrace the idea that there's only one person out there that's meant for you and you alone. What about all the people who are widowed and remarry? Is their second marriage a sham? What if your "soul mate" lives on the other side of the planet and you never meet them? Are you doomed to live alone your whole life? Lust, love, and all that jazz are just chemical reactions, anyway.

"This food is delicious. Thanks for the great idea." I flash a quick smile at Garrett.

"Thank Google not me. I did a little search. All the people who have been here before and left a review are the ones who did the legwork."

"Aren't we lucky to have been born now? I mean, even with the trolls and cat memes, it's still pretty amazing. We could be living in the dark ages with no indoor plumbing." My face squinches up in disgust and a laugh spills out of Garrett.

"Definitely, I mean we have all the world's information available at our fingertips if we take the time to sort through the crap, too bad most people don't bother with the sorting part." Garrett says passionately. He truly is a man after my own heart.

The bill arrives and Garrett swipes it up even as I reach for it.

"How much do I owe you?"

"It's on me."

"You don't need to do that." I sort through his actions. I've never really thought about what I expect from a guy. My mouth pulls down at the memory of my dad opening doors for my mom and me. I guess I don't mind the gentlemanly gestures as long as he still respects me as an equal.

"I want to."

"Fine, I'm going to run to the washroom before we head out. Oh, and I'm leaving the tip. Meet you at the door." I slide a couple of bills to the middle of the table before I gather my coat and take the long route to the washroom to avoid Logan.

A few new hipster types occupy the bar when I pass it but thankfully no Logan. That's a relief. At least I think it is.

I wash my hands and take a minute to compose myself. I touch up my lipstick and scrutinize myself in the mirror. The smooth calm on my face hides the anxiety swirling through my body. When my reflection in the mirror doesn't reveal the answers to any of my problems, I take a few deep breaths and count to five before I exit.

Tension emanates from me in waves as I walk to the Dark Horse entrance. I'd be surprised if no one else in the restaurant can feel it. I spot Garrett's beachy hair across the crowded room.

Before I was glad of the warmth, but now the tiny restaurant feels oppressively hot. I join him at the door, where he tentatively takes my hand. He has smooth skin and long, elegant fingers. It feels strange to be holding someone else's hand. I don't think I've done it since I was a kid crossing the street with my parents.

The walk to his car feels far too short. He opens the car door for me, and I climb in, settling my skirt neatly around my legs.

"I hope you had a nice time," he says.

"It was great, thanks so much."

Conversation is sparse on the car ride home. I'm not quite sure what to say to him. This boy seems like he'd be a perfect fit for me, but I'm not feeling the urge to kiss him. Maybe attraction is a thing that grows on you, though. What do I know? I shoot him a guilty look from under my lashes. I don't want to lead him on if he's more into it than I am.

"Will you be at the Regional Qualifiers in Brentwood next week?" he asks.

"Wouldn't miss it and you?" In all the craziness of the last couple of days, I had forgotten the debate qualifiers were coming up so soon.

"Of course."

The silence that settles back around us has a weight to it. It's heavy with anticipation. Of what I don't know, but I think my night of attempted normalcy is over. Tomorrow I'm going to have to face my new reality.

My limbs ease a little at the twin lines of solar lights lining the path to my front door, but a frown pulls my mouth down when the dark takes over at the front porch. It's not like me to forget to leave the front light on. I see my lonely car resting in the driveway. Mom must still be at work.

I turn to face Garrett when the front door creeps up on us sooner than I'd like. He clasps my hands in his and I can see thoughts passing behind his eyes as he considers his options. I glance over his left shoulder and narrow my eyes when I spot a familiar looking dark SUV with tinted windows pulling up to the curb down the street. It's gotta be Logan. I turn back to Garrett and lean into him, closing my eyes. One kiss. Maybe that will jump-start a spark between us.

His soft lips meet mine tentatively at first. His hands settle around my lower back, and he pulls me in a little closer as he deepens the kiss. My mind betrays me, and I imagine it's a pair of stronger arms around me and blue-green eyes gazing into mine. I shake off the disturbing thought and pull away. I definitely should not be thinking of one guy while kissing a different one. What is wrong with me? I fumble with my purse to unlock the front door as my heart sinks to my toes. The kiss was nice but that's it. No racing heart or clammy palms. None of the chemical reactions that lust is supposed to induce.

"Thanks for dinner. I had a great time." I pause in the open door to glance back at him.

"I had a fantastic time. I hope we can do it again. I'll text you tomorrow," Garrett says.

"Night."

I shut the door and lock up behind me before heading upstairs to get ready for bed. I definitely need to decompress with my current book candy before attempting to sleep after that wild roller coaster of a day.

After performing my bedtime ritual and throwing on some fuzzy pink pajama pants featuring rocket ships and a matching tee, I lay down on my bed with my novel.

I toss the book aside with a sigh when I realize I've read the same page five times without absorbing any information. Too many thoughts are fighting for space in my head. I've gone from no plans to date–until, I don't know, after grad school?–to maybe lusting after a hot guy that I don't particularly like while going on a first date with a guy that is quite possibly perfect for me. Beating these other ideas into submission is the overwhelming discovery that magic is real, and I am involved with it. I try to untangle the thoughts one at a time.

Logan's eyes and dark spiky hair slide into my head, and I cannot imagine what is drawing me to him. I've never thought of myself as shallow, not my style at all. He's kind of sullen on the surface and seems to think I'm some sort of annoying job, but I feel like he genuinely wants to protect me. I need to scrub these lustful thoughts out of my brain. Even if it was a good idea to pursue him, he has shown no reciprocal interest whatsoever.

Garrett, on the other hand, makes logical sense as a boyfriend. He's cute, into the same things as me, and also clearly a normal person not involved in this crazy world of magic. Having seen with my own eyes what Logan can do, I can no longer deny the existence of magic, but I don't know what my role is yet. Maybe it's still possible to extricate myself from this world. After all, my magic was blocked for the first seventeen years of my life. Can I find someone to do that for me now? It must be possible. The hope that brightened my mood for a moment shatters when I think of what happened to the woman who bound my magic. They killed her. They murdered her to get to me. It's my fault. I shiver at the chill that slides up my limbs, taking residence in my bones. I can't let that happen to anyone else. I'm going to have to deal with this myself. Or I guess with the help of Logan and Liz. They are after all, the experts on this subject. Just as I've resigned myself to this inevitability, a loud crash yanks me out of my thoughts.

My head whips to the window and a shriek escapes at the sight of a creature peering through the glass. It's bat-like with a triangular fanged face and leathery wings, but are those feathers? I squint at the weird animal. It's larger than the Silver-haired or Big Brown Bats that are common around here. Huge, luminescent eyes stare at me and a shiver runs through my body as it claws at the window.

That is definitely not a local animal. Maybe it's gotten lost or injured along its migratory path. It doesn't look like any bird or bat that I've ever seen, but I'm no wildlife expert. The shock of surprise wears off and my heart slows to its normal steady rhythm, however there is no way I'm getting to sleep with the sound of its nails on the window stabbing me in the temporal lobe.

I'll just go outside and check it out. I can probably scare it off or call animal control to come collect it if it's injured. I grab the emergency flashlight and a broom from the hall closet, throwing on my warm jacket and boots this time. From the front lawn, I peer up at my bedroom window. The creature perches on my windowsill, still clawing at the glass.

When the flashlight beam illuminates it, I can see that it's about the size of a Cocker Spaniel with tufted, owl-like legs and glossy blue-black feathers. Its head swivels all the way around like an owl, and that's where things get weird. Cause, of course they weren't weird enough already. Dark fur covers its face, and its pale green eyes reflect the light of my flashlight. The creature is staring at me like it recognizes me. But that's impossible. I'm clearly losing it.

I jump as it leaps from the windowsill and swoops toward me. I bang the broom against the house to scare it off, but it keeps coming. The claws extended in front of the bat-thing look a lot more vicious than they did from the safety of my room. It's coming straight for me, so I jump to the side. It veers unnaturally fast, landing on my shoulder. Sharp talons bite into my skin. I cry out in shock and pain, and a tingle runs down my arm. A ball of white light shoots from my hand and I jerk my arm back in surprise. The light hits the side of the house. Meanwhile, pain rips my neck as it sinks its fangs in and latches on. I scream and try in vain to swat it away, causing myself more pain as the fangs tear at my tender skin.

A figure tears across the lawn and grabs hold of the beast. Amid a flash of light, it releases my neck and I stumble as it pushes off my shoulder, its huge wings beating the air. Logan chases after the creature and launches a jagged blue streak of lighting after the bat-bird thing. A curse escapes his mouth as it flies off unharmed.

I'm still standing there frozen in place when he lopes back a few minutes later empty-handed with a frustrated growl.

"Let's get you back in your house."

"What was that thing?"

"Now." His tone brooks no argument as he grabs my arm and practically drags me back inside my house.

My knees give out as soon as the door clicks shut, and I collapse to the floor in a shivering heap as the delayed fear slams into me.

"Shit don't...." He trails off before he looks around the room and grabs a blanket off the back of the couch.

The comforting weight of the blanket settles around my shoulders, followed by a pair of solid arms.

"We need to get that sorted. Do you have a first aid kit in here somewhere?"

"Upstairs bathroom…first door on the left, under the sink." I manage to get the words out with a breathless gasp.

He unfolds himself from the floor and disappears upstairs. A bone deep cold seeps in and I hug myself to try to ease the shivering.

When he returns, he takes my hands in his and pulls me up from the floor. He leads me to the couch and settles beside me. Warmth slowly seeps into my body as his leg presses into mine.

I inhale sharply at the vicious sting as he presses a towel to the wound on my neck.

"This is pretty nasty. Usually they leave a cleaner wound. Little punctures, like a vampire."

"Usually? You mean you see a lot of vicious bat-bird bites?" I infuse the comment with sarcasm despite my pain. "Don't tell me vampires are real, too. I don't think I'm ready for that. Wait, was that a vampire in bat form?"

He snorts. "Well, not too many, but I've seen some." He says this in such a matter-of-fact tone I'm taken aback. "And no, no vampires, but these guys are definitely one thing that helped fuel the vampire stories."

I'm kind of relieved at the thought that there are no vampires out there. "Really? Ok, well then what the hell was it? Yeouch!" He's dabbing at my wound with an antiseptic wipe.

"Sorry, trying to be gentle. Let me just finish this up and then we'll talk." He places a gauze pad on my neck and tapes it down. His long fingers brushing my neck send a different shiver through me as he pulls his hand away. "Did you need another blanket?"

"Uh no, it's fine." I duck my head, hoping he doesn't catch the real reason for my shiver. That wouldn't be at all embarrassing. He is being surprisingly nice at the moment, though. His usual angry sarcasm seems to have vanished for the moment at least.

"Why don't I make us some tea and we can talk after. You could probably use a hot drink. I don't want you going into shock."

He leaves me before I can tell him where to find the tea things, so I hear every single cupboard in the kitchen open and shut (along with a few frustrated growls) as he conducts his search.

Exhausted after a couple of restless nights and the traumatic attack, I lay my head on the couch cushion and slip into oblivion. As I'm drifting off, the soothing scent of the deep woods with a hint of lime settles over me and I feel a whisper of a touch on my forehead.

CHAPTER 8
Logan

I set the cup of tea I scrounged together in her kitchen on the table beside the couch where she's passed out. My hand strays toward her face to take her glasses off. Can I do that without waking her up? Probably not. Shouldn't risk it. Her long hair is tangled around her face and small snores escape her lips. An uncomfortable anger pushes up through me at the thought of those lips kissing that tool she went on a date with. I start pacing her living room. I have zero right to that anger. She can kiss whoever she wants. I shouldn't even be thinking of her in that way. My job is to protect her. Keep her safe, like I couldn't do for Ivy.

Ivy's face drifts into my mind. Her straight black bob and deep russet eyes with hints of gold around the pupils. Her name matched her affinity with plants perfectly. She was a Bio Mage and could make anything grow.

We'd grown up together. The magic community was tight where I come from, but she, Trey and I were super close, with Liz constantly tagging along. Younger sisters can't always keep up with their older siblings, but that's no problem when you've got her speed. She could run circles around us and constantly did.

The day things changed is so clear it's like it happened yesterday.

It was Ivy's fifteenth birthday, and we were at a party in my parent's backyard. Everyone always ended up there. Alternately letting the sun bake us and jumping into the pool to cool down. Trey and I were rolling around like idiots fighting over some stupid thing until a wave crashed over us as someone cannonballed into the pool. I pushed him away, spluttering and sending droplets of water over the girls lounging behind us.

"Hey, cut it out, idiots!" Ivy peered over the top of her ridiculous shades, and my eyes met hers. Her slender hand was absently trailing through the grass under her lounge chair and clover was rising up under her touch.

Sophia mutters something and I'm pulled out of my memory to glance over at her. I'm sure she'd have no problem telling us off for acting like fools. She's like Ivy in that way. Speaks her mind. Sophia's face blurs back into Ivy's as I remember the look on her face.

Her heart-shaped face was squished up in annoyance as she glared at me, but the heat in her gaze wasn't anger. There was something else there. Something I had never seen before. I'd seen all kinds of looks on her face. Anger, laughter, teasing, and joy but never that look. That appraising look of attraction.

I had always known she was pretty, but I'd never thought of her in that way. Not until that moment with everything sharper in the bright sunshine.

That was it. We kissed that night and started dating. Trey was, of course pissed, because he had it bad for her too, but she chose me. Bad decision. She should have picked him. Maybe then I never would have had to experience the nightmares of her lifeless body.

I can't do that to Sophia.

My ears twitch at the sound of a car pulling up. Her mom must be home. I've got to get out of here. Somehow, I don't think her mother will appreciate a guy lurking over her daughter's sleeping figure.

CHAPTER 9
Sophia

I wake with a start to a loud bang from the front door slamming. I'm alone on the couch and my mom is hanging up her coat.

"Oh hi honey, I didn't expect to see you up," she says.

I blink blearily. The events of the evening shock away the grogginess. I'm not sure who she'll kill first if she finds Logan here. I scan the room but find no sign of him. He must have left. Thank goodness for both of us. "Long day. I must have fallen asleep on the couch."

Sharp pains shoot through my neck and shoulders as I stand up and look down at my torn and bloody shirt. Probably not the best idea to let Mom see that. It will only freak her out and I'm pretty sure that I'm freaked out enough for both of us at the moment.

I mummify myself in the soft blanket to conceal my wounds and give my mom a quick side hug with my left arm to avoid exposing my bandaged neck. I'm definitely going to have to delve into my turtleneck and/or scarf collection this week, as I do not want to be answering questions about my sketchy neck wound. I have a lot of questions that I need answered though.

I tilt my head and study her. How much does she know already? She was being super evasive about my biological parents. Does she already know the truth? I thought I knew my mother, but I'm not so sure now.

"I really am wiped. I should head up to bed. How was your day?" I ask.

"It was great. I worked late and then met David for dinner. It was really nice. How about you?" Her eyes shine as she says David's name whisper-soft, like it's breakable. This recent development is going to take some getting used to.

"Crazy busy at school and then I went out with a friend for dinner. You'll be home in the morning, right?" I'm so not getting into my date with her despite her advice yesterday. In fact, after the events of this evening, the date feels like a distant memory.

"Yes, I will. We can talk then if you're tired. Love you so much." She pulls me in for a big squeeze and kisses the top of my head. "Night sweetie."

"Night, Mom. Love you too."

I head for the stairs before she can delay me any further. Despite the brief nap, I'm dragging myself up the stairs. Where did Logan disappear to? If it wasn't for the painful bandaged neck wound, I might have thought the whole incident was all in my head.

I flop down on my bed and spot Logan sitting on my floor with his knees pulled up to his chin. An undignified squeak escapes. Luckily, my mom has turned on the TV for a little post-work unwind so she won't come running to defend me from a burglar. Now that I've seen him, I wonder how I could have missed him at all. He seems somehow too large for my room. Taking up more floor space than any one human has a right to.

"What are you doing in here?" I hiss.

"What? Did you want me to nonchalantly stroll out the front door when I heard your mom pull in the driveway? Ok." He pushes up from the floor.

"No, no! Sit back down! How did you even know which room is mine?" A guilty look passes over his face for a flash.

"I've been keeping an eye on you. I told you that. And even if I hadn't, I would have figured it out pretty quickly. I don't think your mom has a stuffed unicorn on her bed." He gestures toward my fluffy pink stuffed unicorn and his mouth quirks up on one side.

"Hey, I've had Mr. Sparkle since I was a kid." I grab him up and give him a cuddle.

"Mr. Sparkle? Really?" He shakes his head.

"Leave him out of this. He lives here. You're the one intruding in my private space."

"I couldn't exactly leave you alone after that. And I diiid promise to tell you about the Ferrebat."

"Ferrebat? What is that?"

"Big black, vicious creature made a snack out of your tender neck. Ring any bells?" He gives me a duh look which I don't appreciate in the least.

"Cut the sarcasm. How on earth would I know what that thing is? I thought it was some sort of creature lost on its migratory path. Now I assume it's some sort of beast that your community might be familiar with?"

"Your community? I think you mean *our* community, sweetie. And you can use the *m* word you know. Magic. You're going to have to say it eventually."

I lift my chin and shoot him my best intimidating glare. "Don't call me sweetie."

He has the grace to look contrite. "Sorry. Anyway, it was definitely on the hunt for you. Ferrebats…they're kind of messengers. They're excellent trackers. Once they've tasted the blood of a person or animal, they can track it across really far distances, so they're often used by bounty hunters and other baddies to help hunt down their targets."

"Umm, so this thing is going to track me now that it's tasted my blood?" I pull my knees up to my chest and hug my legs to still the tremble in my arms that has started up again at this info.

"I think they sent it to find you and now that it's tasted you, it will bring its master back. The big question is, who does it belong to?"

"How did they find me to send that thing in the first place?" I glance at the window. Is someone out there now waiting for Logan to leave?

He pulls at his hair. "I'm only guessing right now, but I suspect Helena let something slip before she died. Maybe just enough to pinpoint your general location. And once you started flashing your magic, they were able to narrow it down. That's why I told you to keep the magic under wraps in public for now. Each type has its own signature. Since your magic is unique, you pretty much leave a beacon out there when you use it. They'd have to be close to detect it though. As for who's looking for you, it could be anyone. There are lots of bounty hunters for hire in the supernatural world and lots of rich fucks who would want you either dead or under their control before you have a chance to develop your powers."

"What exactly are my powers?" I ask.

"As an Archimage you could have abilities from any of the four power groups. The biggest problem is that it's going to take you a while to develop those powers and they may manifest slowly over time, which is something that we don't have on our sides with bounty hunters already after you."

"What if I don't want these powers? Can't I just not develop them? Block them again?"

"While that would make my life easier, I think it's a little late for that. There are artifacts and spells that can block your powers, but that's not going to stop whoever's after you. They already know your name and your location. Unless you plan on entering witness protection, you're out of luck. You don't strike me as the type to run from your problems, anyway." He tilts his head and issues me a challenge with his eyes. "Probably best if you cut off that thing with the mundane boy as well. Don't want to put his precious neck in danger, do you?"

Dread wells up in me at the realization that he's right. Not about telling me who I can date or not, but the rest for sure. And it's not even about me. My mom, my brother, my friends, even Garrett are all in danger thanks to me. I can't hide in the library and pretend I'm safe. I can't hide from reality. I have to embrace this truth and get a handle on my powers, whatever they might be. I have to learn to defend myself and my family. The fear didn't go away. It's still lingering in every trembling limb, but grim determination is settling in alongside it.

"I get it. You still don't get to tell me who to date, though." My glare might fall a little flat, accompanied as it is by my watering eyes, but I need to show him that he doesn't get to control me.

"Ease up, princess. I'm only suggesting it for his sake. I mean, do you really want to put him in the path of your enemies? He's just a regular guy. He can't defend himself."

"Well, neither can I! I'm not some ninja super wizard or anything." He snorts.

"Wizard, really? This isn't a movie."

"Well then, enlighten me. How exactly am I, a high school senior with a gift for debating, going to fight bat monsters and magic-powered bounty hunters? Did you perchance, want me to present them with rational arguments about why they shouldn't hunt/attack/kill me? Cause let me tell you, I don't think that bat creature is going to listen to my logic. I can run, but somehow I don't think that's going to help me if someone's shooting a fireball at my back." Saying this out loud, I realize the enormous stupidity of running out of the house with a broom to scare it away. To be fair, at the time, I had no idea it was a vicious supernatural creature.

"It's a Ferrebat and you're not supposed to defend yourself. At least not at first. That's my job. Liz and I will start training you to fight and to control your powers, and I'm here to protect you in the meantime."

"Well, you can't exactly be with me twenty-four-seven. What happens if something comes to attack me at night in my home?"

"I'll be around for the foreseeable future." My eyebrow lifts at his vague words.

"You can't move into my house. Pretty sure my mom would notice. I mean, she works a lot, but she's a smart lady."

"I sleep in my car on my watch nights. That's where I was when you got attacked earlier, hence the speedy response. And Liz will trade off a few nights. She's a bit younger than me, but she's well trained in both offensive and defensive magic. There are definitely some perks to being a Phys."

"A fizz? Refresh me here."

"A Phys, that's what we call Mages who fall into the Physical Magic spectrum. They can control things to do with their bodies. Some can travel extra fast, have super strength, agility, levitation, teleportation, enhanced senses. Stuff like that." He says this nonchalantly, as if the ability to levitate is so trite, but I guess if that's what you grow up with, then it is your reality.

"So, your sister can fly?"

"No, she can't fly." He rolls his eyes at me like I should have any idea of what's possible. "She's still young and developing her powers. Right now, she has enhanced speed and strength, plus she also has better-than-average hearing. Some of these abilities will get stronger as she reaches maturity, and a few other powers may manifest. Usually, we achieve our full power set and strength by the time we're eighteen or nineteen."

"If she's got all this superhero strength and stuff, why were you sent to protect me and not her?"

"Well, for one, I'm an adult and already finished school. Like I said, I had plans to go travel and meet some Mages in other parts of the world when my plans were rudely interrupted."

"Oh yes, your plans were interrupted by a murder and the apparent death threats directed at me. Plunging me into a world I had no clue about until now. How inconvenient of me to interrupt your travel plans." I inject as much frost into my tone and glare as I can. "Why couldn't they just send someone else?"

"It's complicated." Of course it is. "Our family and a few trusted members of the council are the only ones who know about your existence at all. During the years around your birth, the council was in a bit of upheaval. They'd moved on from the archaic ways of the past, such as killing or imprisoning Archimages at birth and were being led by a much younger and more progressive leadership. However, there were still powerful and wealthy older families who had influence and opposed these views. Your parents feared there were some on the council who would go behind the backs of the others to hunt you down. They only ever told a select few trusted members, plus my family. We've worked for years to keep your secret." His eyes dart away for a moment before landing back on me. "Then there was the bond thing. That's why I lucked out. Trust me, I wouldn't be here if I didn't have to be."

"How flattering. You really know how to make a girl feel good about herself." I know I shouldn't care, but his reluctance to be here still manages to wedge a knife between my ribs.

"Whatever. I'm not here to feed your ego, just keep you alive."

"Awesome, looking forward to spending more time with you. What was that bond thing you skipped by?" His shady attempt to drop that in and his slippery gaze set off my internal radar. The creak of the fourth stair interrupts my inquisition. Logan shoots to his feet with the impressive speed and stealth of a cat. I guess I'll just have to pursue that line of questioning at a later date.

I place a finger on my lips and Logan stumbles as I shove him into my closet. I hear my mom pause at my door and hold my breath until she moves on to her own room. I wait until her door clicks shut and I heart the water running in her bathroom before releasing Logan from the cramped closet.

"Seriously?" He raises one sexy eyebrow at me. I need to quash those thoughts asap. I have never thought of eyebrows as sexy before.

"My mom can't find you in here or you won't need to worry about bounty hunters killing me. She'll do it for them preemptively," I whisper. "You too."

"Okay, I'll head out for the night, then." He swipes my phone off the dresser. "I'll add my contact info, so call right away if anything else sketchy happens."

"Sketchy like a giant bat-bird attacking me? Gotcha. Are you really sleeping in your car outside my house? You know that's super creepy, right?"

"Well, I could sleep in your bed if you'd prefer." His eyes leave a trail of heat as they meander down my body.

"I did mention my mom and the whole murdering us thing, right? Get out of here." I hurry him toward the door.

He veers off and heads for the window instead.

"You can't go out the window. There's nothing to climb!"

"Oh, don't worry princess, I've got a few tricks up my sleeve." He winks at me and slides the window open before folding himself out of it.

I peer out to see him kind of floating down to the ground. My eyes widen and I give my head a shake in disbelief. He gives me a backward wave and jogs off.

I drop back on my bed, exhausted from the fear and pain of the attack. Two days ago, my life was on track. Science was the answer to everything, and I could fix most of my problems with hard facts and hard work. I was well on track to getting my much-needed scholarship. Now I've been flung into this crazy world of magic and learned the truth of my biological parents. Not to mention lusting after a guy who considers me an inconvenience.

As the foggy embrace of sleep is pulling me under, the thought floats by that he never got around to explaining that bond he was talking about.

I search for Logan's SUV in the morning, but it's gone. He must have headed home to change, or perhaps he was joking about sleeping in his car to keep an eye on me. A shiver races down my spine at the thought of being left alone. I scan the trees and bushes surrounding my house, but don't see any sign of anything or anyone lurking in the shadows.

A hot shower eases the chill and soothes my sore muscles, but I wince as the steamy spray pierces my neck wound like sharp needles.

My mom is humming to herself while she stirs batter in a big silver bowl, dumping in a pile of plump blueberries. My mouth waters at the sight. She's in a suspiciously good mood. Usually, I throw some breakfast together for us while she makes coffee. It's been years since she made my favorite blueberry pancakes for us. Maybe even since Dad.

"Good morning, honey. Nice scarf." I let myself sink into her comforting arms for a moment before pulling away. I have to force my hand to stay at my side rather than tug on the scarf concealing the bandage. "What's up with you? Who'd you have dinner with last night?" My mom gives me the single raised eyebrow that always makes all my secrets tumble involuntarily from my mouth. I guess the pancakes are her way of softening me up to move in for the kill.

"A friend?" I say, blushing, while totally aware that is not going to suffice. "Okay, so I went on a date." My eyes scrunch up and my voice raises to a pitch only dogs could hear as I say the word date.

"A date?! That's fantastic, honey. So, you maybe decided my advice the other night was worthwhile? Who with?"

"His name is Garrett. He goes to Sherwood. We went to Dark Horse." I lay out a mere skeleton of the details. Honestly, the rest of the evening seriously overshadowed the date. And I'm feeling a little guilty about that kiss. It was nice, but my heart wasn't in it. And Garrett seems like a nice guy. I shouldn't be dating him while someone else is consuming my thoughts.

"Really honey? You think you can get away with that? I need some details. Where did you meet? What does he look like? Did you have a nice time?"

"We met at the debate on Monday and went out for coffee with Xavier and a couple kids from Sherwood afterward. They teamed us up for the debate. He's tall, hazel eyes, sandy hair. And yes, we had a nice time." I scratch at my arm and avoid eye contact. I've never talked about guys with my mom other than the embarrassing, but obligatory, sex talks I would rather expunge from my brain forever.

"I'm so glad. Are you going to see him again?"

"I don't know. I mean, I like him. He's really nice and smart, but you know school and debate take up so much time."

"That sounds like an excuse. You have to make room in your life for actual living. You're always so serious and focused on your schoolwork. You should go for it." That sounds so weird coming out of my mother's mouth.

"The thing is. Stuff is a bit complicated right now. Getting a scholarship. I really have to prove myself. You know, lots of pressure." I trail off. I'm not ready to go into details about what's actually complicating my life at the moment. My hand strays to the gray patterned scarf I threw on to cover up the evidence of those complications.

"I can only advise you so far, but please remember what I said about your dad. I wouldn't change anything. Love is everything." She gets a misty look in her eyes and fades away into the past for a moment.

"Thanks for the advice, Mom. Gotta run to school now." I give her a quick kiss and duck my head, hoping she doesn't notice me wince at the pain in my shoulder when I swing my backpack up over it.

I can't face the thought of walking with my bag rubbing the wound the whole way, so I decide to take my car to school. The infrequently used car grumbles in protest as I cautiously back out and head for school. Relief fills me when I spot the dark SUV tailing me.

It skids into the spot beside me in the student parking lot as I'm collecting my school stuff from the trunk. The big black SUV invades my space. Logan hops out of the driver's seat and slams the door a little louder than necessary. He leans against the back of his vehicle, one leg crossed in front of the other, eyeing the scarf on my neck.

"You okay?" His tone is a little gruff this morning.

"I'm fine." I fiddle with the strap of my backpack. I don't think I actually am fine with everything that's going on right now, but I don't really want to get into the details.

My buzzing phone provides me with the excuse I need to avoid his searching look. It's a message from Garrett.

Had fun last night. Wanna do it again? Does Saturday work for you?

I pause. Should I? I don't really know how I feel about Garrett, and I really don't know how I feel about dragging him into my mess. I shudder at the memory of the Ferrebat swooping down on me.

"Who's that?" Logan puts his arm on the roof of my car, leaning in a little too close and glancing at my phone. "Floppy? Make sure you say no. Like I said, you do not want to be bringing mundys into your life right now."

"Seriously? You think you can control who I see?" Angry heat climbs the back of my neck. "I will see who I want, when I want."

Defiantly, I text Garrett back.

Saturday works for me. 7?

His reply is immediate.

Perfect. I'll pick you up. Smiley face.

"Whatever, don't blame me when you get him killed." Logan says.

I'm now mentally smacking myself. I already said I wouldn't lead Garrett on. How do I make it clear that I just want to hang as friends? Inspiration strikes.

Mind if I invite Xavier and my friend Charlotte? You can invite Emily too if you want?

That should make it clear, right? This is a just friends thing.

In the meantime, Liz has climbed from the car to join us. "Don't let him get to you. He's just pissed he wasn't there in time to protect you before you got hurt. We should talk at lunch today." Her eyes are soft with concern for me.

"Only if you lose him." I gesture at Logan.

"Of course. Girls only." She laughs.

Liz slings her arm around my waist, and we leave her brother behind. She blows him a kiss over her shoulder as we swagger away. For some reason, it's far easier to forgive Liz for being the bearer of mind-expanding news than her brother. She's easy to like with her quicksilver smile. It's so genuine flowing right up to her beautiful eyes, which unfortunately remind me of her brother's.

The morning passes by quickly despite the now expected presence of Logan in all of my classes. We seem to have formed an uneasy alliance after the incident last night. Under the glaring fluorescent lights of the school, it's hard to believe it ever really happened. If it weren't for the tug of pain whenever I move too quickly, I might think it was just a dream. For me, everything has changed and yet while I'm in this place, it's easy to forget.

True to her word, Liz steals me away at lunch. She leads me to an empty classroom on the second floor with a lovely view of the forest behind the football field. The crisp emerald grass contrasts with the leaves that look like a riot of flames celebrating the fall.

"Are we allowed to be in here? Although you do have better taste than Logan. He dragged me into a literal broom closet." I glance uneasily around the empty classroom. It looks lonely, bereft of desks, chairs, wall charts, and technology, not to mention the chatter of bored students.

"It's fine. I'll hear if anyone is coming. Plus, no one is going to get you in trouble. You're like the star pupil. All the teachers talk about how amazing you are." Liz gives me a wink and pulls me down to the floor, sitting cross-legged across from me.

"That's right, you've got supersonic hearing, don't you? That must be weird."

She shrugs. "It's actually pretty cool now that I have solid control over it. It was harder when I was younger and didn't know how to block certain things out or focus on others. I accidentally eavesdropped on way too many convos between the parental units." Her face squinches up at the memory.

"And what else can you do?" I'm genuinely curious. Liz is so approachable she seems a much better choice to learn from. Logan is too unpredictable. I never know if he's going to be frustrated, bored, or sympathetic.

"I'm super fast, not like the Flash, but the mundanes would def get suspicious if they saw me run at my top speed. They can be pretty good at ignoring things that don't fit into their worldview, but they're not that oblivious. I'm also really strong, quite handy if the bounty hunters catch up with us. And of course, the supersonic hearing, as you called it. I could develop a few more in the next couple of years. We'll see."

"That's pretty cool. I'm still trying to wrap my head around all of this." I still kind of wish this was all a dream I could wake up from at any moment, but I have to face the reality. I need to learn as much as I can from Liz while I have her to myself.

Her eyes soften. "I can't imagine how hard it must be for you. And I know my brother has been acting like a first-class jerk. I'd like to kick his butt for the way he's been acting, but his life just got turned upside down, too. When Helena was murdered, the spell to contain your magic broke, and it invoked the bond on your end. I know it's not an excuse, but he definitely wasn't expecting this so soon and he's dealing with it in his typical dumb boy way by lashing out."

"What bond was invoked?" I play innocent. This must be the bond Logan was talking about. Maybe I can wheedle some answers out of Liz.

"Oh ummm maybe he wants to tell you himself. We should probably get back to class." She's getting all shifty eyed and glancing at the door.

"Not gonna happen! You are staying here and filling me in. Your brother said something about this the other day and then got all shady on me. If this is something that concerns me, isn't it important that I know about it? I feel like I've been kept in the dark my entire life."

"I'll get the full Logan jerk store treatment for at least a month if I tell you. Maybe for the rest of my life. All cold shoulder one minute and stern karate master the next. I can't handle a month of extra training sessions." She pleads dramatically with me.

"I thought moody was just his standard personality. I don't want to be responsible for you getting in trouble, but I need to know Liz. Please. No more secrets." I reach out and place a hand on her knee.

"Okay fine, you're right. It is your life." She leans a little closer. "Start at the beginning, I guess. You know about our parents and how close they were. Well, your parents wanted to be able to keep track of your well-being when you grew older and moved away. Sort of like an insurance policy. Before they sent you away to your new family, they had my mother perform this Guardian spell. She's a powerful Psychic Mage. We couldn't get away with anything growing up, but that's a whole different story."

"What's a Guardian spell?" I ask to pull Liz back on track.

"It's a bonding spell. Lets you kind of keep track of the other person. You can feel their stronger emotions, and even locate them from distances. Since hardly anyone knew their secret, they had limited choices about who to bond you to soooo….” Liz trails off, giving me the side eye.

“LOGAN!” I yell. “I’m bonded to him? How come I never felt him before? Is that why I feel that tingle when he’s around?” Anger flares up hot, but reason soon kicks in. At least this means the feelings I’ve been having for him aren’t real. Right? They’re just a bad side effect of magic. But what else does it mean? A flash of the lustful thoughts I’ve been feeling around him flits through my mind. Did he feel that? Oh god, I can never face him again. Wait, has he been manipulating my emotions or thoughts? Is that possible? Unease slithers down my spine.

“Yes to the first. I’m sorry. I wasn’t even born yet, otherwise maybe it would have been me. As for the second, I expect you didn’t feel it because your magical abilities were suppressed. He’s always felt it. I don’t think it’s a physical thing, though. I think he’s described it more like feeling emotions in his head that aren’t his and kind of a magnetic pull at his mind in the direction you’re in. I don’t know all the details. Logan and I are tight, but I’m still just the little sister and he’s not much of a sharer. I know maybe you don’t want to right now, but you will have to talk to him to get more details about it.”

This is all a bit much to deal with. I jump up.

“I think I need to go process this. It’s a lot to handle right now on top of everything else. Don’t worry, I’m not mad at you. I don’t think I can even look at Logan right now, though. Call me later.” I rush out of the room. Liz doesn’t stop me. I like that she gets my need for some time to freak out alone.

CHAPTER 10
Sophia

I blunder toward the closest exit. I'm dimly aware that I'm skipping class, but I'm too frazzled to care. I burst out the back door into the field where a gym class is playing soccer. I rush past the jocks dominating the field while the nonathletes hang back, chattering and "guarding" the goal. There's even one pair fully sitting down off to the side, arms around each other's shoulders. Mr. Tanaka, the gym teacher, only has eyes for his stars, so he doesn't notice me darting by.

I make it to the groomed turf of the empty football field and plop down on a bleacher. I've never been a sports fan and can't muster up enough school spirit to attend games. Give me a science competition or a spelling bee, though, and I'll be right in the middle of it.

My mind races with the plethora of new information I've acquired, and for the first time, I feel like I need to try some sort of magic of my own. On purpose. This bond thing has really tipped me over the edge. I don't want to be tied to Logan. I definitely don't want to have to rely on him to protect me. That's not who I am. I need to learn to look out for myself. If an Archimage really is so powerful, I shouldn't need the protection of someone else. Right? I just need to learn how to harness this power, whatever it may be. I can protect myself and everyone I care about. My mom's face flickers in my mind. She may or may not have been hiding information from me, but that doesn't change the way I feel about her. If she got hurt because of me, I'd never forgive myself.

Tension is vibrating inside of me craving release. The problem is, I don't even know where to start. Do I need to say words, wave a wand? Nobody has filled me in on those details. Maybe I should have brought Liz along for this adventure. I think back to the times I've seen Logan perform magic. The fire had just appeared on his hand with no incantations or rituals. I guess I just have to use my mind. Yeah right. Easy as that.

I glance around to make sure I'm truly alone before tentatively holding out my right hand. It looks so normal, capable of holding a pen, typing on my keyboard, and texting on my phone. Not creating fire or electricity. I shake off the wonderings and clear my mind. I channel my inner yogi and suck in a deep breath. The air travels through my nose, down my throat and into my lungs, expanding them with life. Opposite process for the exhale. Eventually I reach that empty white room in my mind that I like to be in before tests or competitions. Free from distractions.

Once there, I slowly open my eyes and focus on that hand. I picture a ball of flame sitting on it with red, orange, and yellow flames dancing gently on my palm. Nothing happens. I try again, getting more senses involved this time. I try to feel the heat from the flames, smell the campfire smell that feels like summer at science camp. Sitting around and singing songs, roasting marshmallows, telling ridiculous ghost stories. A jolt shoots through my arm, taking me by surprise. Not the mild tingle I've started associating with magic. It's like a lightning bolt searing down my arm, contracting the muscles and then bursting through my palm.

A basketball sized ball of flame rips from my hand and slams into the metal bleachers in front of me before snuffing out as quickly as it appeared. My mouth gapes open in shock at the scorch mark marring the silver bench in front of me. Crap, what did I do?

I don't know how long I sit there, starting at my hands and shivering, when someone settles down beside me. The tingle at the base of my neck identifies my new companion as Logan. His thigh brushes mine and the heat increases tenfold, which reminds me of how cold the rest of me is. I definitely should have grabbed a coat on my way out.

My elbows rest on my knees while propping up my head. A weight settles on my shoulders, helping ease the chill. I'm enveloped in his distinctive scent of cedar with an interesting hint of lime. The shivers slowly ease up as the warmth from his coat settles in.

We sit like that in silence for a while. It's as if he knows I need some processing time and exactly when I feel capable of human interaction again. Is he reading me somehow? Liz didn't seem to think he could read my thoughts, but she wasn't super clear on the details either.

"Liz told me about your conversation. I figured you were pretty pissed, so I was going to leave you alone for a while, but then I felt a whole whack of magic building up, followed by a black cloud of fear. I didn't know what was going on. I was worried you'd been attacked, so I tracked you down." The concern in his eyes looks genuine, but I'm conflicted. I don't know what his motivations are, and I still don't know if he's capable of manipulating my thoughts.

"No, I just decided to prove that I don't actually have any magic. Epic fail on that point. No turning back now, I guess." I shoot a sideways glance at him to see if he catches the lie. Doesn't look like it, but maybe he has an amazing poker face. I close my eyes and focus on his presence next to me. Maybe I can read him too. A dark cloud of fear. That's all I'm getting. Is that him? Or me? I don't even know at this point.

"I don't think there was ever any chance of that. I understand why you did what you did, but next time you decide to explore your abilities, please come to me or Liz. We can help you learn how to control them. I really don't want you getting hurt on my watch. And like I said before, other Mages can track you by your magic signature." I notice his eyes are constantly scanning the field. "What exactly did you do, anyway? That was a hefty jolt of magic I felt." His words remind me in a rush of embarrassment that he can feel my emotions.

"Remember when we were in the closet, and you showed me that fireball trick?"

"You tried to harness fire? What were you thinking? You could have fried yourself or someone else. What actually happened?" He looks angry again. Good for him. I'm mad too. I'm mad that our parents decided to tie us together with this bond without our permission. I'm mad that I'm just finding out about my heritage now. I'm mad that my life has been turned upside down in such a short period of time. Worst of all, I'm mad at how out of control it all feels. I crave order in my life, not chaos.

I wave guiltily at the scorch mark on the bleacher. "Um well, instead of a nice little fireball, I made this huge basketball sized one. It felt like it was being ripped from my body. Does all magic hurt like that?"

"You actually did it? Shit, I'm impressed. That's a pretty advanced ability. The reason it hurt was because you don't have control of it yet. Your powers are just surfacing. They're stronger than they would be if you developed them younger, and you're pretty special to begin with."

"Awww, you think I'm special?" I try to make a joke about it, but my voice falters and I pull his coat tighter around me.

"That's not what I... Never mind. We need to work with you right away, otherwise your power is going to start escaping at random moments and causing havoc among the mundanes. We've got some pretty strict rules about secrecy."

"Well clearly. I would definitely have found out by now if there were any evidence of you guys...us out there to be found."

"Look, about the bond? Did you want to talk about that?" He's rubbing his leg as his eyes dart around anywhere but at my face. He looks like a new boyfriend who feels obligated to have "the talk".

"Nope, need a few days or maybe lifetimes to sit on that one. How about the rules you were talking about?" I'm freaking out enough about it without putting the words out there in the open. I also need some time to figure out my feelings for him. Is the attraction real? Because it sure hasn't disappeared. Is it because of the bond? How does he feel about me? I don't think I can talk to him about it until I have my head on straight.

"I know you mentioned a council. How does that work? Do you have jails, schools, I dunno magical government?" The questions spill from my lips in a rush. I want to learn as much as I can about the structure and rules of this strange new world. Maybe I'll be better able to cope with the unexpected when I have some more information.

"That's a lot of questions. Umm, The North American Magical Council is the overall ruling body for Mages here. They have their own in Europe, Asia, Australia, and Africa. Then we have local branches. We have prisons equipped to deal with supernatural criminals that regular jails can't hold and a policing body to enforce the rules. There's a lot of info, though. Books about magical history and governance through the years. Boring."

"Any chance I can get my hands on some of those?" The thought of actual books with facts and history where I can do research lights me up with the hope that I might actually be able to get a handle on this.

"Really? Yeah, I can pick some up for you. Our parents have a pretty intense library. Wow, you are really excited about that, aren't you?" He crunches his brow up at me.

"Are you like, reading my thoughts?" Anxiety has turned my stomach into a tangled mess. I'm paranoid about how much of my mind he has access to.

"No. Your whole face sort of got all lit up like a light bulb when you asked about the books. I can't straight up read your mind, Sophia. It doesn't work like that. My mom, on the other hand… Don't let any stray thoughts loose around her."

"Oh. I'm glad. That would be way too weird."

"We are going to have to talk about it, eventually. I know it feels strange for you right now because you're new to all this, but I've been living with it my whole life. And let me tell you, not always a picnic for me either."

I analyze that. Put myself in his shoes. What would it be like? Maybe you'd be having the best day ever. I picture myself winning the regional debate last year. I can feel the eyes of the crowd, the tension waiting for the results, and the exhilaration when my name is announced and my teammates cheer for me. It isn't exactly a sold-out stadium concert, but it was an amazing day for me. Then I imagine what it would feel like if I had someone else's emotions in my head. What if they were sad, lonely, angry? Would that dampen my joy? Pull me down from my high? A trickle of sympathy for Logan sneaks in. Before I just thought he was angry about being pulled away from his travel plans, but in reality, he's been dealing with this bond and its ramifications his whole life while I lived in oblivion.

"I'm sorry," I say.

"Sorry for what?"

"For judging you so harshly. This has affected your whole life, and it's not like you had a choice in it either. I can't imagine what that must have been like." I place my hand on his in a tentative gesture of friendship and solidarity.

His face brightens, and a big smile spreads across his face, crinkling his eyes at the corners. It might be the first genuine smile I've seen on him. And then he opens his mouth, and the solidarity evaporates like spilled water hitting the sidewalk on a sweltering summer day.

"If you wanted to hold my hand, you could have just asked. Didn't need to set the football field on fire." His smile twists with snark, and he raises a suggestive eyebrow at me.

I jerk my hand away. "Oh my god, totally not what I meant! I'm out of here. When you get those books for me, have Liz pass them on." I stand up to storm off, but Logan grabs my hand, causing that infernal heat to creep up my arm.

"I'm sorry. I was just trying to lighten the mood. It was getting a bit heavy. Forgive me?"

"Ok. I may have overreacted a bit. I'm pretty on edge right now." I sigh and reclaim my hand. This boy is going to cause me no end of grief.

"Promise me you won't try any more magic on your own. I don't want you getting hurt."

"I won't, don't worry. I'm not going to risk repeating that disaster in my own house." I gesture at the glaring black mark on the bleacher. I look up at him. "Are you…" I wave in the vague direction of the parking lot, not sure how to word my question. I want to know if he's going to be watching out for me tonight, even though I hate the idea of him having to sleep in his car for me.

He cocks his head. "What?"

He's going to make me say it. "Are you going to be around?" I hate that I have to rely on him for protection, but until I get my own powers under control, I think I'm going to have to learn to lean on him.

"Of course. I wouldn't leave you on your own. I have a few things to do at home, but I'll be swinging by your place to keep watch soon. You should be fine to drive home. Nobody is going to attack you in broad daylight in your car. Don't leave your house after you get home, though. Please."

"I won't. See you tomorrow?"

"Yes. I can drive you to school if you'd like."

"Sounds good."

I leave him sitting on the bleachers. At this point, I've missed most of the day, so I decide to head home early. Maybe

I'll ask Charlotte to come over after school. It feels like the only way to survive is to somehow keep my old life running smoothly in between learning about the new one.

I know she's in class, but I send her a text for when she gets out.

Had an appointment and missed my afternoon classes. Want to come by for a study session after school since you missed Monday?

It's amazing how easy it is to lie to one of my oldest friends, but there's no way I can tell her the truth of why I've missed class. She's probably already in danger from our friendship. I don't want to make it worse by spilling magical secrets. I should probably find out the consequences of telling non-magical people about us.

My car purrs to life, and I decide to take a drive before I head home. That's okay, right? Logan said I would be safe in my car in the daylight. Driving around the country roads helps me clear my head, which is something I'm badly in need of right now. The endless stretches of green and gold dotted with grazing horses and cows are soothing. Plus, there's the bonus of very few other cars on the road to stress me out. It's not really the driving so much that bothers me as the traffic. Other drivers are unpredictable.

I pass through the city streets first. Tree-lined roads divide a mix of small, older homes with peeling paint and missing shingles mingling with the shiny new monster houses that are springing up to replace them. I don't understand why people want to cram the largest house they can onto a plot of land until they're a foot away from their neighbors. There's something to be said for a little breathing room and a nice yard to enjoy in the summer.

I think of all the fun times we had in my yard this past summer. Hanging around the pool laughing and talking with my friends. Summer is the only time I ease up even a little of the constant pressure I put on myself to succeed. I don't even know now if my life plan is feasible anymore. Will I be able to go to a regular university without putting my classmates in danger? I don't want to involve more people in my problems. I'm already worried enough about my mom and my friends here. It's the first time I've been relieved that my brother chose a university on the other side of the country. Normally, I'm not a pessimist, but things are looking pretty uncertain at the moment.

I pass my favorite farm. It has a beautiful black iron gate guarding its entrance with a keypad to gain access to the privileged world beyond. A long driveway is graced with maple trees decked out in bright colors like ladies at a masquerade ball. There's a fountain at the top of the drive circled by clean white barns. Sometimes horses peek their curious heads out to study the passersby, but today they're out grazing the fields wearing multi-hued blankets to ward off the chill. I always wanted to take riding lessons as a kid, but it never happened when I was younger and then after dad died my mom got rather overprotective about dangerous activities.

The peaceful drive takes me back to a similar one, years ago. I had to have been about ten years old. I was in the passenger seat of my dad's old white Buick. He loved that car. It was older than me, but he refused to get rid of it. "Why would I get rid of a perfectly good car? It runs fine." He'd say this right before spending hundreds of dollars on whatever fix it currently needed. He was generally a practical man, but he certainly had his moments of illogical nostalgia. I can remember the leather and pine smell of that car and the way I would sink into the seats. This was a special day, just me and my dad. My brother must have been at a soccer game or at a friend's house.

We drove by red barns with white trim, long lines of wood plank fences and content horses and cows munching away. I ogled the horses as I always did. There was just something so graceful and mysterious about them. I longed to get out and lean over the fence to see if I could tempt them over with grass. Almost as if Dad could read my mind, he pulled over to the side of the road and climbed out, coming around to my side to release me into the wild as well. I rushed to the nearby white fence and climbed onto the bottom board hanging over the top rail with a handful of grass.

"So Pumpkin, what are you going to be when you grow up?" Dad asked.

This was a favorite game of both of ours. I changed my answer without fail every time. Sometimes my answer would be completely out there and sometimes it would have a grain of truth.

"Hmmm. I think I'll be one of the first astronauts to step on Mars."

"A noble goal. And how are you going to make that happen?"

That was always his follow up question. Impossible dreams weren't a problem for him. You just had to have a plan to realize them. I guess that's where I got my penchant for goal making and life planning from.

"I could go to school and become an engineer. They'll definitely need engineers on Mars. And of course, pilot training. I'll need to be able to fly the shuttle, obviously."

"Definitely. Engineering skills will be essential. That's a brilliant plan."

The memory fades away. That was my dad, constantly encouraging us to pursue our dreams. He always took us seriously and then encouraged us to think about how we would achieve our dreams. When I was younger, I wanted to be a ballerina, police officer, author, astronaut, paleontologist, and many more things. It was only after his death that I decided to follow in his footsteps and attend medical school. He always said that we should be open to new opportunities because we never knew where they might lead us. The unexpected might be the place we were meant to be all along. I loved that about him.

After aimlessly driving for a while, I find my car heading in the direction of Ridgewood without ever consciously making the decision to go there. Once the little shops of Main Street creep up on me, I drive until I get to Arabica Nights. I glance at my watch and realize that school will be out by now, so before I can change my mind, I text Garrett.

In the neighborhood. Want to join me for a coffee?

Sure. His reply comes back.

I'm at 1001 Arabica Nights.

I can be there in 15. Can't wait.

A flash of guilt hits me when I think of my promise to Logan. Technically, I did say I wouldn't leave my house after I got home, right? I'm not really breaking my promise. And no one is going to attack me in a public place like this. I'm not even sure why I ended up here. I think I'm still clinging to Garrett as a tie to normal life. Plus, he doesn't know me, so he's not likely to figure out there's something going on with me. Charlotte or Xavier would totally dig around trying to figure out what's wrong.

There are a few tables occupied with a mix of harried university students in casual clothes with tired eyes and messy hair, and businesspeople in sharp suits and professional skirts. The high school crowd hasn't arrived yet to order their sugary blended concoctions.

I take advantage of the relative quiet to order myself a drink and a sandwich. I realize that I never ate lunch due to my girls' club meeting with Liz. The barista behind the counter today is blonde and excessively bubbly. Being mostly an introvert myself, I'm somewhat suspicious of people of the overly bubbly nature.

I thread my way through the tables and settle in the same cozy spot we enjoyed last time we were here. That's when the nerves set in. Why did I come here? I sit with a jittering knee and mind full of thoughts.

Garrett walks in and strides over to me with a smile rising up his face like the sun in the sky. People talk about lighting up a room, but I never knew what that meant until I met him.

"Hi Sophia, it was such a nice surprise hearing from you." He brushes his floppy hair back off his forehead as he greets me.

"Hi Garrett. I just had a bit of a day and wanted to see you." The words come out even as I question the intelligence of coming here. Am I just clinging to him as a way to hang on to my humanity? I'm not even sure anymore.

It's not like I can tell Garrett what's got me so messed up. 'So, here's the thing, I got attacked by a Ferrebat after our date, found out I'm being hunted by magical murderers and have a weird bond to another guy, oh and I literally shot an out-of-control fireball from my hand.' Yeah, that's not happening. I think I've been deluding myself into thinking that if I have a normal conversation with a normal person, maybe my life will make sense again.

"Can I order you something?" he asks.

"No thanks, I already ordered. Sorry, I should have waited for you, but I didn't have time for lunch, so I was starving."

"It's fine. Too engrossed in your schoolwork to take the time for a lunch break?"

I pause for a few long seconds before answering as I remember the conversation that stole my lunch hour. "Yeah."

"Well, you won't be sorry about the sandwich. They bake their own bread. Delicious. I might even grab one myself even though I didn't skip a meal. Unless you feel like dessert. We could share something? The PB & J Chocolate Cake is amazing."

My mouth waters at the thought of that, but I hesitate, thinking about the implications of sharing a dessert.

"Sure, I'll share with you." I rush the words out before I can change my mind. He brightens.

"Well, I'll probably be a few minutes." The line has stacked up while we were chatting as high school kids stop in for some caffeine and socialization after being trapped behind desks all day.

Before he heads to the counter, Garrett leans down and brushes his lips softly against my cheek. I close my eyes and imagine the past few days never happened. I think about introducing Garrett to my friends. Hanging out with him on weekends. Studying together. A regular but still extraordinary life flashes before my eyes, and then I open them up to my new reality. I sigh, tucking that alternate future away and decide that I'm going to have to let Garrett down easy today.

My sandwich and Hazelnut Americano arrive just before Garrett does, but my appetite has vanished with my dreams. I take a sip of my drink, inhaling the therapeutic aromas of hazelnut and coffee and stare glumly at the sandwich.

"Aren't you going to eat that?" Garrett asks as he slides onto the couch next to me.

"I'm not so hungry anymore. Did you want some?"

"I'm good, but thanks anyway. You can get it wrapped up before we go. Did you want to talk about your day?"

"Not so much. Why don't you tell me something? A story or something funny that's happened to you recently." I know I'm only putting off the inevitable.

"Funny, I've got funny." Garrett says before launching into a story about how he went out for dinner with some friends a couple of weeks ago, only to be abandoned by their waitress. It turned out she was making out with her boyfriend in the next booth. I laugh until tears leak from my eyes as he recounts the incident in graphic detail.

"Well, thank you for that. Definitely took my mind off things." I wipe tears from my eyes.

We chat for a little while longer while we enjoy our coffees and I even manage a few bites of the cake. It's amazing. The perfect ratio of moist chocolate cake to smooth creamy peanut butter and tangy raspberry jam. Whoever made this should definitely be inducted into a baking hall of fame if there's such a thing.

When we finish, I glance at my watch and then at the sky outside. I need to get home before it gets dark.

"I should definitely head out." Dread has been slowly building, leaving a pit in my stomach at the thought of my task. It's necessary, but that doesn't make it any easier to do.

I pretend to not notice his offered arm and march ahead of him into the chill evening. The street is strangely empty.

I'm all keyed up during the walk to my car. I can't stop thinking about what I'm going to say. How can I explain that my world has taken such a sudden turn and there isn't room for romance in it? Not with someone who has no chance of defending himself.

When we arrive at my parked car, he leans toward me. I put my hand on his solid chest.

"Wait, I just need to talk to you about something."

Before Garrett can reply, a huge arm grabs me roughly by the shoulder. Suddenly I feel like I've been picked up by a tornado whirling frantically as I'm battered about in darkness, and then the world goes black.

CHAPTER 11
Sophia

My body aches all over as if I've been hurled about by a storm, and my brain is fuzzy. I can't move my legs or arms. I peel my eyes open to assess the situation. I'm definitely not on Main St. anymore.

Something is chafing my wrists and my arms ache from being twisted behind my back. My legs are equally stiff, and I seem to be tied to an uncomfortable wooden chair that presses into my back.

I squint around to see that the room I'm in is large and lit by a few dim bulbs. No fancy light fixtures for this concrete hole I've been dumped in. It looks like some sort of warehouse or industrial space, judging by the high ceilings and lack of furniture. The smells of dust, mold, and some sort of pungent animal infestation assault my nose. I shudder at the thought of rats. They carry so many diseases. Then I realize that rats are the least of my worries and the cold fingers of panic creep up my spine.

I've been kidnapped. I don't think they took Garrett. I hope not. I'm sure he's called the police. At least there's that. But then, what can they do about a magical attack? I've been taken by supernatural means. That smoke cloud that concealed us was definitely not natural. How long was I unconscious for?

A loud creak announces the arrival of a pair of hulking figures. They stroll toward me as if they have all the time in the world to cause me pain. I cringe back against the chair and yank at my bonds. This does nothing but cause a sharp pain as the ropes dig in deeper.

"She's awake. Time for some fun," says the one on the left in a deep, growl. He looks like a pro wrestler. Grotesquely muscled arms, not enough neck, and blond hair shaved into a short buzz. The one on the left is still well-muscled but more of a regular working guy kind of muscle. He's also tall, with a few days' worth of dark beard growth and a sharp look in his eyes.

"Now, now. You know we're not allowed to play with the merchandise. Otherwise, no payday." He chastises the jacked one.

Muscles just grunts in disgust and gives me a look that sends my heart racing once again while my palms get all cold and clammy.

"Where am I?" I ask in as forceful a tone as I can muster. It comes out closer to a whisper than the demand I was trying for.

"A better question would be, where are we taking you?" Scruff laughs in a creepy clown-serial-killer kind of way.

"Well then, where are you taking me?"

"Never you mind," he replies, before turning back to Muscles. "The rendezvous time isn't until tomorrow morning. I would kind of like to enjoy myself a little before we hit the road for the drop spot. I saw a few juicy looking morsels when we were casing the town earlier."

I have a sick feeling that he isn't talking about food.

"Can we just leave her like that?" asks Muscles.

"Well, she's tied up, and we were told she can't control her magic yet, so I think we're safe. Unless you're scared of little girls. And don't worry, we'll make sure to knock her out before we go." The trembling kicks up a notch. If they knock me out, I won't have a chance to escape.

Rage bursts upon me hard and fast, heat flooding my chest. It feels like more than I'm capable of producing myself. It doesn't match the blind panic I was feeling a moment ago. Could that be Logan? If only I could control my magic. Previous experience indicates that I might set myself on fire if I try anything. If I can't fight, then maybe flight it is? Is there any way I can escape from this place?

"Excuse me," I say in a voice as soft and pitiful as I can muster. The weaker they think I am, the better. "Could I use the bathroom before you go?"

"Fine, take her. I don't want her in my car if she's pissed herself. Remember, we've been warned, though. No touching." Scruff waves at Muscles to handle it. Muscles looks peeved at the direction but still obeys.

He unties my legs, pulling me up with a rough tug that throws me off balance with my arms still tied behind my back. He grabs me by the elbow and drags me down a long hallway with several doors branching off on both sides. I walk as slowly as I can with him tugging me along while my eyes dart around searching for an exit. All I can see is aging concrete, old broken wooden pallets, dust, and cobwebs. I guess I'll have to take my chances that I can hide from them long enough to find an exit. If I can get away.

Muscles stops in front of one of the doors and shoves me in. I stumble into the dim room. A small window high on the wall lets in some light from the outside world. It is definitely still night, and the artificial quality has the look of streetlights. At least it appears like I haven't been unconscious for too long. The height of the window makes me think I'm probably in the building's basement, which isn't great news. There's no way I can climb up and get through that tiny space, even if it does open. And if I do manage to get away, I have to find and make it up a set of stairs before they catch up to me. I search my mind for the moves I learned in the self-defense classes Mom and I took at the community center. Groin, foot stomp, knee to the nose. That's the one that's always stuck out in my mind.

"Hurry it up in there! I haven't got all night. If you're not out in thirty seconds, I'm coming in."

That would ruin the element of surprise, so I brace myself and swing open the door as quickly as I can. I burst out to the right where Muscles has been waiting impatiently and knee him in the groin as hard as I can. While he's bent over in pain, I whip my knee up into his nose. He howls in pain and rage as he flies backward, crashing into the wall. My mouth drops open in shock at how far he flew, but I shake off the surprise and make a break for it. The tingling buzz of magic sparks through my veins.

My heart is pounding faster than my legs are pumping as I make tracks down the long hall, moving awkwardly with my hands tied behind my back. A loud crack rends the air as I trip turning over my ankle. My stomach drops and my ears ring from the pain, but I force myself to keep moving. When I turn around to open the door, I spot Muscles pulling himself up with a murderous glare in his eyes. I make it out, breathing hard and find myself in a stairwell. Bingo. I push as hard as I can to get up those stairs and limp through the door on the first landing I come to. I hear the pounding of heavy feet on the stairs in close pursuit.

I'm in another large, empty room with generic doors branching off on either side and no obvious exit. I'm going to have to pick a door and hope I don't trap myself. I take a chance and dart through the middle door to the left. I've heard the general consensus is that people tend to turn to the right. I can only hope that my kidnappers go with this instinct.

My heart sinks at the empty stretch of walls devoid of any windows or another door. At least there's a cluster of broken shelves and piled boxes at the back of the room. I can temporarily hide here.

I wedge myself underneath a fallen shelf, gagging at the smell of moist rotten wood. I take deep breaths in an attempt to slow my breathing, but I'm hit with another blast of rage and panic. The foreign feelings mingle with my own fear and pain to overwhelm my mind. The throbbing in my ankle brings tears to my eyes.

A loud bang vibrates through my eardrums, and shouts of rage ring through the deserted walls. Scruff must have found out, and they're both hunting for me now. Great. I cower in my hiding spot, trying to think of any next move that will get me out of this. I wish I was more into chess. Maybe some strategic thinking would help me out in this situation.

A magnetic pull in the center of my being tugs at me, and the feelings that don't belong to me intensify. Is it Logan? I hope so. It sounds like a stampede of wild horses is charging through the building. The crashes, bangs, and explosions are so loud it feels like the old building might come crumbling down around me.

I need to get out of here, right now. Debris rains down on me when I shove the shelf away. I scrabble out of the corner I've jammed myself into and roll over to scramble up from the floor without the use of my hands. Fire shoots up my leg at every step on my injured ankle. I make it to the door and press my ear against it. The room next door has grown quiet, and I can only hope that the winner of the battle is on my side.

"Sophia?" Desperation tinges Logan's familiar voice.

My head feels light, and I lose the feeling in my legs as relief crashes over me. I throw my shoulder into the door to swing it open. Logan stands there in a fighting stance with a sword casually hanging by his side. A sword? I thought his hands were a weapon on their own. Why does he need a sword? Like he's not bad ass enough without it. His black hair is pointing in all directions and there's blood trickling from a wound on his forehead. My kidnappers are down. Muscles is slumped against the right wall his head dropped onto his chest. Scruff is lying directly in front of Logan, as if just vanquished. I have a very uncharacteristic urge to kick them.

Instead, I crumple to the floor, my ankle finally giving out. Logan closes the distance between us in a few strides. I wince as he lifts his sword, but he's very careful as he slices through the ropes that still bind my hands behind my back. My arms are numb and stiff from being trapped for so long. He drops to the ground next to me, his sword clattering to the floor, and pulls me into his lap, holding me tightly in his arms and brushing his lips against my forehead. I throw my arms around him and squeeze, finally feeling safe.

The trembling eases, and a wave of relief flows over me.

"I thought I'd lost you." His voice is thick with gravel.

He tilts my chin up to look me in the eye. Too many emotions are fighting for space in my head. Our faces are inches apart and all the heat that's been building since the first moment I stumbled into him outside the coffee shop reaches a peak. I lean in, pressing my lips to his. It's a gentle touch at first, then he deepens the kiss. His hands rub up and down my back as if to reassure himself that I'm really there. Heat flows back and forth between us in a constant flow, and the dual sense of passion is intense. Until he jerks away, shaking his head at me.

"I'm sorry Sophia. I shouldn't have done that. I'm not even sure what possessed me. I lost control after the panic of losing you."

I give him a puzzled look. I'm the one who kissed him. Did he not like it? Humiliation washes over me, adding to the fear, pain, and anger. This should be the least of my concerns at the moment.

"What are you talking about? I kissed you."

"But I shouldn't have returned it. You were terrified and traumatized. You just got kidnapped."

"That doesn't mean I didn't want to do it." His words aren't really clearing anything up. He may be right, though. I don't think I would have initiated that kiss under normal circumstances. It was the desperation and relief and fear that drove me to it.

"Okay. We should talk about it, but maybe we can do it somewhere less awful." His lip curls up as he glances around at the dimly lit warehouse. "We need to get home and clean up, get some rest. Plus, they're waiting for us," he says.

"Who?"

"Liz and…Garrett. They're in the car."

"Garrett? What's he doing here? Why didn't Liz help you with those guys? Are we just leaving them there? They're not dead, are they?" The questions tumble over each other on the way out of my mouth.

"We called in some help. They'll take care of these assholes. They're not dead. They'll question them and lock them up in a secure facility. As for the rest of your questions, I'd like to get you out of here and safe before we tell you the whole story."

"What about my mom? She must be so worried! She's probably called the police by now. What time is it?" I fret, picturing my mom wondering where I am. She isn't always around, but I know how much she truly loves me.

"It's 11 o'clock. Don't worry about her. We took care of it. Liz had my mom call her. She told her you were staying over at our house for a marathon study session."

"Oh, that's good. She was ok with that? Not even hearing from me herself? She doesn't even know you guys, or your parents, for that matter." I'm confused at this easy acceptance from my mother, who has never let me stay over at a friend's house without first interrogating their parents.

"Our mom, wellll, she's got above average powers of persuasion, you might say." Logan looks mildly sheepish at this.

"Did she meddle with my mom's mind?"

"Just a little mild persuasion, like I said. We couldn't have the mundane cops getting all up in our business. Got to keep the secret, you know."

"I get it and I'm glad she's not worried, but it's not going to mess with her head, or anything, is it?"

"No, of course not. My mom wouldn't do anything to hurt her." Logan stands up and reaches a hand down to help me up. "C'mon, let's get out of here."

I inhale sharply, crying out when I put weight on my left foot.

"What happened?" Logan glances at Scruff with a dark rage in his eyes, as if he's contemplating breaking his ankle in return if he's hurt mine.

"I turned over on it while I was running away. Probably just a sprain."

"Could be, but we should err on the side of caution in case you broke something."

Without a moment's warning, Logan whisks me up in his arms.

"I can walk." My protest sounds weak even to my own ears. My whole body is still shaking and I'm cold all over.

"I'm sure you can, but it will be slow and painful, and we don't want to cause any more damage if we can avoid it. Also, I don't know about you, but the sooner we're out of this hellhole, the better."

I can't argue with that, so I place my arms around his shoulders and drop my head on his chest. The tension in my muscles eases up a little more with every step we take out of the creepy old building.

Liz and Garrett spill out of the car and rush us as soon as we're in sight. I release my hold on Logan guiltily at the sight of Garrett's concerned expression.

"Easy," Logan says. "She's fine. Hurt her ankle. Let me just get her in the car before you get all up in her grill."

"I can talk for myself." I might be exhausted, hurt, and in a situation totally beyond my understanding, but I'm still my own person.

"I'm well aware of that." Logan gives me his classic eye roll that's starting to grow on me.

He settles me in the passenger seat. Liz and Garrett climb in the back.

"Are you hurt? What did they do to you?" The first questions come from Garrett. It's weird seeing him here in the car with Logan and Liz. It's like they come from different planets that should never collide.

"I'm ok. Exhausted. After he took me, I felt like he zapped me. Then I lost consciousness. Other than tying me up and being a little rough with me, they did nothing else to me physically. I twisted over on my ankle while I was running away from them. I'm exhausted though." A huge yawn escapes me.

I let my eyes slip shut and lean my head against the car door, falling asleep for the rest of the car ride home.

I wake up with a startled gasp as the car slides to a stop. I panic, thinking I'm still back in the warehouse. Someone reaches out to me, and I slap at them.

"It's okay Sophia, it's just me." Logan says in the softest tone I've heard out of his mouth.

I stop slapping and my shoulders droop in relaxation.

As I finally blink myself awake, Logan comes around to my side of the car and I realize we're in an unfamiliar driveway.

"Where are we? I want to go home." My voice rises anxiously.

"We're at our house," Logan says, gesturing to Liz and himself. "We can't take you home, remember your mom thinks that you're staying with us tonight. Plus, you want to hear the story and we want to make sure you're protected."

"Ok," I say in a small voice.

Logan helps me out of the car letting me lean heavily on him to limp the brief distance to the door. It's too dark to catch any details, but it looks like a typical two-story suburban house in a typical neighborhood. Like, pretty much the opposite of the pair of them. Garrett looks out of place too as he trails after us toward the Armstrong's house.

"Where is it?" I need some grasp of the situation and at least a location is something. Too much of my life has flown wildly out of my control over the last few days. I need to at least know where I'm staying the night.

"London St, just a couple of blocks from your house," Liz answers.

At least it's close enough to home that I can walk it if need be. Not that I'll be walking anywhere alone any time soon. I shiver.

"Are you cold?" Logan asks. I blink at the sudden onslaught of light as he helps me through the door. My eyes protest the brightness after being stuck in that warehouse for the last several hours.

I take in my surroundings, trying to ground myself as we slowly make our way through. It looks comfortable but more like what you'd see in the house of a bunch of college students than in a family home. Assorted random furniture of the well-loved variety. None of it matches and there isn't quite enough to fill up the space.

Logan settles me on an overstuffed tan couch that consumes a large part of the room. It has a friendly quality with its puffiness and soft suede-like fabric. My battered body is grateful for the comfort. He sits beside me, a little too close for friendliness, and I shoot a covert glance at Garrett from under my eyelids. He just looks shell-shocked. Why was he still even here? Not that I'm trying to be a jerk or anything, but preppy Garrett doesn't seem to fit in with the magical bad asses.

Liz passes me a soft cranberry blanket, and I pull it in tight, craving the comfort it offers.

"I'll grab you an ice pack for your ankle," she says, trotting off in what I assume is the direction of the kitchen.

"How did you wind up here, Garrett? I think I probably need your side of the story," I ask.

"I wanted to make sure you were ok. I can take you home if you don't want to stay here. No one can force you to." He shoots daggers of resentment at Logan. I can't blame him. Hours ago, we were out together and now Logan is sitting so close to me we're almost melding into one person. I should push him away, but I just don't have the strength right now.

"I should stay. I don't want to freak out my mom in the middle of the night. What time is it, anyway?"

"Midnight," replies Garrett.

Wow, it's only been six and a half hours since we left the coffee shop. I realize I never even got the chance to tell him we can't see each other. Not romantically, anyway. Probably not even as friends the way my life is going right now. My gaze shifts from him to Logan, and I squirm a bit. I just kissed Logan. And now the two of them are in the same room.

"He's just going to stay here the night as well. He left his car in Ridgewood, and after he saw you vanish into thin air, we had to bring him along. I filled him in on the truth. Technically, we're not supposed to tell mundanes, but there wasn't any way to cover that one up," Liz says.

"Wait what? You told Garrett about the magic stuff?" I stare him down. He doesn't look like his world has just been blown apart. How is he acting so calm right now? And he just believes them? Two strangers he's never met before.

"Yeah, they did. I mean, you and that guy just disappeared. I thought I was going crazy, and then she came roaring up like the hounds of hell were after her. The way she was moving…it wasn't normal."

I stare at him, openmouthed. It took me a while to accept this whole thing. I'm not sure what they did to convince him so quickly, but it must have been intense. Maybe he's still in some sort of shock about it, though, and he'll freak out later when he's alone.

"And how did you guys find me?" I turn my attention to the siblings.

"Liz was already there in Ridgewood. She had to wait for me to get there to track you to the warehouse. I sent her to follow you home after school, since I had some things to look after."

"I was hanging around outside pretending to window shop rather than broodily staring at you in the coffee shop like he would have done." She tosses a thumb at her brother. Her face falls. "I should have been there, though. I might have been able to stop him. I was too far away when he grabbed you. I couldn't get to you in time. I'm so sorry. I should have been there."

"It's okay Liz. He teleported her. There's no way you could have gotten there in time. She called me, and I broke every speed limit to get there. Luckily, that guy didn't take you farther than the bond could track you. It took us too long, though." His face twists in anguish as he pulls at his hair. "Liz had to stop Garrett from calling the police. She had to swipe his phone. He was in complete shock, freaking out that you vanished. I dragged him to my car to keep him from going to the police or telling anyone else." I'm glad I'm not the recipient of the angry glare Logan turns on Garrett. He's being pretty unfair, though. Of course Garrett was freaking out.

"How did you find me? Who were they?" I'm still exhausted but my car nap gave me enough juice to get through the explanation and there's no way I can sleep until I have some answers.

"I used the connection between us. It's more precise the closer we are, so at first it was a vague pull in your direction. It's not like I have a Sophia GPS in my head. I mean kinda, but I don't get exact directions."

It's the first time I've felt thankful for the bond. If not for it, who knows where I'd be right now? I think back to the corner I had trapped myself in and can almost feel the weight of the shelf pressing down on me as I breathe in musty air. My breath speeds up and another chill spreads through me.

Logan glances over and rubs his hands up and down my numb limbs. "It's okay, you're safe now."

I nod at him and try to slow my breathing to match his.

"We drove for about an hour before the pull got strong enough to pinpoint the abandoned warehouse. When we got there, I told Liz to stay in the car with Garrett."

"I totally would have busted into the place if he hadn't been back quickly enough," Liz interjects.

"As if I'd need your help to manage those two morons."

"Are you ok? Did you get hurt badly in the fight?" I ask, my hand involuntarily rising to softly brush the skin beside the slice on Logan's forehead. At least it's stopped bleeding. It can't be that deep.

"I'm fine." He brushes off my concern but not my hand. "Usual bumps and bruises, but those losers were no match for me."

"Why exactly do you have a sword, anyway? Can't you just shoot fireballs at them and be done with it?" I'm genuinely curious about this point.

"If we're going to be at all involved with taking down the baddies, we have to train physically and learn weapons as well. Our magic is like any other ability. You can tire and drain yourself, so you have to be able to fight in the more traditional way. Usually, we try to either end a fight quickly by magic or fight physically and conserve the magic for key blows. Depends on who you're fighting. Regardless, you have to know how to fight both ways. Liz and I have been training our whole lives. Kind of the family business."

I file that info away for later. Good to know our magic is not an infinite resource. No wonder I was so exhausted after the fireball incident.

He gives me a speculative look. "And how exactly did you escape from them?"

"Oh, I fought dirty. No regrets. I asked them to take me to the bathroom and then I kneed Muscles in the groin, tromped on his foot, and then bashed his nose in. Then I ran. Unfortunately, I cornered myself. Then I just hid. I'm certainly no ninja master. That's my one move from self-defense class. I think the only reason it worked was that he wasn't expecting it at all. Plus, I'm pretty sure my knee-to-the-groin move had a little extra magical boost."

"Muscles?" Garrett quirks a brow at me.

"He was one of the bad guys. Muscles and Scruff. That's what I called them in my head."

Logan laughs and gives me an approving look. "You have some fight in you. I like it. That's hot."

Heat floods my body. He thinks I'm hot. I shift my glance, wincing at the murderous look on Garrett's face.

"You'll fit right in. Also, don't be such a pig." Liz gives me a high five and then wrinkles her nose in disgust at her brother.

"Uh no, I won't. I want nothing to do with whatever it is you guys do. I want to learn more about my magic to defend myself and my family, but I definitely do not want to make a career of it. I have NEVER been in a physical fight in my life. Even when Christina goaded me nonstop in grade nine and then threw a soccer ball at my head. Words, not fists. That's my superpower." I shake my head at them emphatically. I'm trying not to think about how comfortable the fiery ball of rage that twisted my stomach when I was fighting for my freedom felt.

"And those guys, they're just low level hired thugs. No one important. It's a good thing too. If they had more juice, they might have been able to take you somewhere too far away for me to track. Teleportation is actually pretty rare. I'm surprised one of those idiots could do it. It's a good thing I caught them by surprise and knocked him out before he could teleport again. Although, he might have already been out of juice after the one."

"About that. Are there limits to how far you can teleport? Is that why he stayed so close?" This ability piques my curiosity. What if I could do that? That would be pretty cool if I could appear at school in the blink of an eye.

"Definitely. A couple hours' drive tops for most. Less for weaker Mages. No one is teleporting to Australia or anything." Logan explains that mystery.

"So, who hired them?" I ask.

"No idea yet. Our local enforcement crew picked them up and took them to the nearest facility. They'll lock them up and question them to see if they can squeeze out a name. If I can get out there and get my hands on them all the better. We need to find out who hired them. On the plus side, we know he doesn't want you dead."

"Comforting," I say dryly. My life has been reduced to being thankful someone wants to capture me alive. What's the alternative? Imprisoning me, stealing my powers? Trying to control me?

"We can protect you from getting captured again now that we know that's endgame. If there'd been a kill bounty on your head, well…I don't want to think about that." A pained look spreads over his face before he quickly blanks it out.

The events of the day catch up with me and a wave of exhaustion leaves my muddled brain struggling to absorb all the info. "I think I've had about enough of today. I need to get some sleep."

"You can sleep in my room if that's cool with you." Liz grabs my hand. "I have twin beds in there."

"Fine with me." My mouth gapes in an enormous yawn that I don't have the energy to politely conceal.

I yelp as the weight on my damaged ankle darkens the edges of my vision again when Logan helps me up.

"That's just not happening. I'll take you up."

For the second time that day, I'm swept up in his arms. This time I catch Garrett's jealous expression and he looks at me as if to gauge my willingness. Like I would have chosen to be in this position. I mean, sure it's nice, but my inner feminist doesn't want to play the helpless maiden.

Garrett stands up and grabs my hand as we walk by. It looks like he might have gotten a bit more daring and leaned in for a kiss, but Logan scowls at him. Logan is intimidating on his best day, and today is most definitely not his best day. Boys are so dumb. I'm not planning on being their chew toy to fight over, but I'm too tired to get into it right now. I'm already torn up enough with guilt over leading Garrett on and then kissing Logan. To be fair, we really only went on a couple of dates. I'm not sure he even has a right to this level of protectiveness. Plus, I fully intended to let him know my feelings before the kidnapping.

"Night." A tinge of sadness colors his voice as he squeezes my hand.

"Night," I reply. "I'll call you tomorrow."

My head feels as if it's being dragged down by an invisible anchor, but I wait until we're out of sight of the rest of the crew before I let it drop to Logan's shoulder. Waves of warmth and comfort flow into me along with a nervous energy. He must still be worried about my safety.

He lays me on the spare bed in Liz's room and smooths the hair back off my forehead. My stomach is buzzing with anticipation. Will he kiss me? I'm disappointed when he backs away.

"Good night, Sophia. I'm right across the hall if you need me."

"Night, Logan," I murmur.

Great, the visual of him lying on his bed is now stuck in my head. I flash back to the kiss and analyze it. Was he actually into it? Is he into me? I don't know how to read the bond well enough to untangle my feelings from his. That thought is terrifying, and now my brain is stuck in a loop. Why am I even worried about a boy when I got kidnapped today? I got kidnapped. That doesn't feel real. How is this my life?

CHAPTER 12
Logan

My nerves are shot, and I drained my energy reserves wearing down the carpet with my pacing last night. I should never have left her alone with Liz. It's my responsibility to protect Sophia, even from herself, and I failed to do my job. My father is never going to let me hear the end of this.

I yank on the first clothes my hands touch, run a hand through my hair, and head downstairs to plan. Also, have to get rid of that guy. All we need is a mundane blabbing about us to get into some serious shit from the council.

I take the carpeted stairs three at a time as I head down to scrounge some breakfast. This house is adequate but still feels unfamiliar. Liz and I have only been here a couple of weeks. I'm not surprised that my sister is still in bed. She's such a slacker. She'd sleep until noon every day if she could. Sophia gets a free pass after her crappy day yesterday. Of course, the one person I have zero desire to see is casually sitting at the breakfast bar sipping my coffee.

"Garrett." A grunt is all the attention he deserves.

"Logan. What exactly is going on between you and Sophia?" I'm surprised he's so blunt with me. I thought he would be more of a politician than that. He seems like a smooth talker.

"None of your business." Maybe I can cut this conversation off altogether. Probably wishful thinking, though.

"Actually, it is my business. Her and I are dating and if you're trying to steal her from me, I have a right to know."

"No offense, but I don't see that lasting. Her life is different now, and there's not going to be room for mundanes like you in it. It doesn't matter to me, though, I'm here to protect her, not to date her." My head knows this is the sensible course of action. Unfortunately, other parts of me are not onboard. I can't afford to be distracted when I'm trying to protect her. The words are out of my mouth when her presence tugging at the back of my neck causes my stomach to lurch.

She comes limping around the corner, and her face crumples. That look doesn't last long, as I can basically feel the lasers shooting out of those big brown eyes now.

"As if I was asking." Her tone is scorching. "And by the way, my life is not up for your discussion. Don't talk about me like I'm a possession to fight over."

Shit, I had not meant for her to hear that. I have no intention of hurting her. I'm just trying to do the right thing. All either of us needs right now is for things to get too intense. There are too many people out there trying to take us down to worry about that, too. Her soft lips draw my eyes to them, and a bolt of lust shoots through me at the memory of them pressed against mine.

"I didn't mean it like that. Let me help you." I hurry my stupid ass over there to offer her a hand, but she just brushes me off and proceeds slowly over to the table. Her short, tentative steps cause me pain to watch, and it's amplified by her actual pain shooting through the bond.

A couple of agonizing minutes later, she settles heavily into the chair with a small sigh. Garrett pulls out a spare chair for her to elevate her leg and hurries off to collect a blanket and an ice pack for her. Chivalrous bastard. I would have done it given half a second. Whatever, I don't need to impress her. Why is he still in my house?

"I'll go make some breakfast." I mutter and leave the two of them alone.

I make more of an effort than my usual protein shake with a side of peanut butter and jam on toast. There are drawbacks to moving out of the family home. I really miss my mom's excellent cooking. She would have made us waffles with fresh strawberries and homemade whipped cream after the absolute shit storm of a day yesterday was. My mouth waters at the thought.

Luckily, we have the ingredients on hand to make my one good meal. I scramble up some eggs, even getting a little fancy with some fresh chives, onions, and cheese. The crackle of bacon sizzling on the griddle makes my stomach growl, so of course, I scorch my mouth with a bite. Not smart. The English muffins are the perfect shade of golden brown when they pop out of the toaster.

One of Liz's infernal beasts saunters into the kitchen, weaving between my legs and tripping me up as I head over to the toaster. It's Colby. He yowls at me, demanding his own breakfast. I curse Liz and her cats. She insisted on bringing a couple with us from our parent's house. I grab the bag of kibble and pour some in his bowl to keep him quiet and also to prevent death by cat. That would be an embarrassing way to go.

I load up plates for Sophia and myself. The conversation at the table dies away as I approach.

"Did you want some coffee or OJ?" I ask Sophia.

"I'll take a coffee please." I recognize the gleam in her eyes at the mention of coffee. Clearly, we agree on the best way to start the day.

"Help yourself." I vaguely wave at Garrett before I head back to the kitchen to grab coffee and condiments.

When I settle back at the table, Garrett gets up to help himself to some breakfast.

"Look Sophia," I say. "I wasn't trying to stake my territory or anything. I know you can make your own choices. It's just that mixing with a mundane like that is only going to put him in danger and little as I care for his well-being, I'm sure you are probably not into him getting damaged."

"You made yourself clear. I get it. I was planning on breaking it off with him last night anyway, right before I got snatched. I'm a practical person and I can see that it would be a bad idea to get him involved. Not that it has anything to do with you!" She hisses this at me under her breath with extra emphasis on the last word. I guess she doesn't want him to overhear and get his feelings hurt.

"I got it. So, how are you doing this morning?"

"Sore, tired, emotionally drained, terrified, and resolute." She lays out her list in a straightforward way, as if cataloging the feelings of someone else.

"Ummm, can I do anything for you?"

"Teach me how to use my magic, and how to defend myself. I don't ever want anything like that happening again. Teach me. It's important to me to be able to defend myself."

"Teach you what?" Garrett asks, catching the tail end of our conversation. I eye his full plate. How long exactly is he planning on staying here?

"About, you know, the magic stuff," Sophia says sheepishly. She sounded so strong before, but now faced with Garrett, she's retreating again into doubt.

"Maybe you should just avoid it. Seems like it's only brought danger into your life," he says. What an idiot. Not helpful.

"Not a chance," I snort derisively.

"You, what did we just talk about?" Sophia points a finger at me with a glare. "And you." She turns her attention to Garrett. "I don't have a choice. I wish I did, but people are going to come after me, whether or not I accept the magic. There's no escaping it. My only alternative is to fight back. Honestly, you're probably in danger by association." Her eyes plead with him to understand.

"I'm not afraid. Pretty shaken up about all this stuff, though. Now that I know magic exists, I don't think I'll ever be able to just forget about it."

"I know. I feel the same way. I think we should probably talk about all this craziness, but maybe not here," says Sophia.

"I agree. It's kind of toxic in this place. Can I call you later?"

How dare he call my house toxic? Well, maybe to him. He's overstayed his welcome. Sophia, on the other hand, is safest here.

"For sure."

"Great, glad we got that sorted out. Don't you have somewhere to be?" Logan says.

"Is it completely necessary for you to be such a jerk?" Sophia asks.

"It's kind of my thing." The corners of my mouth creep up into a lazy grin.

"There's something in your teeth," Sophia says bluntly. She isn't even discreet about it. Guess I had that coming. I suck on my teeth to remove the offending object and then channel Colby and pretend like it never happened.

"As charming as the company is, I really have to head home. Any chance someone can give me a lift? My car is still downtown near Arabica Nights."

"Don't leave on his account." Sophia tosses her thumb in my direction.

"Maybe you can grab an Uber?" I'm not driving him home, forget that. I didn't want him here in the first place, and I'm definitely not leaving Sophia again. My insides are already shredded that I let her get kidnapped yesterday. A red rage is simmering under my skin and I'm itching to punch something, or someone.

Liz walks in to save the day in a fuzzy, black cat onesie before I get myself any deeper in the muck with Sophia.

"Stop being so Logany. I'll give you a lift, Garrett, once I've had a coffee and maybe some toast." She looks like the cat she's impersonating with the size of her yawn.

"And change into some, like, actual clothes?" I suggest without much hope. My sister is her own weird little colorful island in an unending bland desert.

"Nope, it's Saturday, cat onesie is not coming off." She smiles gleefully at me. Completely unashamed, and also happy to heap embarrassment on her poor brother.

"Fine by me. I think it's cute," Garrett says. He's being way too smug about it.

I roll my eyes. "I'm heading up for a shower. I'll be down in a few, and we can plan our day. Can you keep an eye on Sophia until I get back down?" I try to communicate to Liz with a look that I want her to watch out for her safety as well as Garrett's intentions. I don't know what it was about that guy, but I can't stand him. He's just too nice or perfect or something. Something is off. Grates on my nerves like no one else. I think I'd prefer the company of one of those bounty hunters to him. At least I can take out my frustrations on their faces. Sophia would probably be pissed if I did that to his pretty face.

I hop in the shower and let the steaming water soothe all the aches from the fight last night. I wince as my fingers brush the bruise that stretches up half of my left rib cage, where the muscly one slipped a solid punch through my guard. My forehead has a clean knife slice running from my hairline to my right ear. Nothing I can't handle.

My family has always been on the more active side of the magical council. We go way back. Founding members. Some of the council members these days are politicians, high-powered executives, and academics. Soft. The council used to be made up of warriors. I guess it's necessary to keep up with the times. My family are still warriors though and we're trained from our childhood to defend ourselves and police the dangerous elements of the magic world that threaten our safety and secrecy.

I always knew I would slip into my expected role and join the Magical Enforcement Division, but not so soon. One year, that's all I asked for. One year of freedom. Freedom from family obligations, council assignments, and magic squabbles. After two weeks in Paris, I got called home to look after Sophia. It shouldn't have happened for years. Helena should have been safe. I don't blame Sophia, but it still chafes that I can't just have that brief period of time to call my own.

Liz, on the other hand, is happy to be here. She's still in high school, anyway. This is just a fun assignment and a new friend to her. She's always been curious about Sophia anyway, ever since our parents told us about her powers and her parent's death. We'd been told once our parents felt we were old enough to be trusted with the secret. We're good at that, anyway. All kids born in magic families are. We learn from a young age that you can't show your abilities in front of mundanes.

Now that we're here, though, I've felt a fierce need to protect Sophia. The problem is being so close to her I'm having a hard time distinguishing whether my feelings are the result of the protection bond or even if they're my own. The closer we are physically, the more our feelings mingle together. Lust, protectiveness, anger, jealousy, concern. They all get mixed up into a big, tangled mess. Like that swamp water we used to drink when we were kids, you couldn't even remember which drinks you'd mixed in by the time you finished.

My mind slips back to the kiss. Her lips had been so soft and desperate. Her hands tangled in my hair, pulling me closer. Heat races through my body at the mere memory, so I know how I feel about it. Sophia's feelings I'm not so clear on. Was she responding to my desire, or was she grateful for being rescued? It doesn't matter. I shouldn't have responded like I did.

I can't deny to myself that she wanted it, but she was scared and vulnerable and I was a dick for taking advantage of her in that state. I can't let it happen again, because I'm not sure I'm strong enough to stop it a second time.

I towel myself off and my mind wanders, picturing they're Sophia's hands on me instead. Shit, I have to stop thinking things like that. It shouldn't happen. I run a replay from the fight last night in my head to see where I could have done better. My traitorous mind, however, just keeps drifting back to Sophia. I picture the terrified look on her face when I first saw her covered in dirt with tear streaks running down her face. I never want to see her in that state again.

I sink on my bed with my head in my hands until Liz yells oh so subtly up the stairs.

"Heading out now, big bro! You can come out of hiding!"

Sisters are the worst. The best, but also the worst.

I still don't go down until I hear the slam of the front door. Only then do I head down the stairs, my steps muffled by the carpet.

Sophia made herself at home in the family room. She's sitting on the poufy couch with her legs pulled up beside her and a blanket draped from neck to toes. She looks so innocent resting there that the protective instinct flares up. She glances up as my weight sinks onto the couch next to her.

"Can I get you anything?" I ask.

"No, I'm good, thanks. Liz and Garrett got me all set up before they left." She lifts the blanket to reveal an ice pack soothing her ankle and tilts her head toward the coffee mug sitting near her head. It's one of Liz's. It has a cat on it with a rainbow unicorn horn. Caticorn is emblazoned underneath in rainbow letters, so I'm assuming that's the name of this unnatural creature. I find it completely ridiculous, but maybe Sophia needs a bit of ridiculous right now.

"Did you want to talk about last night?" I try. I have no idea what I'm gonna say if she wants to talk. Sharing my feelings? Really not my favorite thing.

"Not really. Why do you have to be such a jackass to Garrett? He never did anything to you, and it's not his fault that he's gotten mixed up in this business."

She's nothing if not direct. I like that about her.

"I don't know. Something about him just gets to me." I say gruffly. I don't really want to think too closely about why he's getting to me so hard.

She raises an eyebrow at me, causing more to spill out than I intended.

"I just don't like seeing you with him. He's a liability. He can't protect you from anyone." Who am I kidding with this crap?

"Uh huh. And was there someone else in mind better suited to the task?" She stares me down.

"Look, Sophia. The kiss last night. I shouldn't have responded like that. You were scared and traumatized, and I should have known better. I really do like you."

"I sense a but here."

"But I can't protect you if I let myself get too close. That's how mistakes happen."

"Well, what if I don't need your protection? What if you teach me how to handle my own powers? If I really am this all powerful Archimage, which I have serious doubts about, by the way. But if it's true, then I'll be able to protect myself."

"It's going to take time for your abilities to surface and even more to learn to control them. I'm talking years until you're really up to speed. Liz and I, we've spent our whole lives training and enhancing our abilities plus learning physical fighting skills."

"You know my superpower is studying, right? I'm an excellent student. Look, if you're not into me, that's fine. I get it. Just thought we should try it out. I mean, you infuriate me, you can be such a jerk, but then you let your real self out." She waves her hand at me. "I'm drawn to you. Every time you're near. I can't help it, but I'm confused. Is the bond causing these feelings?"

"It doesn't work like that. The bond doesn't force you to feel anything. It lets us feel what the other is feeling and gives us a connection and awareness of each other."

Her head tilts to the side and my gaze falls to her bow shaped mouth as it drops open. "Oh," she says. "So that means…"

I lean in, ignoring all the alarm bells in my head. Our lips touch and a live current zaps through my body. The skin-on-skin contact brings her emotions into even sharper focus. I tangle one hand in her hair and let the other slide down until it connects with the bare skin of her lower back. My hand slides up the soft, heated skin under her shirt and I pull her closer. She yelps in pain.

I pull back and jump up, tensed to fight.

"Calm down, it was just my ankle you leaned on." Her breath is coming in quick gasps.

"That's why we can't do this," I say, taking my frustration out on my hair and starting to pace. "I can't let my defenses down like that. What if someone had snuck up behind me?"

"You would have handed their ass to them, I assume." Her confidence fills my hardened heart with a fuzzy warmth. "Don't push me away. I get to make my own decisions. I don't need you to do that for me."

"I know, but I can't risk your life out of my own selfishness." I have to force the words out.

She pulls away and the tension ratchets up. We sit there silent for a moment, avoiding each other's eyes until she breaks the awkward silence.

"Well, if that's going to be how it is, fine. Teach me. We can't avoid that."

"Teach you what?" All the things I could teach her race through my head. None of them dim the fire that's raging through me at the thought of the kiss.

"My training. You said I need to be able to defend myself. That this can't happen while I'm vulnerable. Fine. Teach me. Help me figure out my magic."

"Now?"

"Yes, right now. You say it's life or death, and I never want to be in a situation like last night again, so we have no time to waste."

"Um okay. I thought maybe you could work with Liz first, though." A flash of panic eats at me. I knew this was coming, but I was hoping I could put off my involvement at least at first. I think of my father pushing me far beyond my limits and driving me to exhaustion. With him as my role model, I don't know that I can be the right teacher for Sophia.

"She can help, but I want you as my primary teacher. Nonnegotiable. I can tell that where Liz will take it slow and easy with me, you'll push me to learn as fast as I can. No mercy. That's what I need right now."

"But after last night... You need a day off at least to recover." I want her to learn to defend herself, but I can't let her cause herself unnecessary pain. Or me, for that matter. When it comes right down to it. Her pain is mine as well, felt through the bond between us. And that's just another distraction I can't afford right now.

"I'm sure we can work on some basics with me sitting down, can't we? I'm not looking to go running around chasing monsters, but I need to get a handle on this," she says, her face a mask of determination.

"If you insist, but it's physically and mentally draining. Don't say I didn't warn you."

"Okay, but should we be keeping quiet down here? Are your parents still in bed? And are they ok with you randomly bringing people home to sleep over?" The confusion on her face matches the wave coming through the bond.

"My parents don't live here, Sophia. I thought you knew. They're still back in Port Grand. They run the Magical Enforcement Division for our area from there, so they have to stay close. Liz and I were sent here on assignment and since I'm nineteen, they're fine with us staying alone. It's not like we came here to throw wild parties or anything. I'm not sure I would even know how to do that." I laugh. All the training, both magical and physical, plus the fact that we aren't really allowed to make friends with the mundane kids means we grew up faster than most.

"Oh. We're alone here then. My mom would so not approve." Sophia squirms a bit and pulls the blanket up to her neck as if that'll protect her from whatever she thinks is going to happen with no parental supervision.

"It's fine. We're just doing a bit of magic. I mean, unless you were thinking of something else?" I wink at her, trying to dispel the tension a bit.

She flies right over my innuendo. "Right, so where do we start? Is there a book I can read?" Her eyes light up. It's pretty cute how excited she is about a book. I kind of want to bring her home a pile of books, so that I can be the one to put that look on her face. I try to shove the errant thought to the deepest crevices of my brain.

"You can't learn magic from a book, at least not our kind. Maybe that's what witches do. Hell if I know." Her face falls and my mood dips with it.

"Witches?"

"Yeah, humans who do magic. Not important. We can talk about that another time." She looks like she's about to argue but reconsiders. "We need to take this downstairs, though."

Her brow crunches up with a quizzical look. "Downstairs?"

"Yes, magic blocking wards line the basement walls. Nobody can sense your magic while we're down there."

"Oh. That's cool. How does that work?" Her curiosity is endless, unfortunately our time is limited right now.

"I promise I'll hook you up with some books as soon as I can. For now, though, we need to focus on your magic."

"You're right. Let's go."

I think the trip down the stairs causes me more pain than her. I let her lean on me, but she still winces with every step. She gives me a concerned look when we reach the foreboding metal door at the bottom. My eyes flick around, seeing it from her eyes. Heavy door leading into a basement room with no escape route protected by keypad entry. Great, it looks like some kind of serial killer cave.

"This is not what it looks like." I rub my hands up and down her arms in an attempt to reassure her. The touch has the unfortunate side effect of sending flames licking through my body. I fight the urge to turn her around and continue what we started upstairs. That would be the opposite of helpful.

"What, you mean like you have the heads of your former girlfriends hanging up in there?" I wince and pull back at the thought of Ivy.

She must catch a hint of the regret and pain tearing me apart as she drops her voice and cups my cheeks. "I was kidding. I trust you."

I duck out of her grasp and punch in the code to open the door. It swings open to reveal the setup we have here. We don't have the full gym like at my parent's house, but Liz and I have set up a mini training zone in the basement. We have to keep our skills sharp no matter what.

I lead her past the mat and through a regular door into the office area. My lips curve up as Sophia heads straight for the bookcase on the back wall. She runs her hands down the spines like she's petting a favorite dog. The collection here is limited, but we brought along a handful of reference books Mom thought might come in handy. I ignore the unused desk and help Sophia get settled on the couch nestled against the left wall.

The biggest problem is that I really have no idea where to begin. As an Archimage, she should have access to all the four types of magic, but which abilities does she actually have? It's all just trial and error. I guess I should start with what I know.

"Ok, so Elemental Mages like yours truly can use their energy to manipulate things like fire, water, metal, wood, electricity. All sorts of things. Maybe we should try water first. Less destructive than fire, right?"

"Yeah, I'm not too eager to try that one again." She laughs.

Probably should have planned this better. I have to run upstairs to grab a bowl of water. I hold my hand over the bowl and focus on the ever present current of power flowing through my body. I let it flow through my right hand to pull the water up into the air, creating a column before releasing it to let it splash back into the bowl.

"Your turn," I say. Yeah, I was right. My teaching skills are nonexistent.

"How? Isn't there some magic spell or word or something? Don't I need a wand?"

"Only no-talent hacks and humans need a wand to direct the magic flow. It's a part of you. Don't you feel the tingle of power coursing through your body? For me, it's kind of like..." I have to pause to think about it. "...a low-level electric current, but I think there are different ways people feel it."

"A couple of times lately I've felt a tingle when I did magic or someone else did."

"Perfect. You need to find that and use it. You harness it to your will."

She gives me an uncertain look. "It's just not there all the time. I've never felt it unless something weird is happening. I don't just feel it, whatever it is." Her hands cup the air in front of her as if she's trying to grab something tangible.

It's frustrating because my magic is just part of me, and it always has been. I take a minute to focus on her. Maybe I can help her find it and connect with it. I close my eyes and grab onto the bond that ties us together. I follow it back to her, searching for her magic. It's elusive. I can't quite grasp it at this level of connection.

"You need to open yourself up to it. Magic is part of you. Like the blood flowing through your veins. I can probably help you. You know, through the bond, but you'd have to trust me."

I hate the way a wave of uncertainty flows across her expressive face. I want to prove to her I'm the kind of guy she can trust. I'm kicking myself for acting like such a jerk when we first met. "How?"

"We can connect mentally, and I can help you get in touch with the energy inside." I don't really know how to explain it, but I try my best.

"I guess." She sounds reluctant, and I'm not going to force it. We'd have to completely open ourselves up to each other. Let go of all our shields. I'm not even sure I'm ready for it, but I'd do anything to keep her safe.

"Are you sure? I'm not doing this if you're not fully with me. It will leave us both open to each other's thoughts and emotions." It would be a total invasion of her mind if she doesn't actually want me there, and I would never do that.

"Is that different from usual?"

"Yeah. The effects of the bond are more intense the closer we are to each other. Like if someone yells from across the street, you can hear them, but you can't hear if they whisper. If we're far apart, I get a vague impression of an emotion. It's stronger if we're in the same room, but I don't get any of your thoughts unless we're physically touching, and we drop our shields."

"Oh, right. That makes sense. What do you mean by shields, though? I don't have shields."

"Everyone has shields, magical or not. It's subconscious."

"Ok. Then yes." The steel is back in her tone. "This needs to happen. I need to figure this out, so yes do it. I'm in."

"Okay. Grab my hands. Physical contact will help."

She shifts on the couch to face me and places her small hands in mine, tentatively wrapping her fingers around them. The contact creates instant heat that spreads up my arms. I'm momentarily distracted by thoughts of what it would be like to twine our whole bodies together. I try to shove that thought to the back of my head and clear my mind like my father taught me to do. Sophia definitely doesn't need to hear that.

I pull myself back together and focus on the bond between us. It lives inside me as if it's a part of my consciousness. I picture my own magic inside myself as a red light and the bond as a golden glow. Once I grasp it in my mind, I trace the thread of it back to her.

With the extra focus and physical contact, her emotions kick me hard, and even some of her thoughts come to me in fragments. She's feeling pain and fear, yet there's also that resolve and calm in her. She's so strong. I catch her thinking of me and our kiss, wanting to repeat it. That almost breaks me. Her lust piled on top of my own is kind of overwhelming. I almost forget what we're doing this for and pull her in for a kiss.

I pull myself out of it, though, and search for her magic. It's there but very dim. I catch a glimpse of a soft pink glow, but instead of flowing through her body, touching all corners of her being, it's just faint flickering lights here and there. Like the stars trying to shine through a cloud and only managing occasional peeks.

I pull at these sparks as if I'm picking at a piece of thread that's unraveled from a well-worn sweater. Her energy responds to me slowly getting drawn out until more and more of it is visible. It flows faster and faster until there's a bright pink glow touching every part of her. A rush of adrenaline sends my heart racing and my magic responds, setting my body on fire. The intimacy is incredible.

She gasps and jerks away from me. The breaking of the connection is almost painful, and I feel a deep sense of loss.

CHAPTER 13
Sophia

A shiver runs through me as I disconnect from Logan, but that was too much, too intense. His feelings and mine folded together like a woven basket until I couldn't distinguish them from each other.

Now that we're apart, I start to get a sense of self back but with a new addition. An energy force is crashing through me like water released from a dam. It's like a constant buzz vibrating through my whole body. It's overwhelming. My breathing comes in quick pants and my vision tunnels as my head grows hot.

"Sophia, Sophia, are you ok? Just breathe." Logan's voice is hollow and quiet as if he's far away. He reaches for my hand, and I jerk away. My nerves are raw, exposed. I don't think I can handle his touch right now. This is enough to disperse the light-headedness, and my breathing settles back into an easy rhythm.

"I'm ok. Just need a minute." I lay my head on the arm of the couch and take a few deep, calming breaths, focusing on the air as it floods my lungs, filling them with life.

When I finally get my regular senses back under control, I'm able to feel the new energy buzzing inside me, but it's no longer violent. It's calmed to a low vibration.

"I can feel it. The magic. My magic." That is pretty freaking awesome and terrifying at the same time.

Logan's face is etched with relief.

"That's a great first step. Now comes the hard part. Learning how to harness it with precision and purpose. That's one of my dad's favorite sayings: Precision and Purpose." Logan drops his voice a register.

"What are your parents like?" I'm curious to know more about Logan and where he came from, and I need a minute to gather myself back together before we try any more magic. My senses are heightened, and I need a distraction. The reds, blacks, and golds of book spines, Logan's sea-blue eyes. All the colors are a little too bright.

"Well, my mom is a Psyche, so we could never get away with anything around her. She's softer on us than my dad but strong. Comes from a very old Mage family so she's got lots of pull in the community and with the council. My Dad is tougher, he'll push us to learn and isn't afraid to let us fail so we can learn from our mistakes. He's been training us ever since we were kids, although we have some outside teachers, too. His family has always been mostly warriors. Always defending against Mages gone bad, protecting the secrecy of the magic world, and various other monsters."

"When you say various other monsters…." I trail off, kind of reluctant to pursue this line of questioning. Do I even want to know what else is out there? I shudder and my hand drifts to my neck when the thought of the Ferrebat's teeth sinking into my neck intrudes.

"I wouldn't even know where to start. There's definitely a book for that. For now, it's just important to defend you from the immediate threats and see if we can track down whoever is behind the kidnapping. At this point, all signs point to another Mage."

I'm doubtful, as I do like to have all the information on hand ahead of time, but I let it go for now.

"Ok, what do I do with this energy now? And also will this weird feeling go away, or am I stuck with it now for good? There's like a constant buzz humming through my entire body."

"I guess it's probably pretty overwhelming at first. You'll get to a point where it's just there in the background and if it was gone, you'd miss it. I don't know what I'd do if it was just gone one day. Would probably feel like losing your vision or hearing. It's like a sixth sense to me."

I'm skeptical that this constant tingle will ever feel normal, but I guess he has a lifetime of experience to my nil.

"We can do one small test of your magic today. But then I think you need to rest. You need to heal, and draining your body isn't going to help," he says.

"Yes, doctor." I roll my eyes, even though I know he's probably right.

"You said you can freeze objects, right?"

"I think so. There was the vase, and maybe the dog, but I dropped the vase pretty quickly."

"That's because you had no idea what was going on. It was all subconscious. Remember, Precision and Purpose." He laughs, then glances around the room before grabbing a gray throw pillow with a white cat silhouette on it.

"That doesn't exactly look like your style." My eyebrow quirks up.

He looks at it like he's never seen it before. "Liz. One benefit of living with my sister. Cat accessories everywhere."

"And if you were accessorizing the house, what would it look like? All black with maybe some weaponry hanging from the wall." I tease.

"Accessorize, what's that?" he asks with a puzzled look.

"Ah, good to know you're capable of a joke or two. Lame as it may be."

"Enough fooling around. We have work to do." He gives me a faux stern look, but I can feel his amusement. "Here's the deal. I'm going to drop the pillow and you are going to focus your energy on freezing it. Like so." He lets go and with no apparent effort it drifts in midair before he snatches it back.

My mouth drops open as I stare at the pillow rocking gently in a nonexistent breeze.

"Sure easy." I make sure to inject some decent sarcasm into those two words.

"Your turn. Full disclosure. I used the element of air to kind of levitate it, but you should be able to straight up freeze it." He grins and drops the cushion without warning. I just stare at it as it hits the floor.

"No effort at all there, princess. Want a hand?"

I pull back as he reaches for my hand, but then capitulate and clasp one of his calloused palms. The connection immediately snaps back in place and his emotions and magic mingle with mine. It's less intense this time.

"Dropping the pillow." He at least gives me some warning this time, directing his own energy at it while pulling mine along for the ride. Together we freeze the pillow and I let out a surprised yelp which breaks the spell and releases it to fall to the floor. He laughs and retrieves the pillow.

"I totally felt that." My heart beats faster with the energy still coursing through my veins.

"Of course you did. Ok, let's try one more time. This time, you direct it. I'm just along for the ride. Concentrate on that feeling and use it." He squeezes my hand in his warm one and an embarrassing emotion heats my body. Crap, can he feel that while we're connected like this? "Focus."

He releases the pillow and this time I picture it freezing in midair and direct the buzzing magic inside me toward it like a swarm of bees pulling his current along with mine. I jump up and down with glee at Liz's frozen cat pillow. This time, he uses his lightning-fast reflexes to snatch it up before it falls to the ground.

"Ok, I'm going to let go and you're going to do it all on your own." His confidence in me gives my own a boost. "Ready?"

"Yes." I can totally do this. I have to do this.

The pillow falls from his hand and, just as before, I focus my thoughts and it works. I did it all on my own. Excitement bubbles up inside me and I throw my arms around him. The contours of his well-muscled abs press against me, and his arms pull me tighter. I pull back just enough to gaze into his eyes and unthinkingly close the space between us. My lips meet his and my arms travel up his neck tangling in his hair. He shivers and opens up, deepening the kiss and sliding his hands around me.

They leave a trail of heat as he slides them up my back. I lean onto the arm of the couch, bringing him down with me.

"Hi guys, am I interrupting?" Liz's bright question hits me like a bucket of ice.

"Shit!" Logan springs back, running a hand through his hair. The sudden absence of both his body and his energy leaves me cold.

I'm pretty sure my blush would be identifiable from space.

"Don't stop on my account." Liz teases. At least she doesn't seem angry. "Actually scratch that. Please stop. I don't need that picture seared into my brain for the rest of my life."

"I've gotta go… Going to do a sweep." Logan mutters without looking at either of us before bolting. I hear the front door slam as I pick at the fringe on the blanket, studiously avoiding looking at Liz.

The couch bounces next to me as she flops down practically on top of me.

"So, you and my brother? That's an interesting development. Although I could sense it coming."

"Like, magically?" I ask. I don't know if I can handle both of the siblings able to read me like that.

"No, I'm not a Psyche, but I'm also not blind. I can see the way he looks at you. And vice versa."

"Oh. It's nothing, though. He helped me with magic, and we just got caught up in the moment. It's probably just the bond, right?" The flutter of hope that rears up at her words is disconcerting.

"That's not how it looks to me. I think it's a good thing. My brother could use a smart girl in his life. He hasn't seriously dated anyone since Ivy." She slaps her hand over her mouth as if to keep any more words from spilling out, piquing my curiosity.

"Ivy? Who's that?"

"Uh, his first girlfriend, they dated for a couple years when he was 15/16. Please don't tell him I mentioned her name. He really doesn't like to talk about her. I shouldn't have said anything." She glances around as if Logan might be lurking in a corner somewhere.

Of course, her comments have fired up a burning desire in me to know more about Logan's ex, but I don't want to get Liz in trouble, so I nod.

"Like I said before, he's actually a nice guy underneath that top crusty layer, and you seem like an awesome person, so I totally approve."

"The thing is... It doesn't feel real." I'm glad to have someone to talk to about it. Even though she's his sister, we're becoming friends too, and I really like Liz. She's easy to talk to as if I've known her for years.

"What do you mean?"

"Well, with the bond, you know. Sometimes I can't tell which feelings are mine and which are his. I don't know if I like him because of the bond or if it just intensifies feelings that are already there. It's just really confusing, and I've never really dated anyone before other than a few hang outs with Garrett, so I have like zero experience to compare it to." I don't want to sound like a loser to Liz, but the truth spills out of me.

"Oh. I'm surprised you haven't dated before. I mean, you've got it going on. What about Garrett? Have you still got feelings for him?" She asks this last question with more intensity than I think it merits.

"I just never wanted to take the time from my studies. I need to get a scholarship. There's no way I can afford med school without one. Boys are an unnecessary distraction. And then Garrett asked me out. He's smart and cute and seemingly perfect for me, but there's no like heat or whatever. But once I met Logan, I was drawn to him. He's totally wrong for me and sometimes he acts like a bit of a jerk. And I worry I'm throwing away something that could be great with a normal guy for this thing with Logan that might not even be real. It might just be the bond."

"It sounds to me like you're not into Garrett in the dating and kissing way. If you were, you would definitely know. Honestly, I have no experience with this bond business. It's not a very common spell among Mages anymore. I don't think it forces you to feel things though, just lets you feel some of your partner's emotions and their location. Logan has felt it his whole life, and he never seemed to have any of that kind of interest in you until after you guys met."

"Ok," I say, not entirely convinced. "Logan himself doesn't want this to happen. He said he can't protect me if he's distracted by a relationship, so that's that. I'm not going to force anything."

"Not what it looked like that when I walked in on you. Was this conversation before or after I caught him on top of you? Also, just got a flashback, ew gross. That's my brother." She shudders dramatically and rubs at her eyes.

"See? He's totally messing up my head. I don't have time for this." I'm deluding myself. I'm starting to realize that the couple of dates I had with Garrett were easy. He doesn't come close to touching my heart. Logan, on the other hand, he could have the power to destroy me.

"Yeah, I think we both need some distance from this right now. In fact, I might need to go stare at some pics of Danny Griffin to scrub that image out of my head. You hungry? I can go make us lunch if you're up for it."

A pang of hunger pulls at me. I didn't even realize I was hungry until she mentioned it. It's not unusual for me to get so wrapped up in my head that I forget to eat. "Yes please. Want me to help?" I half-heartedly offer when, really, I just want to regenerate some energy on the couch after the exhausting morning.

Liz's hair is a black and teal blur as it bounces around her face at her emphatic shake. "I'm just making grilled cheese. That ok with you?"

"One of my faves." Nothing more comforting than gooey cheese and carbs.

Liz darts out of the room faster than I can track her, and I realize that she's let down her magic guard around me. It's easy to forget that little Liz is also a Mage since I haven't seen her powers in action. I recall Logan telling me she's a Physical Mage which basically means she has cool mutant super strength, speed, and hearing. Weird. It's hard to imagine I'll ever get used to that sort of thing.

I take my time getting up the stairs and relocate to another couch before opening my Kindle app. I can't concentrate and keep skipping paragraphs and having to reread them as my thoughts bounce around the events of the last couple of days.

I shudder as my mind drifts back to the dank warehouse where I was trapped. I wonder what my life would have been like if my biological parents weren't killed. If I have to be this Mage, or whatever, why can't I just be a regular one with like normal powers? Why do I have to be this weirdo with extra power and a huge target on my back? If only I had family to help me deal with this. I don't think I can turn to my mom, though. I can't tell her about magic and tangle her up in the perils of my new life. Will she be in more danger if she knows or if she doesn't?

My thoughts drift to my dad. That awful day Mom got the call from the police. While suffering her own intense grief, she had to then break my heart with the news of his death. I can't put this on her. She's just started pulling herself back together. She seems happy for the first time since that moment.

What would my dad have thought about the magic? He was always so curious and interested in the world around him. I bet he'd be excited about the new experience. He'd want to learn every aspect of it and find out what all his abilities were. That thought finally straightens out my head. Thinking of how he would have dealt with such a strange situation, I can do the same. I'm going to embrace it.

This revelation finally stills my busy mind and solidifies my determination.

I blink my eyes groggily with hunger knocking on the door and the sun considerably lower in the sky than when Liz left to make lunch. I must have fallen asleep. Seems like that's all I've been doing lately. This magic stuff is exhausting. Liz is sitting in the comfy black leather recliner across from me with a book in hand and a stripey orange furball curled up in her lap purring. She glances up.

"Oh hi. I couldn't bring myself to wake you up. You definitely needed that sleep."

"I know. I'll feel better once I shake off the fuzzies. Exactly how many cats do you have?" In addition to the adorable fluff in her lap, there's a sleek black one lounging at her feet. It lifts its head and blinks at me with disdain, almost as if it understands.

"Right now? Four. Cats just seem to find me. My mom always thought I'd be a Bio when I was a kid because of my animal obsession but turns out I can kill a plant by looking at it. Imagine her surprise when I lifted a boulder the size of Logan's colossal head and dropped it on his foot when we were kids. It was so gross. He lost a toenail. So much blood."

My stomach contracts at the thought of Logan hurt like that even though it's a distant memory. "Ok, enough of that. What are the names of those fuzzballs?"

"This is Cheddar." She indicates the small one in her lap, then points at the black one. "That's Voodoo. She doesn't like strangers. Colby is the black and white one, he's a little overly friendly and Blue is the gray one. You'll see them around when they want to be seen." I'm a little dizzy trying to keep up with the whirlwind that she is. "You must be starving. I did make you a grilled cheese, but I ate it when you didn't wake up. We have some leftover pizza if you like. And I cut up a bunch of fruit and veggies with lunch. Do you like hummus?"

"Mmmm, love it. And I'll take a couple of slices for sure." I unglue myself from the couch, tentatively testing out my ankle. Still pretty sore but I can make it to the bathroom.

Cheddar hisses at Liz as she unceremoniously dethrones it. "I can get it for you. Stay there. Do you like your pizza hot or cold?"

"Hot definitely. Cold pizza is ick!" Disgust wrinkles my face up. "Just going to hit the bathroom."

"Gotcha. And I totally agree with you on the great pizza debate. Logan likes it cold, though. Perhaps we should just disown him." She giggles.

I laugh and make my awkward way to the bathroom. I grimace at the horrifying glance of myself in the black framed bathroom mirror. I can't believe I kissed Logan looking like this. How traumatic, for us both.

"Hey Liz, got a hairbrush I can borrow?"

Silence is the only response until a loud crash and a scream break it. My stomach drops and I limp back out toward the kitchen. Edging my way along the wall, I reach the kitchen door and peer in.

Liz is locked in battle with a huge guy sporting some gross, greasy black hair and an epic mountain man style beard. He looks like he's come right out of the ring from one of the pro wrestling matches my brother used to love so much when we were kids. Seriously, his arms are the size of all my limbs put together and are straining against the black tee shirt he's wearing.

I have no idea how tiny Liz is going to beat this guy, but she's darting around faster than my eyes can track, so I assume he isn't landing too many of those punches. I could try some of my magic, but I figure the chances are equally good that I'll hurt either myself or Liz instead of the thug. I wince as he throws one more left hook at her, but she slides deftly under his arm. He turns around at a normal human speed only to meet her foot crashing into his big ugly nose. It looks like it's suffered a few breaks already, so this will not be a novel experience for him.

He flies backward several feet before crashing to the floor unconscious, I hope. Holy crap, Liz is strong. I think about when I kneed the guy in the warehouse when he flew back a few feet. Maybe I've got some of that super strength, too. That will come in handy.

"Lunch is ready," she chirps at me, shaking out her fist. "Let me just tie this asshole up and call the MED team first."

Now that the excitement is over, I slide down the wall, my legs folding under me. I shake my head, trying to make sense of what just happened. Liz was like a blur for a moment. MED team. That must be the Magical Enforcement Division Logan mentioned.

"Do you know that guy?"

"Nope. Just an uninvited houseguest. Definitely overstayed his welcome. He's not even magic, though. That's the weird thing. They just hired a human thug to take on a house full of Mages and an Archimage."

"I don't know that I would actually classify myself as an Archimage. I can't even control my powers yet." I hug myself around the middle. I'm so vulnerable right now. There is no way I could have fought off that guy on my own. What would I have done if Liz wasn't here?

"This is true, but they must know you're staying with Logan and me. Why would they send a mundane?"

I shrug at her. "How did you… What was that even?" I look at her through narrowed eyes, trying to connect her with the huge guy passed out on the floor. "Where did Logan go? He said something about a sweep, but that was hours ago."

"Yeah, he did a sweep of the neighborhood to make sure no one was lurking about. While you were off in la la land, he stopped in and said he was heading out to find info about the imprisoned bounty hunters who kidnapped you. They must have been watching the house and attacked when they knew he was gone. Serious underestimate of my abilities. Big mistake." Crazy girl actually looks happy about the home invasion and attack.

"Tell me about it. I certainly wasn't expecting that from you. I wish he would have taken us along. Then maybe that wouldn't have happened." I point a shaky finger at the huge guy Liz has tied up neatly against the wall.

"No way he would have done that. It's too dangerous for you to be anywhere near the rest of the magical community. Not until we figure out who's behind this. How about you eat some lunch now? It's super important to keep well fueled when you're using your powers."

"I guess." I grab the yellow flowered plate that managed to survive the fight and munch unenthusiastically on a baby carrot. I sit down to eat, but I'm still trying to wrap my head around the fight and the fear and adrenaline have chased away my hunger.

CHAPTER 14
Logan

I squeal out of the driveway and hit the road at speed after filling Liz in on my plans. My gut is clenched with anger at myself. I've had self-discipline drilled into me my whole life, but something about that girl is eating away at it, taking me back to the reckless year when I was sixteen and started taking unnecessary risks. Risks that other people suffered from.

My mind travels back to one of my many training sessions with my dad. The last one before he passed me off full-time to an official council trainer, so I would have been fourteen.

We were sparring in the training room in the basement of our house. I can almost smell the mix of salty sweat and lemon cleaner that permeates the walls.

The basement consists of a large gym with the usual accoutrements: punching bags, mats, weights, weapons, and exercise equipment. The locked door into the library is the reason for all the security, though. The ornately carved mahogany door leads into a good-sized room lined with bookshelves. These shelves contain books on magic, spells, monsters, and the history of the magic community. There are also various family heirlooms and items of power or value. I used to love sitting in that room on the floor while my dad or mom did council work at the desk. I would find any excuse to hang out there. Sometimes Liz joined me, but more often than not, she was hanging with her friends of the magical or mundane variety. She was constantly getting into trouble for that. Strictly speaking, we weren't supposed to hang with the non-magic peeps.

On that day in the training room, I was angry. To be fair, I was angry a lot of the time. I don't even remember why. Something happened at school. A mundane was bullying another kid, and I stepped in. I hate seeing jerks bully those who are weaker than themselves. I knocked the bully out with a single punch, which got me suspended for the rest of the week despite my good intentions. The situation filled me with such anger that I came home spoiling for a fight.

My father's solution was to take me right down to the training room. He didn't let me rage and pound on the bags like I wanted to. Instead, he sparred with me and took me down harder than usual, which just made me angrier and more frustrated. After a third pin, he said to me, "Rage will never win a fight. Emotion makes you weak and vulnerable to your opponent. Precision and Purpose win every time." My father always says those two words with such weight that I can't think of them without capital P's.

I drag a few deep breaths down my lungs as I drive the car and center myself before I reach my destination. It would never do to run across any council members, Reds, or more importantly, my father while I'm wound up. He'll spot the emotional agitation immediately and not let me talk to the bounty hunters. He might even pull me as Sophia's protector if he suspects we're getting too attached. At least that would be a hard one to justify, since our bond makes me uniquely qualified to look out for her. I've always resented the bond, but the thought of anyone else getting that close to her makes my stomach churn.

By the time I arrive at the compound, I've calmed myself and slid my poker face into place. I pull up to the black iron gates and buzz the gate guard, looking directly into the camera so they can identify me.

"Name and pass code?" A brisk voice crackles through the speaker.

"It's Nomad." I give her my code name and type in the current pass code to enter the council compound. You can't be too careful when dealing with Mages or Witches since there are those out there who could change their appearance or create illusions.

"Oh, hey Logan," says the guard, as she buzzes me in.

I stop at the gate house for a chat. Cecilia's manning the gate today. She's only a couple of years older than me and we've known each other forever. We even had a brief fling a few months ago.

"Hey, Cecilia."

"How's it going? You in town for long?" Cecilia tosses her long dark ponytail over the shoulder of her red uniform, giving me an appreciative look.

We had a few fun nights, and she is stunning to look at it, but I cut it off before she had a chance to form any attachment. We'd both been on the same page about keeping it casual. My current assignment is top secret, so she won't know where I've been.

"No, just came for a visit and to talk to some thugs that were brought in the other day. Heading out right after." I give her the bare amount of information.

"Gotcha, well have a good one and make sure to look me up when you're in town next." Her lips curve in a wicked smile that spreads a little heat through me, but hot as she is, I don't think I'll be calling her soon. I give her a wave and crawl up the winding road. My fingers drum a soft beat on the steering wheel as I chafe at the speed limit within the compound grounds.

The compound is just outside of Port Grand in the middle of farmland. Trees surround the grounds, and a fence runs around the perimeter of the property. It's unassuming but offers protection in the form of magic wards as well as an electric current. Best of both worlds to keep out curious mundanes and the bad elements of the magical crowd.

As I clear the treed area, the buildings come into view. I wonder what Sophia would think about it. It looks less like government or military and more like an expensive private school. There's a series of large red brick buildings covered in ivy, each with their own parking areas. Beautiful gardens line the pathways between each building. They have some skilled Bio Mages that excel in plant life to keep them looking ace even in the middle of the snow blanketed winter months. Sophia would definitely freak if she saw that. My lips curve up at the thought of her amazed expression. It's kind of cool to think about the magic world through her eyes.

I head for the largest building, Wellesley Hall, first. My dad and mom both have offices here.

My family has our own house off the compound, but as a kid growing up, I was envious of those families that got to live here surrounded by others like themselves to play with. As an adult, I'm glad for the privacy and independence that living off the compound offers. If more people were in the know about Sophia, they would definitely try to get her to move in, but with the risk of an insider's involvement, it's not wise. A chuckle escapes at the thought of anyone trying to force her to do something she doesn't want to do. I'm kind of glad that Liz and I get to selfishly keep her to ourselves for now. A dark feeling slithers through me at the thought of some of those other goons here getting their eyes on her.

I nod at the two door guards and punch in a different code to enter the imposing front door. I head straight for my dad's office first. He can help me gain access to the prisoners, and I'll never hear the end of it if I come here without stopping by to check in with him first.

I roll my eyes at the sweeping staircase in the main hall that looks like it belongs in the home of a 19th century British duke. This place is so pretentious. I lope up the stairs two at a time, turning right at the top to head down the long hallway lined with pictures of former council members. Mostly a bunch of old white dudes with sticks up their asses. I reach my dad's office and stroll in. A huge grin stretches my cheeks at Rose's kind, round face and short cap of neat silver curls. It's been too long since I saw her.

"Logan, what a nice surprise," she says with a genuine warmth in her voice. "We weren't expecting you today." She glances down at her calendar as if to verify I'm not on the agenda, but we both know very well how efficient she is. She's been my father's assistant since I was a little kid and she still treats me like one, but in a good way. "Would you like a cookie?" She holds out a basket that's filling the room with the warm scents of vanilla and chocolate. Reminds me of Sophia for some reason. Never one to pass on Rose's delicious baked goods I grab two.

"Chocolate chip, you do know the way to a guy's heart. Don't suppose you're single yet?" I flash her a teasing grin.

"Shame on you! Gary and I are doing just fine. Have you found yourself a lovely little Mage to settle down with yet?"

"Rose, how could anyone else possibly measure up to you? If I can't have you, I guess I'll have to settle for the bachelor life." I let loose a dramatic sigh, while trying to keep my mind blank and away from thoughts of Sophia. Rose might look like the fairy godmother from a story, but she's a solid Psyche. An excellent quality to have in an assistant.

"Stop it with the charm, young man. You kids these days are too flippant about romance. Always a new girl on your arm every time I see you." She gazes at me sternly, but her indulgent tone gives her away. Her and Gary have been married for like forty years or something, so she's definitely proven that young love can last.

"Is Dad free?"

She glances at the phone to check if he's on the line. "Yes, he's in his office right now." She gives him a buzz on the intercom. "Logan is here to see you."

"Send him in." My dad's voice crackles back on the ancient phone. They spent a fortune on the latest security tech for the place, but my father still hasn't gotten rid of the phone system that's older than me. Typical.

"Thanks, Rose." I give her a wink and brandish my mouth-watering cookie in her direction before I hit my father's office.

Nothing's changed here either. Boys' club all the way with a hunter green carpet, ornate cherry desk, and chairs upholstered in green leather pulled taut by brass buttons. The bookshelves lining the back wall snag my attention. I wonder if any of them would be useful for Sophia?

He looks at home in the manly room. His slicked back black hair has silvered a little more at the temples since the last time I saw him, and he's sporting a neatly trimmed beard on his usually clean-shaven face. I always find it strange to see him in his expensive three-piece work suits. I'm used to him at home in training mode. He would definitely fit in at the snootiest of country clubs in that getup though. I'm not sure how they'd feel about admitting a Mage, though. Probably have rules against that. Old money mundanes aren't known for their tolerance of those who are different. Although, come to think of it, if they thought he could give them more power, they might second guess themselves.

"Hey, Dad." I greet him with a handshake. He isn't really the hugging type.

"It's a surprise to see you, son. What brings you out here? Is everything alright with Sophia? Why aren't you with her?" Doubt tinges his formal tone. Of course he doesn't think I'm doing a good enough job, and after last night he's probably right.

"I left her in Liz's capable hands while I came out here. She was resting when I left. After last night, she needed some time to recupe."

"And did she sustain any serious injuries at the hands of those men?"

"She hurt her ankle, but it looks like it's just a mild sprain. She should be ok with a few days to rest it."

"You should have been there with her. They never should have been able to lay hands on her in the first place. You knew your responsibility. I'm tempted to send someone else in as back up."

Of course he doesn't trust me to handle the responsibility. He's spent my whole life training me to be stronger, faster, and better, but it's never good enough.

"I can handle it, Dad. It took her some time to believe us and to trust me. She's at our house now and we'll watch her every second from now on."

"Well, it's on your head if anything happens to the girl."

"I know," I say, as if I don't feel guilty enough. The thought of her in the hands of those assholes is like a punch in the gut.

"That's the reason I came here, though. I want to talk to those bounty hunters, see if I can get any info out of them."

"I've interviewed them and had one of my most trusted men try as well. We're not getting anything out of them. You wasted the drive here."

Nice to see you too. I think, but I'm careful not to let the retort slip out my mouth. It won't do to piss him off when I need to get in to see those guys. "Since I'm here, you might as well let me talk to them. It can't hurt, and even if I don't find out who hired them, I might be able to gain a little more insight into how many others might be out there. Please Dad. Anything to help me do my assignment to the best of my abilities."

A sour taste fills my mouth at the ass kissing coming out of it, but he can't say no when I put it like that.

"I will have Trey escort you down." He hits the intercom. "Rose, please have Collins report to my office." Then he turns back to me. "Have a seat, son." Of course, he's going to send Trey.

I settle into one of the chairs across from my father. They match his desk chair but are smaller and lower to the ground. If he wasn't born a Mage, my dad would have fit right in as the CEO of some huge mundane company. Intimidation and mind games are almost automatic to him.

"How's Mom?" I ask, the icy wall I've put up to talk to my father melting a bit at the thought of her. I've been talking to her on the phone regularly, but it's been a couple of days since we last chatted.

"She's doing well. Up to her usual clubs when she's not working. And your sister? Are you looking after her?" He steeples his hands in front of him and gives me an appraising look.

"Of course. Although you know Liz, she's pretty self-sufficient."

"That may be, but she is still not of age and she's under your care. I hope you're not letting her mix with mundanes as she's prone to doing."

"Well, we are attending a high school full of mundanes, so we can't avoid speaking to them altogether," I say, hoping my dad won't catch the sarcasm. "Liz, however, has really taken her responsibility seriously and is spending a lot of time with Sophia."

I might not care about getting myself into trouble with my father, but I would never try to sink my sister along with me.

"Good. I'm glad to hear she's maturing and growing out of that mundane fixation of hers."

I go off to the blank place in my head to avoid rolling my eyes at him. Seriously, he needs to get over his biases. We're living in the 21st century, after all. I know we can't reveal the truth to mundys, but there's no need to treat them like lower beings.

A murmur of voices sounds in the outer office, and I'm almost relieved that Trey's arrived. I'm not looking forward to spending time with him. Probably one of my dad's endless tests. He knows I can't stand Trey but wants to see if I can control my emotions around him.

The door to my father's office swings open, and Trey swaggers in. He looks older than the last time I saw him. It's probably the uniform and the douchey buzzed haircut.

"Good afternoon, sir." He's all that is polite when he addresses my father, holding his hand out for a handshake. "Logan." He adds that for my benefit, offering his hand as an afterthought. An evil delight flashes through me at the glint of anger I catch in his eyes when I leave him hanging.

"Trey. Let's get to business. I don't have all day. Bye, Dad." I start walking before I finish my sentence without a backward glance for either of them.

Trey is the son my father wishes I had become. Polite, obedient, robot-like in his ability to control his emotions, and dedicated to the council. Dad always wanted me to become a Red and rise through the ranks, but I'm not the blindly obedient type. I know I'll have to find my place here, but the thought of a foot soldier role makes me want to crawl out of my skin.

We would have been fine though, if not for a girl. Trey and I grew up together and were close when we were kids. We grew apart as we hit the high school years and I took the path more reckless. I wanted to enjoy my life before they conscripted me into service to the council for the rest of my days while Trey was the perfect Straight A student who never stepped a toe across the line. He was a good-looking guy though, so I've been led to believe, and there was no shortage of girls into both of us.

There were enough to go around, and we never had a problem until we both fell for the same one. Trey never forgave me after Ivy chose me, and he still blames me for her death. Our already poisoned friendship went toxic after that. Part of the problem is that I blame myself for her death too, and the double dose of guilt drags me down like a drowning man when he's around.

Trey has to jog to catch up to me as I power down the hall.

"How did you get assigned to such an important mission? You're not even with the MED." He's probably assuming, like everyone else, that I got it through nepotism, which I guess is partially true. I mean, that's why I got bonded to her in the first place. Because our parents were tight.

"Top secret. You don't have the clearance." I let him mull that one over. Clearly my father has told him about Sophia but kept the info about the bond on the down low.

"Yeah right, I heard you were traveling and wasting time this year. Probably messing around with more girls, too. There must be a reason they pulled you into service early." He's a little sharper than I expected. A little too curious for my liking. I shouldn't have expected that. Trey may irritate me like a pebble in my shoe, but he's a smart guy.

"Like I said, top secret, but the job does have its perks." I smirk at him, knowing how much it chafes that they gave an important assignment to me instead of him. He doesn't need to know that I didn't earn this job through my skill or dedication, but a spell I was burdened with before I could talk.

"Whatever, you're all talk, man."

We spend the rest of the walk in silence, probably for the best, as the words would have only come out sharper until they potentially turned into fists. Trey's way too into his job for that, and I don't want to mess up my chance to talk to Sophia's attackers.

We head to the converted old barn that's used to house criminals that can't be turned over to the mundane police. We pass through the old wooden door into the gleaming lobby that doesn't give any hint about the contents of the bonus floors underground.

Trey uses his handprint and pass code to gain us entrance. I'm not a member of the magical enforcement team and thus do not have access. It pisses me off to have to rely on him, but it'll be worth it if I can drag anything out of Sophia's kidnappers.

The black and white tiled floor squeaks underfoot from its smooth polish. I sign in and whip the knives out of my boot and hip sheaths, reluctantly turning them in for the duration of the visit. The constant current of my magic disappears as we step through the steel door. This place is heavily warded to dampen magic, and it's like my insides have been yanked out. No wonder some prisoners go crazy after a while. I can't imagine my magic being gone for good. Once out of the reception area, the reality of the building surrounds us in steel bars and armed guards. The guards in here carry Tasers since they can't access their magic either. It's a depressing place.

Trey leads me to an interrogation room not too far in and drops me in the bland beigeness before leaving to fetch the thugs. There's a single metal table bolted to the ground and a few chairs on either side. I lean against the far wall with my arms crossed, not wanting to be at a disadvantage when they bring them in. My father arranged to have all the recording devices turned off and for only Trey to be present at the interview.

Trey marches them in, flanked by two beefy guards. They cuff them to the chairs and Trey waves them off. I realize I don't even know their names. Sophia referred to them as Muscles and Scruff, for obvious reasons. I plop down in the chair and put my feet up on the table, ignoring Trey's glare. I'm not a Red…yet. I don't have to act like I've got a stick up my ass like him.

I wait until the door slams shut behind the guards before I speak.

"Who hired you?" I ask, not expecting an answer. They sneer at me in silence, as expected.

"Look guys." I pull my feet off the table and lean forward with my palms on the table. "I'm not one of these tools." I jerk my head toward Trey. "You know what that means, right?" I lean in even closer with my best empty psychopath stare. "I don't have to follow their rules. So, it's basically a little cooperation or a continuation of that beating I handed you the other night."

Muscles gives a slightly panicked look to Scruff, who shakes his head. For a big guy, he's a real coward.

"We can't tell you, man. He'll hunt us down and kill us."

"I don't even need to hunt you down." Muscles glances nervously at Trey. "He's not going to protect you. Just spill before I get impatient." I take a little pleasure in his flinch at the sharp crack my palms make when I slap the table.

As expected, Muscles breaks first. "We never learned his name. We never even met the guy. He goes by the name of Zeus, but nobody knows his real identity. He spreads the word through the Darknet when he wants a job done and he pays real well."

"And what's the bounty on this job?"

"A million large man. Who couldn't use that?" Shit, there's a million-dollar bounty on Sophia's head? I glance at the door. An itch tugs at me to get up and boot it back to her immediately. She's far enough away that only super intense emotions will hit me through our bond.

"Well now you've ended up with nothing and nowhere to spend it locked up here. You should consider making better life choices. Anything else you can tell me about this guy? Know anyone who's collected on a job from him? Did you have to take her alive? Why he's after the girl?" I hide this question among the others to disguise its importance.

"No way. Last guy I heard who blabbed about a job he did for Zeus wound up with his head cut off after he got sliced to ribbons. No one's gonna talk. Yeah, he wants her alive. No prize if she winds up dead. And guys like us, we don't ask why, although given that price she must be something pretty special."

"You've got to have some helpful information on how to contact him." The crack of my knuckles echoes in the bare room. I reach for my boot to unsheathe a dagger, stopping short when I remember I had to check it in. Stupid rules.

"There's nothing man. We just keep up on the job postings."

I stand up and walk around the table. I'm really itching to hit one of them for what they did to Sophia.

Muscles cowers back a little at my approach. "I swear, man, there's nothing. Guy is like a ghost. I'm pretty sure he's the one behind all the recent Mage disappearances."

Interesting. I've been thinking the same thing, but I didn't want to freak Sophia out even more. I've heard of at least five Mages disappearing within the last few months and none of them has been found yet. I have no idea how that connects to Sophia, but there must be something.

"Thanks for the lack of enlightenment. Enjoy your stay here." I stretch and make one more quick move toward the pair, just to watch them flinch. "Let's peace Trey. I'm done with this place." Pain shoots through my palms when I clench my hands so tight I break skin.

"Shame I didn't get a piece of the bitch." The mutter behind me grips me in a red rage.

I lunge back, enjoying the thud as my fist slams into the face of the one with the sad excuse for a beard. Trey hauls me back and out the door when I go for the second one.

I speak up as soon as the door snicks shut behind us. "Well, that wasn't too helpful, but it is good to know the price on her head. Basically, that means every baddie on the continent is going to be after her and maybe some foreigners as well. Fuck!" I punch the wall for emphasis. There is no way I can keep her safe where she is, but I don't have a clue how or where we would move her.

"I'm sure taking it out on the wall will solve the problem, dick."

"I'd be happy to take it out on your smug face if you'd prefer." I think that would be a solid step toward calming the rage still burning inside me.

"Don't even think about it, man. Looks like you're not going to be able to do this job on your own. I'll talk to your father about moving her onsite."

"No way is that happening. There could be people on this compound who would not have her best interests in mind."

"Why? What's so special about her?" He really wants to get that nose of his punched in, doesn't he? I stretch out my fingers a few times.

"Well then, I guess we'll just have to arrange a protection detail. I'll speak to Robert about heading it up."

"Oh, on a first name basis with my father now? That won't be necessary. I've got this under control." My jaw pops at my clenched teeth. I know this is going to happen no matter how much I protest. My father will never trust me to protect Sophia on my own with that many people gunning for her. And I want the extra layer of protection. I don't know who I can trust, though.

"Yeah right. Be seeing you soon."

"I gotta get back to her. Check ya later, asshole."

Trey heads off to wherever smug bastards hang out around here and I storm off to collect my weapons, fuming the whole way.

CHAPTER 15
Sophia

A cleanup crew of two men and two women all decked out in black tactical gear with a stylized red M on the back of the vest and a red and gold crest featuring a lion and the same M pulls up. They are definitely not from any police branch I've ever heard of.

They efficiently carry the still unconscious guy out to their unmarked black cargo van.

"Umm, your neighbors are so calling the cops," I say.

Liz only laughs. "Every clean up team has at least one Psyche who can create illusions. Don't worry, any nosy neighbors will just see them as a delivery crew or something."

I'm not sure whether to be impressed or concerned. I'm rethinking my whole life now. How many magical occurrences have taken place over the years without my knowledge?

Logan frantically bursts through the door after the cleanup crew has cleared out.

"What happened? Where's Sophia? Are you ok?"

His eyes lock on me and he rushes over. I let out a squeak as he engulfs me in a hug that pulls me off my feet.

"I'm fine." I say, extricating myself from his arms. If he doesn't want a relationship with me, he'll do well to keep his hands to himself. His hot and cold behavior is making my head spin and not in a good way. I pretty much offered myself up on a platter and he pushed me away.

"Chill brother, nothing I couldn't handle." Liz pipes in.

"What the shit? I knew I shouldn't leave Sophia." Logan is way too bent out of shape when we're both clearly fine.

"A thug broke in who I tidily looked after. No biggie. Yeah…you're going to have to fix the back door, though."

"What was he? A Mage, witch? Some other brand of supe?" he asks.

I shake my head to make sure my hearing is still working. I don't even want to think about what the other options could be. Nope.

"No, just a mundy. I have no idea why they sent him. Clearly, I can handle one mundane thug with my hands tied behind my back."

"Really? A mundane? Could be distraction." His edgy gaze darts around the room. "They must be up to something else. Not a clue what that it is, though."

Logan finally settles down a bit, but I can see the tension lingering around the edges of his ocean eyes and in his tight shoulders.

"Did you learn anything on your trip?

"Nothing too helpful. Nobody seems to know the real identity of this guy. He goes by the code name Zeus." He's going to go bald prematurely if he keeps tugging on his hair like that.

A knot settles into my stomach. We're back to square one in the information department and I have to get home. My mom is going to freak out if I don't show for dinner this evening.

"Well that sucks." Understatement of the millennium.

"Yeah. We'll figure this out. I promise."

"I guess we can get together tomorrow to do some more research. Any chance you can give me a ride home? If not, I can walk. It's not far."

"You can't go home tonight. Call your mom and tell her you're staying another night," Logan says.

I give him an incredulous look. "I can't exactly move in with you guys. My mom is expecting me for dinner. I have to go home."

"No, you can't!" His voice pitches up a bit.

"Dude, this is not the 19th century. You don't get to order me around like that."

Liz jumps in. "Let's all calm down and have a seat. Logan, you stop being a domineering jerk, and Sophia, retract those quills. I'm sure Logan has an excellent reason for wanting you to stay here, even if he has a terrible way of expressing it." I'm surprised the glare she directs at her brother doesn't singe his eyebrows.

I reluctantly do as she asks but settle into the armchair furthest from the couch where Logan plopped down.

Logan fills us in on the details of his inquisition, including the million-dollar bounty on my head. I can't quite get my head around that one. I mean, I value myself and all, but how could anyone possibly think I'm worth a million dollars?

"And now our father is going to send Trey and some loyal soldiers from team Red to provide us with back up." He growls this last part out.

"Trey's coming? This should be fun." Laughter bubbles out of Liz.

"Who's Trey?"

"Logan's archnemesis. And also, our dad's pet soldier."

Logan is almost vibrating. I can feel a whole mess of anger and irritation bubbling out from him.

"He's not that bad. Logan just has an old beef with him, about Ivy…" She trails off with a guilty look on her face.

"What do you mean by team Red?" I ask.

"Oh, Red is like slang for the Magical Enforcement Division agents. They're the police of the Mages. The cleaners you met are a part of them."

"Why do you call them that?" I'm genuinely curious about the etymology.

"They used to wear all red uniforms, but that got to be a little conspicuous as civilization modernized, so now they just have the red M on their back and the MED crest."

"Gotcha. None of this information changes the fact that I have to go home."

"Please, Sophia." I realize how serious he is when a hint of fear peeks through Logan's controlled mask. "Call your mom and tell her you're spending one more night on your marathon study session. You can go home tomorrow evening. By then, our dad will have sent a team and they can keep watch at your house overnight. Until then, you won't be safe there and you'll be putting your mom in danger. They might want you alive but if she gets in the way of an attack, they won't have any problem hurting or even killing her. Anyone who would work for this Zeus guy is a real bad person."

The mention of the danger to my mom is a bit of a low blow, but it convinces me. It also doesn't hurt that he's asking now instead of commanding.

"Fine. I'll call her."

Logan and Liz share a relieved glance.

"Fantastic. You call your mom, and we'll figure out dinner. Noodles or burgers?" asks Logan.

"I think I could use some good, greasy carbs. Let's go for noodles," I say.

"I agree. And you hardly ate any of the lunch I made you." Liz's lower lip pushes out into a pout.

"I don't know. Maybe it was the second kidnapping attempt and kitchen brawl that dulled my appetite." I give her my most sarcastic look before leaving the room to call Mom.

"Glad you won't be alone. I'm going to have to meet this new friend of yours," she says. "They seem like a nice family. Her mother was very sweet when we chatted." She's surprisingly cool about it. I wonder if their mom used a little more of her psychic juice than they originally told me.

"For sure, you'll have to meet them. Love you, Mom. Stay safe." Like that's happening. I try to imagine her reaction if I introduced her to Logan. That's a hard no.

"Love you too. Bye, honey."

"Bye," I say, reluctant to break the connection. Now that Logan has mentioned the danger, I'm worried about her all alone in our house.

"She'll be fine." Liz says, as if she really can read my mind. "You're not in the house, so no one's going to look for you there."

I hope she's right.

"Any chance we might be able to have just a fun, normal night? No epic fights, broken windows or kidnapping?" A girl can dream, can't she?

"I can't guarantee that, but there's no reason we can't try to watch a movie in between brawls." Liz gives me a wink.

Logan swaggers in. "Actually…I just talked to Dad. He's sending a local witch over to put up some extra wards on the house. She'll be over shortly. She's going to do your house as well. We should be safe in here for the night. When you have to go to school and stuff is when we could run into problems. Good thing I'm in all your classes."

"Yeah, about that. How did you pull that one off? There's no way you ended up in all the same classes as me by coincidence."

"That would be the work of our mother again. She might have performed a little of the mind control mojo on the school admin. All on the hush hush though, don't tell anyone." Like I have anyone to tell.

"Is there a difference between a Witch and a Mage?" I ask. I remember he mentioned witches earlier and then didn't have a chance to expand on the thought.

"Oh yeah, huge. Witches are just regular humans who have learned to control the magical energy that exists in the natural world. They don't have any magic of their own, so they have to use spells, potions, and magical objects to capture and harness it. Limiting. Any old mundane can do witchy things with the knowledge and lots of practice. Although some of them probably have a drop of super diluted Mage blood in them."

"So, you think you're better than them, but you need them?" His tone was pretty dismissive.

"I didn't mean it like that. Witches are good at lots of things. Most of them have a specialty. This particular witch is an ace at wards. She'll set up wards all around the outside of the house so no one can pass the threshold if they intend to harm us. There are just quite a few humans who pursue witchcraft to gain power or money. More often than not, they go over to the dark side if their intentions are selfish."

"Ahhh wards, so someone we know then?" Liz gives her brother a pointed stare.

"Uhhh, yeah…" Logan rakes his hand through his hair and a flash of his discomfort hits me. Also what might be embarrassment? "Desdemona." He mumbles, his eyes skating all over the room.

Liz laughs so hard she snorts.

"Shut up," Logan says.

"Oh, you're in for it." She's swiping away tears from her eyes.

"First of all, Desdemona, if I ever heard a witchy name that's it. Second, what's the story?" I ask.

"Oh, just one of Logan's favorite mistakes. You'll see. I can't wait for this one. Can I bring popcorn?" Liz replies.

Well, now my curiosity is at full attention.

The chime of the doorbell rescues Logan from further interrogation on the topic. A switch flips in him and his tight muscles are on high alert, his hand brushing the knife at his hip, which I hadn't noticed until now. He's been wearing a knife around the house? He motions at me to get down. I guess in case the food delivery person turns out to be an evil Mage. Or maybe he carries a knife too. Not something I would have considered in my old life.

Liz ducks into the closet by the front door as Logan peers through the peephole before unlocking the deadbolt and opening the door. Turns out the delivery guy is not a secret ninja assassin, and the transaction goes peacefully.

My stomach growls as the tantalizing scents of ginger and garlic invade the room. Logan drops way too many paper bags on the coffee table, and Liz fetches cutlery, plates, napkins, and a pitcher of gloriously cold water to wash it all down.

I realize how ravenous I am once the takeout containers are spread haphazardly on the table, and I pile my plate high with sodium and fat. Conversation ceases while we stuff our faces. When my stomach is stretched to its limit, I fall back on the couch and groan.

I swing my legs over the side of the couch to get up and help Liz when she staggers up from the couch to clean up the mess.

"No, you stay here. You're the guest, and you're injured." She flashes me a quick smile. "You, on the other hand, can get off your lazy butt and give me a hand," she says to Logan.

"Nope, too full, besides someone has to stay and guard Sophia."

"Oh no, you're not using me as an excuse." I shake my head vehemently.

"Whatever. Guess you're on laundry duty tomorrow," she says to Logan.

"Uhhhh." He groans but doesn't move from his place on the couch. He gravitated next to me for dinner, and I didn't have the energy to protest.

"Soooo, tell me about Desdemona." I narrow my eyes and direct an evil grin at him.

"I should have helped Liz, after all." He drops his arm over his face. "We sort of had a thing. I wasn't in a good place and let her snare me. She won't let it go. I never should have done it."

I'm interested to see the sort of woman Logan's been involved with, but despite his apparent lack of interest in her, a flare of jealousy shoots through me.

The doorbell chimes again and this time Logan is much less SWAT team about answering it. I hear muffled voices before they enter the living room.

I cough to cover up the giggle that almost slips from my mouth. Logan's standing there looking sheepish, and a woman is clutching his arm possessively with her talons. She looks like she belongs on the package of a sexy witch Halloween costume. Long, straight hair dyed blue-black drapes the back of her fitted black dress that bells out at the elbows and flares from the waist to mid-calf. The most eye-catching part, however, is her "assets" spilling from the deep v of the neckline. When my eyes make it to her face, I make the unfortunate discovery that she is gorgeous underneath the excessive makeup and bright red lipstick. She's also at least ten years older than Logan, by my estimate.

"Aren't you going to introduce me to your friend?" she asks Logan, in a sugary sweet voice that belies the hostile expression in her eyes.

"Uh sorry. Desdemona, this is Sophia. She's an old friend of the family. Sophia, Desdemona is here to do the wards I was telling you about."

"Is that all I'm here for?" She coos at Logan, stroking his arm. I don't think I've ever felt like ripping a limb off another person until this moment.

"That's what my dad is paying you for, right?" Logan, master of diplomacy.

I'm surprised at the deep, throaty laugh that comes out of her. I was expecting a cackle.

"Hi Desdemona! How are you doing?" Liz walks back in and holds out her hand for a shake, allowing her brother to slither out of the Witch's grasp and mutter something about the bathroom before ghosting.

"I'm doing better now that I'm here with you and your brother. He's a naughty thing, hasn't been returning my calls. I thought he was away traveling for the year." She gives me a furtive glance, probably suspecting me of keeping him away.

"He was traveling for a little while, but then he got called back on council business. How about I take you out around the house so you can ward it. We can get caught up." I'm eternally grateful to Liz as she grabs Desdemona's arm and half drags her toward the front door.

Once I hear the front door shut, I let the laughter spill out, which is how Logan finds me when he creeps around the corner.

"Not exactly what I thought your type would be."

"Really. And what did you think my type would be?"

"I don't know. Closer to your age, less cartoonish? Do all Witches dress like that? Is there a uniform or something?"

"Well, some Witches are men for a start. So, no."

"Hey, I don't judge. Be yourself. Dress how you like. We can wear pants. Why can't guys wear dresses?"

"She's not from a family line of Witches like a lot of them. She's self-taught, so I think she tries a little too hard. She's not so bad, though. She just swooped in at the right time last year when I was still...whatever. Anyway, I haven't encouraged her, and this was over a year ago. Speaking of types, what's yours?" He asks, in a clear and successful effort to distract me.

I blush. "I don't know. I don't think I have a type."

"No? Not floppy haired and hazel eyed? Perhaps you're into something better. Dark hair and excellent swordsmanship?" He grins wickedly at me.

I get serious. "Here's the deal. I'm done with Garrett. We've talked about that. As for you, don't tease if you're not going willing to back it up. I told you how I feel, and you got all squirrelly on me. It's up to you now. I don't have time for games."

Liz and Desdemona choose this moment to come strolling back in. I'm kinda thankful for the interruption. Saves me from that conversation.

"What did Liz and I miss while we were outside?" She turns her beauty queen smile on him, far too toothy for my liking.

"Nothing. Everything all set with the wards?" Logan asks briskly.

"Yes, they're all in place, and Liz helped me activate them. They'll hold out an angry demon if it comes to that. I'm curious why you need these wards in place. It's not like you two can't look after yourselves." I don't like the speculative gleam in her eyes as she glances at me. She's clearly more cunning than she's trying to appear. I'll have to watch out for her.

"Oh, you know Dad. So overprotective with us out here away from them for the first time. And with his position on the council, he always has enemies, of course." Liz is quick on her feet with the lie.

Desdemona seems to accept this, but then glances at me again. "And I'm doing her house too, right?"

"Yes, like I said, close family friend. She has family on the council, too."

"Of course. Shall I bring her with me to seal the ward around her house then?"

"No. It's fine. I'll come with you." Logan's tone gets shorter with every word.

"Excellent, let's be on our way." She's practically purring and rubbing herself against him as she slides her arm through his.

I almost jump off the couch to pull him back but restrain myself. He's quite capable of looking after himself. Nonetheless, I watch them through a jealous haze as they walk out the front door together.

"Thank goodness." Liz sighs, flopping down on the couch beside me. "I couldn't spend another minute with her. Hopefully, Logan will have the brains to not invite her back when they're done at your house."

"Not a fan? What's the deal with her and Logan, anyway?"

"We've known her for years. She's quite good at what she does. Logan just fell prey to her dubious charms last year, and she hasn't let him forget. I honestly don't know what he was thinking. Boys are so stupid sometimes. My brother in particular."

"I can't tell you what he was thinking either, but I can tell you what he was thinking with!"

Liz laughs along with me, but deep in my heart, worry nags at me. Logan is so experienced with women. I, on the other hand, have only recently had my first kiss. I have no idea what his expectations are or even what I want. What a mess I've gotten myself into. Garrett would have been so easy. Instead, I had to fall for the temperamental, overly experienced, sword wielding complication.

"You know what Liz? I think I should probably do some homework." I've been slacking off all weekend and there's nothing like drowning my brain in facts to distract from the excessive feels.

I should give Charlotte a call, too. I know I just saw her at school yesterday, but it feels like longer. She's sent a few texts, Xavier too, but I've been too busy and distracted to reply. That's no way to treat your friends. I'm not sure what I'll say, though. I'll call them tomorrow. I can send them each a quick reply to let them know I'm still breathing.

"Me too, I guess." She's clearly not as excited as I am about solving physics problems.

We fetch our books and I manage to get so engrossed in my work that I do temporarily forget about all the supernatural and emotional crap I'm knee deep in at the moment. Liz got bored and abandoned me after an hour, but I keep at it well until the moon is gleaming high in the sky.

CHAPTER 16
Logan

I'm reluctant to leave Sophia's side despite the wards that Desdemona erected. I had to get her out of the house, though, before she tried to dig more into Sophia's background or the two of them came to blows. Although…the thought of Des and Sophia in a wrestling match is interesting. I wonder who would win. Des is more experienced, but Sophia seems pretty scrappy, after all she did knee Muscles in the groin to escape. The thought startles a laugh out of me.

"What's so funny, lover?" Desdemona asks in her sultry voice. Man, does she even know how to have an innuendo free conversation?

"C'mon, Des, quit it. You know it isn't like that anymore." I'm frustrated with both her and myself. I never should have slept with her, but she really needs to let it go. It's not like she's pining after me with a broken heart. It was casual on both of our sides.

"Why not? We had so much fun together." Her lips form into a crimson pout.

"Yes, but we both agreed it wouldn't work. I'm not looking for any more flings, and neither of us was interested in anything more."

"I know, but it doesn't hurt a girl to try." Girl my ass. She's a total cougar.

The frosty air numbs my gloveless fingers and stings my cheeks. Luckily, Sophia's house isn't too far.

Her house is dark when we get there. Her mom must still be at work. She seems to leave her teenage daughter at home alone quite a bit. That's a puzzle but also an advantage in the guarding department.

The dark walk with Desdemona takes me back to a similar evening spent with her about a year ago. Since Ivy's death, I had done nothing but party and fool around with any Mage or Witch willing to get with me as well as the odd human I came across. It would be too hard to get involved with a mundane in a serious way, but a casual one-night stand does no one any harm. I particularly liked Witches though. They're involved in the magical community, but I didn't grow up with them and I don't have to work with them or see them at the compound all the time like with the other Mages.

I resisted Desdemona's predatory advances for some time, but on that particular night at the Black Flame pub, I had been knocking back shots with some of the Red crew. She had approached me and between the guys, the ever-present guilt, and the tequila egging me on, I made the mistake of going back to her place with her.

Her lair is as melodramatic as the rest of her persona. Altar in the corner, a pantry full of strange herbs, animal bones, and other potion ingredients, and an excess of moody black and red decor. I like my moody black décor as much as the next person, but she's just beyond. Desdemona just tries too hard. It's like because she wasn't born into a Witch family, she tries to overcompensate by acting like a stereotype from pop culture.

The next morning, I left with a multi-level hangover from a combination of the booze and the bad decision. It was, however, my turning point. When I realized I could no longer keep up that lifestyle. I got my shit back together enough to finish school and stop trying to chase oblivion. It also allowed me to finally let go of Ivy and start living again. So I do have Desdemona to thank for being the catalyst, not that I ever would thank her outright, but I will definitely not be going there again.

Despite the fact that I'm desperately trying to avoid her company, I'm still grateful to her. After all, I wouldn't even have a chance with Sophia now if I hadn't gotten my life back together, thanks in part to Des.

"This is her house here," I say, as we walk up to the darkened facade of the white colonial.

"I'll just get to work then, darling."

She walks the perimeter of the yard, hits up all the doors and windows of the house and does all her witchy voodoo. I guess we Mages could also pull from the Earth's energy to perform spells like this if we needed to, but most of us never learn since we can tap into our own magic at will without learning complicated spells or potions. Plus, we have a decent working relationship with the Witches. This isn't the way it's always been. In the past Mages were very intolerant of humans using magic. The Witches' solution was to turn us over to the mundanes for persecution, while they merrily performed their magic in secret. Some of the Mages still hold a justifiable grudge about that, as do some of the Witches.

We finally overcame our differences by forming the Alliance of Magic Users in 1964. The Witches and Mages signed a treaty and established a committee to encourage and regulate magical relations between the two groups. Other supes had joined in more recent years and with each younger generation, it stabilizes further. There is still intolerance out there on all sides that commit hate crimes or discriminate against those who are different, but we have definitely come a long way. The MED helps keep these skirmishes quiet from the humans and investigates cases.

"And now for a bit of your essence, if you please," says Desdemona as she finishes up her work.

I cringe at her wording, my essence? Does she really have to word it like that? I offer my left arm and feel a sting as she gives me a small slice with her ruby handled athame. A pocketknife works just as well, but she's all about the showy props.

Normally you would use blood from the owner or resident of the building to seal the wards, which is why Des initially offered to bring Sophia. There's no way I'm letting her out of our newly warded house tonight, though. Not while the mysterious identity of Zeus is still unknown, and he has a steady stream of expendable thugs for hire in pursuit of her. Besides, the spell will work just as well with my blood because of the magical bond between Sophia and me. We're tied together. It's a good thing we actually like each other. I can't imagine being tied to someone I couldn't stand.

Once she's done, we embark on our short walk back to my place. I scan my surroundings, aware of every crunch of autumn leaves and small animal darting among the bushes.

"What's going on between you and Sophia?" Desdemona drops her faux southern accident and sounds real for the first time in our acquaintance.

"What do you mean?" I ask cautiously, unwilling to betray too much information.

"I would not be a very good psychic if I didn't notice the connection and tension between the two of you."

Although many of the Witches sell their wards, spells, and potions to make a little extra money, most of them also have day jobs that run the gamut from accountant to tarot card reader. Desdemona is a "psychic" for hire to gullible mundanes. She's a real expert at cold reading and has fooled many a human into parting with their money for her nonexistent psychic abilities. The fake psychics are a pretty good way to deter humans from discovering about real magic though. Excellent misdirection.

"C'mon Desdemona." I roll my eyes at her. "Don't try to BS me. We both know you don't have any psychic powers. You know who my mother is."

"Ah yes, but I haven't convinced thousands of mundanes to empty their pockets without being extremely perceptive."

There's definitely truth in that statement. Perhaps I've let Desdemona's almost cartoonish wardrobe and general air deflect me from her real brains all these years. Interesting. I raise my brow at her in response. I'll have to think about that. I always try not to underestimate anyone. Look what my sweet little sister is capable of.

"Are you and her in a relationship?" she asks.

"It's complicated."

"Love always is. That doesn't mean you should shy away from it."

"I can't really give any details, but I have to protect her, and I can't exactly do it if I get too close." The explanation falls flat even to my own ears. I know by this point that there's no way I'm backing out on Sophia. I don't even know why I'm trying to deny it.

"Don't let the loss of Ivy keep you from experiencing love again. It was an unfortunate tragedy, but everyone except you knows that it wasn't your fault." I'm shocked that these insights are coming out of her crimson lips rather than her usual aggressive seduction. I guess I really have underestimated her.

"Thanks for the advice, Des." I'm not sure if I'm being serious or sarcastic.

Her comments bring me back to Ivy and her loss. I've tried hard to bury that one deep, but it always comes back to haunt me at the worst times. I guess I'll never really be free of it.

Ivy and I dated for almost two years. We'd been like the power couple of the magical youth. We grew up together and formed a deep friendship that turned into more when I finally manned up and asked her out on her fifteenth birthday. I picture her black hair and gorgeous dark chocolate eyes set in her pixie face.

She had said yes immediately, and we spent the next two years studying magic and training to be the next generation of the Council. Although I never had political aspirations, with Ivy to spur me on, I could picture myself shaping the next generation of magic. She and her parents were always so positive and optimistic about how we could shape the future and continue to build relations with the other supernatural factions.

I never doubted her vision, but I had eventually started to doubt our future together. I never stopped loving her, but I realized that the love I felt for her wasn't the deeply romantic love she deserved. A few months before her death, I started making excuses and distancing myself from her. Perhaps looking for an easy out.

Then came the day her ideals caught up with her and I wasn't there to save her, because I was off with some guy friends avoiding the conversation I was too much of a coward to face.

Despite her popularity, she gained some enemies because of her radical views on inter-supernatural relations and even those about mundanes. She believed that we all needed to work together and was even lobbying to reveal ourselves to the mundanes.

The Reds took me in for questioning about her murder, but I was easily cleared. That night in the blank interrogation room at the compound, though, I wished they would just detain me and give me the punishment I deserved. I was responsible. I had canceled our plans that night. I should have been there with her. I could have protected her. They still haven't discovered her murderer yet. He or she covered their tracks too well.

Everyone told me it wasn't my fault. They would have gotten her another time if not that night. I couldn't spend all my time with her. I don't believe them, though. I'm as guilty as the murderer for her death and also for the lack of honesty with her in the last few months of her life. I didn't deserve her, and I certainly don't deserve Sophia.

Ivy's face morphs into Sophia's in my head. I picture black hair bleaching to golden blonde and Ivy's glassy eyes staring up at me in death, morphing into Sophia's. I can't let the same thing happen to Sophia that did to Ivy. I have to protect her at all costs. I deserve the pain, and I don't deserve the girl, but I'm that much of a selfish jerk I don't think I can help myself.

I pull Des into a spontaneous hug.

"Thanks. See you later." The genuine warmth that creeps into my voice surprises even myself.

"You're always welcome. And…if it doesn't work out with the blonde, you always know where to find me." She reverts back to her faux Southern drawl and gives me a suggestive wink. I smile back this time before I head inside, grateful for her advice.

Liz is yelling at the Real Housewives on the screen when I get in.

"You have the worst taste in TV, sis. Also, you know they can't hear you, right? Where's Sophia?"

"She's studying in the kitchen. I was with her, but I got bored hence I'm studying the ways of mundanes. You know, for research, gotta blend in." Her teal ends bounce on her shoulders as she shrugs.

I eye the grown ass women on the screen, pulling each other's hair. "Sure, that seems like a great way to learn about human nature. I'm sure no one will mind if you turn the school into Beverly Hills High."

I pause in the doorway to the kitchen when I spy Sophia slumped on the table drooling on a fat textbook. I gently brush some strands of blonde hair from her face, admiring her smooth skin. My heart pulses with need.

"Sophia." I whisper, gently shaking her shoulder to wake her up. "Sophia."

She lets out a cute snort and startles awake, blinking her long dark lashes at me. The gold flecks in her brown eyes dance under the kitchen lights.

"What time is it?" She tucks her face into her elbow to hide a yawn.

"It's only ten o'clock, but you've had a long day, so why don't I help you upstairs."

She reaches out for my hand to pull herself to her feet and takes a couple of tentative steps on her own before leaning into me for help. She smells different. Woodsy and masculine, not like the usual vanilla cloud that surrounds her. She must have borrowed my shampoo instead of Liz's. I kind of like my scent on her, as weird as that sounds. It triggers some sort of caveman reaction inside me. God, no wonder women get sick of us idiots.

I've never felt like this about a girl before. She's driving me crazy.

"Did you want to stay in my room tonight?" My dumb mouth says the words before my brain catches up. She gives me a trapped deer kind of look. All wide eyes and open mouth. "Fully clothed." I'm fumbling this hard. "I think I would just feel better if you're close."

She hesitates for long enough that my leg starts jouncing up and down. This nervousness is completely out of character for me. I'm used to walking into a bar or classroom and having my pick of the ladies. The uncertainty is new, and it makes me uncomfortable in my own skin.

"I don't think that's going to be very helpful in the staying apart department."

I pause to think about my words this time. "Well, maybe I don't want to stay apart."

Her eyes narrow and she shakes her head at me. I don't like that my actions have filled her with this doubt.

"How do I know you mean it for real this time?"

I lean in until my lips are a breath away from hers. My hand drifts down to clasp her palm, bringing it up and placing it on my cheek. "You can feel the truth when we're touching. I want you, Sophia. I need you. I've never felt like this about any other girl. You own my heart."

"Wow." Her voice is a bit shaky. She drags her hand down my cheek, leaving behind a sensitive tingle.

"Is that a yes?"

"Did you ask a question?" The left side of her mouth pulls up just a touch.

"Right. Will you Sophia Rose Tennant go out with me?"

"How do you know my middle name?" A laugh breaks the tension. I love her curiosity, but maybe not so much when I'm trying to be all romantic. "Never mind. Yes. I'll go out with you."

"Awesome. Now is it inappropriate to ask you to spend the night in my bed on our first day officially going out? Purely for protection purposes, of course."

"It totally is, but okay. I'll probably feel safer with you anyway."

"Perfect." I'm almost purring as I lean in to plant a chaste kiss on her lips. "I can keep my hands to myself." The thought of running my hands over her soft curves gets me overheated again. This is probably a bad idea. I certainly won't do anything she doesn't want to, but having her next to me all night so close and not being able to touch her is going to be torture.

"You can get ready in Liz's room, and I'll meet you in mine in a few." I squeeze her around the waist one last time before releasing her.

I book it downstairs to fill Liz in on the sleeping arrangements, so she doesn't freak out thinking Sophia's missing when she gets up to her room.

"Hey Lizzie, just a public service announcement so you don't worry because I'm considerate like that. Soph is sleeping in my room tonight." I try to be chill, hoping to slip it by her while she's engrossed in the lives of the disgustingly rich ladies she's so fascinated by. No luck there.

"WHAT?! You'd better not mess around with Sophia and treat her like one of your flimsy floozies. I like her."

"Relax Liz, this will be a clothed and platonic sleep. I would never treat her like a...what did you call them? Flimsy floozy. I just need to keep her close. Protect her in case anything gets by those wards."

"Uh huh. You know that she's going to have to go home tomorrow and sleep in her own bed. How are you going to deal with that big bro?"

My stomach drops. "I don't know. Just let me have tonight, and I'll figure the rest out tomorrow."

"Ok, but just remember your impressionable little sister who is more than capable of kicking your ass is in the room next door."

"How could I forget? Night Liz."

"Night Logan."

I linger a little too long in the bathroom, brushing my teeth. I'm about to flop down on top of my king-sized bed when I actually look around my room and take in the assorted clothes and books strewn casually about. The only organized things in my room are the polished weapons hanging in neat rows on the far wall. "Damn," I swear under my breath. My room looks like it belongs to a serial killer. And a messy one at that. I've never had a girl in here before, so I never thought about how it looks to someone else. I swipe up an armful of dirty clothes and toss them in the lonely laundry basket that inhabits the corner.

"Don't clean up on my account," Sophia says softly, leaning on the doorframe as if she's too afraid to step over the threshold into my lair. She's staring wide eyed at the knives on the wall.

"I'll just pick up these clothes." I continue to clear the room. "Come in."

She looks cute in a pair of pink flannel pajama bottoms with test tubes and beakers all over them. I laugh at her matching top. It says STEMinist on it.

"What?" Her nose crinkles up when she's confused.

"Your shirt, love it. Liz picked up your PJs I see."

She glances down. "Yeah, she picked up a few of my things this morning after she dropped Garrett off. I gave her my house key to grab my school bag and a change of clothes. I hadn't planned on staying the night, but I guess she anticipated that one."

I stretch out and gesture for her to join me. Her weight slowly sinks the mattress beside me as she tentatively sits, keeping her feet firmly on the ground.

"Did you have fun with Liz while I was out today? Before the intrusion, of course." I hate seeing her look so uncomfortable.

"I did. She's pretty fun." She swings her legs up on to my bed and slides back against the headboard, perched as far away as she can get. "Look, I don't want to get into it tonight, but promise me that if we are going to start a relationship, you'll talk to me about your past and stuff. I need to know that you'll be honest with me."

I narrow my eyes, wondering what Liz has shared with her. I know I'm going to have to tell Sophia about Ivy sooner or later. I've just been hoping we could put it off for a while. Then I think about all the other girls I was with in my destructive phase, and I inwardly groan at the thought of sharing that info. It will have to be done, but whether she'll still want to date me after that revelation is anybody's guess.

"Don't worry. We can talk. Let's just relax for this one night, though. I think we both need a good night's sleep." I throw my arms open wide and am relieved when she snuggles in at last.

I'm more complete when she's in my arms, her warm body pressed against mine. I drag the covers up and give her a gentle kiss on the forehead. As I start to pull back, she turns her head up and presses her lips to mine for a brief but sweet kiss. Now I'm never going to be able to sleep.

CHAPTER 17
Sophia

Peace, contentment, and sunshine greet me in the morning. My pillow is harder than usual, though. As it moves up and down in a steady rhythm, I realize my pillow is actually a hard chest and the peace and contentment immediately flips to anxiety and agitation as the events of the previous evening come thundering back.

I'm in Logan's room, in his bed, no less. Can I get up and brush my teeth before I scare him away with my dragon breath? In the bright morning light, this situation is way too intimate for someone I've only shared a few PG kisses with. I wince as he stirs and snuggles in tighter, throwing a solid arm across my midsection. It's dangerously close to my chest and my cheeks flame up. There goes the teeth brushing plan. Dragon breath it is, I guess.

I should shift onto my side, facing away from him so at least I can attempt to keep the mystery of my morning breath to myself. I soak him in a little first. He's pretty cute in his sleep. His black hair spikes crazily all over, and his long lashes rest on his cheeks. The hard lines of his face are softened. He could actually pass for a high schooler right now.

An irresistible urge to kiss him has me dropping a whisper of one on his forehead and before I can pull away, his blue-green eyes lock on mine, and he slides a hand up behind my head to pull me in for a proper kiss. His mouth presses me down as his fingers tangle in my hair and he shifts, leaning into me. I pull him closer, trailing my arm down the muscled ridges of his back slowly. He slides his other hand up under my shirt, caressing my side and sending shivers down my back. I have zero desire to protest as his hand leaves a trail of flames in its wake as it slides up. I groan as he blinks and pulls away, dragging his hand out from under my shirt.

"I'm so sorry Sophia. I didn't mean to…" He trails off, looking contrite.

"It's fine…You didn't have to stop." I look down, suddenly hyper aware again of my toxic breath, my hair, and the sleep crusties that are gumming up my eyes.

Then a terrible thought passes through my over analytical brain. Did he think I was someone else when he started kissing me? The horror of that thought is enough to send me scrambling away. He grabs my arm before I can escape.

"Don't think I wasn't enjoying myself." I can see the truth in the dark look he gives me, though I'm trying not to intrude on his actual thoughts. "I just don't want to take advantage of you. I didn't intend for anything to happen just because you slept in my bed, and I know as well as anyone that our feelings are all tangled together, because of the bond."

My blood cools at the assurance.

"It's ok. I was participating freely. I really do like you, Logan," I say. "Laying all my cards on the table, though, I don't have much experience with this stuff." I wince and drop my voice to a whisper as I say this.

"That's totally cool. We can take things as slow as you like. I'm not in a hurry."

It's nice to hear him say. I've waited and avoided dating at all for so long, but now everything about this feels right. My mom raised me to be responsible and aware of my body and my emotional state. Sex isn't something I've thought a lot about before, probably because I've never been interested in someone like this. I always just figured it would happen one day and I would know when I was ready.

"Thanks. I'm not saying we can't do anything." I glance up at him from under my half-closed lids.

He runs his hands through his hair. "You're killing me. As much as it pains me, we are definitely not doing much with my nosy sister so close. Nor are we going any further until I have filled you in on all the sordid details of my past. You might not even want to date me after that."

"I don't think anything you say could change what I'm starting to feel for you, but I definitely agree that this is not the time or place. Doesn't mean we can't kiss, though." I try to channel my inner siren with an alluring smile. I think my inner awkward turtle heeds the call instead. Not so great at the seduction thing as it turns out.

My cheek tingles as he trails his thumb along it. "We really should get the day started." His actions belie his words as he leans in for a soft and slow kiss.

I ease away. The break in the mood triggers the thought of my troll breath. If anything drives him away, that could be the thing.

"I'll be right back. Have to use the facilities." The sheets attack me on the way off the bed and I hit the floor butt first in an awkward heap.

"Are you ok?" Logan presses his lips together, and his shoulders are shaking.

I drop my head in my hand, wishing there was a handy portal nearby I could disappear into. Is that a thing? Would definitely be convenient. "Mmmm hmmm."

I test my ankle on the way to the bathroom. It seems pretty solid, so I put my full weight on it. Must have been a fairly mild sprain or twist. I'm glad to have my mobility back, what with all the people who are after me. I cringe when I finally see myself in the mirror. My hair looks like it belongs to a mangy lion and dark circles dim my eyes.

I expel the demons lurking in my mouth, desnarl my hair, and put some lotion on the lizard skin I get in the winter months. I'm rubbing my hands up and down my legs as I reenter Logan's room. His unreal abs are on display as he yanks a fresh shirt over his head. Seriously, he must have just grabbed whatever clothes were closest to his hand when he reached into his closet and run his hand through his black spikes. Yet he looks amazing. Guys have it so easy.

He closes the space between us and pulls me into his arms for a minty fresh kiss. "I'll leave you alone to get dressed and start on breakfast. Hungry?"

"Starving. Coffee?" I'll think about full sentences again after the caffeine hits my veins.

"Of course. How do you take it?"

"Two milks, two sugars."

"You got it. See you in a few."

As if it will only take me a few minutes to get ready. He knows I'm a girl, right? He has a sister.

I grab my bag to see what Liz packed for me and find a pair of indigo jeggings, and a black-and-white striped boatneck sweater. Comfy, casual but still pretty. It's like she can read my mind. She unfortunately did not include any cosmetics, so I wander over to her room to see if I can scam some lip gloss or something.

"Go away, Logan. It's Sunday." She groans at my knock, clearly not a morning person.

"It's me, Sophia."

"Oh sorry, you're welcome to come in."

I slip into her room, shutting the door behind me. "Morning. Sorry to bother you. I was just looking for some lip gloss or something. That is, if you don't mind sharing. I know some people are a bit germ phoby."

"No, it's totally fine. I share. You're practically family anyway." She sits up in bed looking as rumpled as I did earlier and slides open the top drawer of her bedside table. "Help yourself, I'm a bit of a lip product hoarder."

She's not kidding. Lip balm, gloss, and lipstick of every shade and style jam up the drawer. I grab a rosy-pink gloss. It's called First Kiss. Great, even the lip gloss is judging me.

"That color looks good on you. Why don't you keep it. I can probably suffer through its loss." Her bell-like laugh tinkles out as she waves at her lifetime supply of lip products. "Also, now that I think about it. Your lips were probably on my brothers anyway, so now his lips are on it, so if I use it again, it'll be like kissing my brother, which is super skeevy. So, yeah. It's yours now."

Her logic is ridiculous, but I feel my face burning up anyway and I look everywhere but at her face.

"I knew it!" She crows. "I'm glad. It's about time he found someone he actually likes rather than the one-nighters he's been indulging in."

"One-nighters?"

"Oh yeah. He's been a bit sketchy the last two years, but I know he's really into you, otherwise there would be no way I would let my brother near my new bestie."

"It's fine."

I knew he was more experienced than me, but it still makes me nervous to think how little I know about guys.

"Shoo shoo, I need the rest of my beauty sleep. You go enjoy your romantic breakfast with your man."

I roll my eyes at her but head down for breakfast. A cloud of vanilla and maple syrup tempts me to the kitchen where I find Logan making…waffles?

"I thought you couldn't cook anything."

"Waffle Sundays are a family tradition in our house. My mom taught us all the delicate art of waffle making so we could all help. Really, I think she was just sick of the job, so she trained us up young." His smile spreads all the way up into his eyes at the memory. "Anyway, my mom bought us a waffle maker to bring with us so we could keep the tradition alive. Liz is a lazy layabout without Dad to drag her out of bed on the weekends, so I've taken over the mantle while we stay here."

"Can I help?"

"Sure, grab some strawberries from the fridge to slice up."

It feels so natural working side by side in the kitchen making waffles. There's homemade whipped cream, maple syrup, and a sprinkle of icing sugar. I let out a moan as the bright red strawberry I snag bursts into an explosion of sweet and tart.

"Can I get a Mimosa with this?" I joke.

"That's only for special occasions," he replies. "No Mimosas, unless you're wearing a fancy hat. That's the rule."

I scoop up a heaping forkful before my butt hits the seat and then inhale a long sip of roasty goodness to kick start the day.

"So, what's the plan for today?" I ask.

The doorbell chimes. Before the sound has stopped echoing, there's a loud knock on the door. I rise to follow Logan, curious to see who's so impatient to visit on a Sunday morning.

"Stay back." Logan warns and pulls a knife out of the back of his pants. What is his life like that he feels the need to be armed even in his own house? What is my life like now?

I hover in the doorway of the living room so I can still see the action but have an escape route if it turns hostile. Nice, I'm using cop words now as if I'm in some crime drama. Supernatural SWAT or something. Good thing my aspirations don't involve TV production, that sounds like an awful show.

Logan peers through the peephole cautiously then eases up, swinging it open. A gorgeous guy is standing there in an outfit like the cleanup crew that picked up the intruder. Someone from their magical police squad. He has dark hair buzzed short at the sides, rich brown skin, and eyes that are a liquid brown so dark they blend with his pupils. He swaggers into the house without waiting for an invite.

Clearly Logan is annoyed, but he doesn't seem to consider the guy a threat, so I emerge from my nook to meet him.

"Well hello, you must be Sophia. Pleasure to meet you. I'm Trey." His face lights up with a blinding smile and he holds out a hand for a shake. It's softer than Logans as if he keeps himself on a regular moisturizing schedule, but there are still rough callouses in spots.

He might have a model worthy face, but he's tall and solidly muscled, so there's no mistaking him for soft.

"We're eating breakfast. Feel free to wait in here." Logan gestures to the living room, not inviting him to partake in our breakfast. He doesn't look back as he walks into the other room.

"Well, that was rude." I smack him on the arm after I catch up. He just grunts and sullenly attacks his waffle.

Trey apparently has no problem making himself welcome and joins us in the kitchen, pouring himself the last of the coffee before settling down at the table with us.

"Your parents would be ashamed of you," he says to Logan.

"Whatever. You think I care what they think?" Logan replies.

"Someone going to fill me in here?" I ask. "Clearly you know each other and I'm getting tired of being constantly out of the loop." Logan doesn't look up from his plate to appreciate the angry glare I pin him with.

"So sorry about that," Trey answers. "I thought he would have filled you in. Logan's father sent me to help protect you, along with a small MED unit."

"MED unit?" I hate that I'm oblivious about all this magic stuff. I'm used to being the knowledgeable one.

"The MED is the Magical Enforcement Department. We're the branch of the Council that looks after policing mages and other supernaturals. I'm a member of one of our local teams. I've known Logan and Liz and their family since we were babies. My family was close to yours as well."

"Oh, so you know about me?"

"Yes, Logan's father trusted me with the intel, but none of the other three team members I brought with me are aware of the details. They're trying to keep it as quiet as possible."

"He knows who your biological parents are and that you're an Archimage, and he knows about the bounty on your head. That's why my father sent him and his team." I wonder why Logan's face is tight with anger. I would think he'd be happy to have extra help.

"After the kidnapping, he didn't think Logan could provide enough protection for you."

"I am fully capable of looking after her and Liz is here too." Logan's voice rises at the dig from Trey.

"Enough boys. Let's get one thing clear. I'm going to go take my chances with Liz alone if you can't keep your hormones in check. I have zero interest in getting caught between whatever is going on between you two." I flap my hand between the cavemen.

Logan looks like he's struggling to control an outburst, but Trey just calmly settles back in his chair.

"Sorry about that. I'll go sit in the living room and when you two finish this up, come join me for some strategizing."

Logan grabs my hand across the table like I'm his lifeline. "I am sorry about that Soph. He's the one person I can't control myself around. We have a bit of a history. I don't want you caught in the middle, though."

"You'll have to share details with me later. For now, let's clean up and go talk to him. I'm curious how any of you think this is going to work. I'm not a YouTube star. I can't justify showing up at school tomorrow with a contingent of bodyguards."

"We'll figure it out." He reassures me.

He pulls me in for a kiss as we tidy the dishes. My eyes are glazed over, and my lips are swollen by the time we get back to the living room to find Trey sitting on the couch with some action movie full of cars and explosions blaring from the TV.

"Where's Liz?" he asks without turning from the screen.

"She's still in bed. What time is it, ten?" Logan glances at his wrist. "She'll probably be up in an hour. Taking full advantage of being off Dad's rigorous training schedule."

"You really should make sure she's staying in shape given the dangers that you're up against right now." A dark look hoods Logan's eyes at the reprimand.

"She's still training. Don't worry about her and don't you dare gossip to my father."

"I'm not going to tattle. I'm not a six-year-old, just looking out for her. We need to talk business. What's the situation like? How many attacks have there been? What's Sophia's schedule like? Is she staying here? I need all the details so I can create a guard schedule." He's laser focused on us now as he shoots questions like they're bullets.

"I'm not staying here!"

"I don't blame you." Trey laughs. "I wouldn't want to be stuck here with this loser, either."

"She's only seventeen and her mom has no clue about any of this, so unfortunately she has to go home tonight. She told her mom she was sleeping over at Liz's house the last two nights, but that's not gonna fly for the school week. As for attacks, there was the Ferrebat scout, followed by the kidnapping by the thugs on Friday, and the hired mundane thug Liz dispatched yesterday. Don't you have all this info in a file or something?"

"Robert wants to keep this as off the books as possible. Very few people know about Sophia so no paper trail."

"I get that, but this secret won't keep forever. How long does he expect we can hide her?"

"Didn't think I would ever say this, but I agree with you. I think if we can at least catch whoever is responsible for these attacks, then your father will have to figure out how to break the news to the council. Once her secret is out, it will spread like wildfire and the magical community across the continent will find out. There hasn't been an Archimage in 50 years," says Trey.

I have no idea what I'm going to do when that happens. My dreams of school are looking hazy and distant. Right now, my focus has to be on survival. Catch the bad guy, then figure out how to avoid magical infamy.

"Desdemona warded her house and this one, so they're both safe havens for now. Sophia has school tomorrow, but Liz and I are both there. I'm in all of her classes and will stick to her throughout breaks and everything. What's your plan, Trey?"

Though the thought of Logan sticking by my side all day at school makes my skin tingly, the fact that he has to do it for protection is a bit of a downer. Why can't I just have a normal boyfriend who I can flaunt at school? One that chooses to stick by me all day because he can't bear to be away from me. Is that too much to ask? Instead, I'm stuck with a boyfriend/bodyguard who's forced to spend all his time with me, so I don't get kidnapped. Sure loses some of the romance. He'll probably be sick of me in a week. Plus, now I have like an actual magical police guard of my own. Way too weird for my liking.

"I've got two teams and we'll split guard duties. Twelve hours on, twelve hours off. Day shift will provide an escort to and from school and keep watch on the building. They'll be there for you if anything happens. Night shift will guard her house."

"Is that really necessary? Since it's warded now?" I ask skeptically. How can I possibly explain magical guards to my mom?

"One hundred percent. We have no idea who they might send after you. They may be able to break the wards and don't get me started on school. We can't ward a public school, so that'll be prime time to get at you." Trey's gone all intense.

That's not terrifying at all. My mere presence at school could endanger hundreds of innocent students and teachers. I feel like the magic version of Typhoid Mary.

"Well, I guess that's it then. We need to find out who's behind this. I can't live like this. Constantly under guard and endangering other people around me."

"That's a job for MED. You can't be involved. It's too dangerous and you're not trained," Trey says.

"Exactly." Logan agrees with Trey, but he gives me a wink to let me know he's not going to sideline me.

"We're staying at the Lunar Inn just outside of town, so I'm going to rendezvous with the team. Squad B will be on night shift 7pm to 7am. I'll send them over to escort you home, Sophia. Squad A will replace them in the morning to take you to school. Stay put here until I send the team."

"Wait, so I'm stuck here until seven this evening?" I ask.

Logan looks hurt, and Trey looks gleeful at my comment.

"Sick of him already? My my, Logan, don't you know how to look after a lady? I can always keep her entertained."

"You keep your hands to yourself," Logan spits out.

Trey looks momentarily taken aback. "Oh, so that's the way it is. I'm pretty sure your father would not approve of you getting involved with your charge."

"If you speak even one word of this to him, I will destroy you." Logan takes a menacing step toward Trey, hands balled up in fists.

"Enough already. I'm not sick of you, Logan, wipe the beaten puppy look off your face. I'm just getting stir crazy stuck here in this house. Also, for the second time, I'm not your property. You don't need to defend me like that. And Trey won't tell your father because I'm asking him very nicely not to." I turn my eyes on Trey and put all of my unpracticed feminine wiles to work pleading with him to play nice and not reveal our secret.

"I'm sorry." Logan kisses the top of my head. While it's nice to feel his warm breath stirring my hair, it also kind of feels like he's marking his territory.

"Ok, I'm out of here before the PDA gets more intense."

"It's not PDA when I'm in my own house! By the way, who's on the squad? Who's going to be showing up tonight for Soph?"

"We got Jeff and Hannah on the night shift. Roxie and I will take day shift."

"Fantastic," Logan says. "Now you can get out of my house. I'm going to have to see more of you than I'd like for the foreseeable future, so you can leave us in peace for the rest of the day."

"Right back at you. It was nice to meet you, Sophia. I'd love to get to know you better. Just because this guy and I have a beef doesn't mean we can't be friends." He leans in for a quick shoulder hug, probably designed to piss Logan off, but I honestly didn't care how he feels about it. His history with Trey has nothing to do with me. I'm more than happy to entertain the thought of getting to know another Mage better.

"You too, Trey. See you in the morning," I say.

"Bright and early. Bye, Liz." He calls up the stairs.

The door vibrates from Logan's slam.

I turn on him. "You are on my side, right? We're going to solve this thing together and return my life to some semblance of normalcy." Well, maybe that last bit is wishful thinking on my part.

"Yes, we are, but let's wait for Liz to get her lazy butt out of bed. She's an excellent plotter. In the meantime…"

He grabs me and slings me over his shoulder, carrying me to the sofa and unceremoniously dumping me there to a chorus of my squeals. I've never been the kind of girl who squeals, but then again, I've never been handled like that before. I'm laughing so hard my abs ache.

"You, my little lamp, need to get off your feet. And also, I've been told I've not been entertaining you enough. Shall I try to fix that?" He looms over me, waggling his brows like an old-timey villain tying a damsel to the train tracks.

"Stop it." I laugh, shoving at his shoulders. "And your little lamp? Have your brain cells started leaking from your ears?"

"Thought we should come up with cute couple nicknames for each other. You know, annoy everyone we know with our adorableness. Would you prefer something else? My sweet smelly shoe? My darling desk? No, I've got it! My lovely dustpan. Any of those doing it for you?"

"Oh my god. Stop, or you'll have to take me to the hospital for a ruptured spleen." I wipe tears from my eyes. I like this playful side of him. It's like now that he's finally given up fighting his reservations, he's letting his real self come out.

Abruptly his laughter cuts off and hunger gleams in his eyes. My skin tingles as he leans in. I sink into the cushions as his weight presses down on me. His heated lips trail sparks down my neck and then back up to meet my lips again. I don't know how long we stay like that. Mouths open, letting each other in, hands exploring every part within reach. It's like forever and the tiniest blip of time all at once. Impatient with his clothes, I slide up under his shirt to feel his silken skin. His muscles ripple as he shudders beneath my fingertips.

"Again! Super gross guys, take it to your room!"

CHAPTER 18
Logan

My sister's screech would be a brilliant method of birth control if I could bottle it. All I want is for every part of me to be in contact with every part of Sophia. Probably good that Liz walked in before the clothes started to disappear though.

"Seriously? You slept through the entire morning and picked now to interrupt us?"

"Like I said, you have a room. How would you feel if you walked in on me in that position?" I shudder at the thought.

"Exactly. Now, where are my waffles?" She sniffs the air as if she can follow her nose to a pot of waffles at the end of the rainbow. Glad her memory is so short.

"Hey, you're way too late for table service. If you want waffles, you're going to have to make them yourself. We've already eaten and suffered a visit from Trey."

"You're supposed to be looking after me. Should I tell Mom you're neglecting me?" She gives me an accusing glare.

"I'm responsible for keeping you alive and whatnot. Doesn't mean I have to bow to your every whim."

"Fine." She sighs. "What's for lunch?"

"Leftover noodles?" Sophia pokes her head out from the blanket she ducked under when my sister got all up in our business.

Liz brightens up. "Fab idea. Also, coffee would be good." She bats her eyes at me.

"I'll make us coffee." Sophia chimes in. "I feel like you guys have been waiting on me the last couple of days, so I'd love to return the favor now that I seem to be capable of walking again. I'll brew us up a batch. Liz can grab some food. I don't know about you, Logan, but I'm still stuffed full of waffles. And then plotting!"

"Ooh, I love plotting. Who are we plotting against?"

"See, I told you Soph. My sister might be a mood killer, but she's also an evil genius. Balance weighted to the evil side. We're going to find the culprit behind the kidnapping attempts before the Reds do."

"Excellent. Let me grab some nosh and I'll be right back."

Liz and Sophia head to the kitchen, leaving me alone with my thoughts. Probably not the best idea. I can't get Sophia out of my head and it's actually worrying me. I should be happy to finally have someone to care about like that, but what if I can't protect her? What if I let her down like Ivy? I mean, I loved her too, except maybe being young I confused the friendly feelings for romantic ones. I honestly don't know if I ever loved her the way I should have.

I drag my hands through my hair. One thing at a time. First, we have to figure out who's after her, then I can take care of him or her. Where do we even start, though?

Sophia returns with a steaming cup of coffee in each hand. "For you sir, black like your deepest, darkest nightmares."

It's like she knows me already. "How did you know?"

"I'm very observant. I saw your coffee before. It clearly had no milk or cream in it, and you don't really seem like the sugar type to me."

"Too sweet already?" I tease.

"Sure, keep telling yourself that."

I wait for her to put the cups down before I pull her onto the couch beside me and am about to indulge in another kiss, but she pushes me away.

"Liz will be here in a sec. Keep your hands to yourself." She's right. It's like now that I've finally given myself permission to be with her, I can't control the need I have for her touch.

Liz meanders in with a heaping plate of leftovers and points her fingers at her eyes then at me in an 'I'm watching you' gesture.

"How's Trey doing?" She's got noodles hanging from her mouth as she talks. Our mom would be so ashamed.

"We didn't exactly catch up on personal news kept it all business."

"Really? All business? I'm pretty sure you'd get fired for talking that way to a colleague at the water cooler." Sophia pipes in.

Liz snorts. "Couldn't behave yourselves even in front of Sophia? Nice one brother. Glad she had the opportunity to see your most charming qualities. Although if she put up with that and is still here, then you've got it made."

"Were you hiding in your room to avoid him?" I'm justifiably suspicious. My sister is not a fan of confrontation unless it's of the physical kind.

"Oh no, I like Trey. I wasn't avoiding him so much as avoiding the two of you together. You just can't keep the testosterone in check when you're in the same room. It's quite obnoxious TBH."

"Whatever. Has your devious mind come up with any ideas for luring out the arch villain?" I ask.

"The way I see it, we have two options. We're probably going to have to either lure him out with Sophia…"

"No way, not an option! We're not using her as bait." I jump in, pissed that she would even suggest it.

"I get a say too. If that's the way to do it, then fine by me," Sophia says. My whole being protests at the thought of putting her in danger on purpose.

"I figured you'd say that. So, my second option is to contact him on the DL, pretend to be interested in a job to arrange a meetup."

"Have you got any shady contacts in the local supe community?" I narrow my eyes at my little sister wondering what she's been up to in her spare time.

"But of course. My specialty is getting to know everyone. You never know when you might need a favor, so yes, I might have some potential contacts."

"Not sure how I feel about that, and pretty sure Dad would lock you in the basement if he found out. Come to think of it, he'd lock me in there with you to suffer an eternity of torture."

"You'll thank me when this pans out." The smile that spreads across her face is all glee.

"How soon can we make this happen? Once Trey and Team Red are in place, it's going to be harder to skulk about."

"It might take me a few days to contact someone, so let me see what I can do. In the meantime, we'll pretend like everything is normal and go to school. Give them zero reason to suspect us."

"Sounds like a plan. What do you think, Sophia?" I want to make sure she's involved in the process.

"Sounds good to me. It's not like I have experience or expertise with any of this. Is there any hope that the Council and the MED will solve this so we don't have to?"

"They could, but I'm not taking any chances with you. We need to get this wrapped up as soon as possible. By whatever means necessary."

"I guess." I hate seeing the disappointment on her face.

Sophia insisted on getting some homework done before we train. I have no idea how she can concentrate on school right now. After my thousandth lap of the house, Sophia tosses her pencil down and throws her hands up in the air. "Fine, let's get started."

"Great. Let's get going."

My mind was racing around while I prowled. I don't want to push Sophia with her recovering ankle, so knife throwing seems like a good option.

I lead Sophia down to the training room and unlock the weapons cabinet to find the perfect set.

"Whoa. I was thinking of you as a ninja wizard in my head after I saw you with the sword, but I didn't know you actually were one." Her eyes widen.

I glance at the array of swords and knives that are hanging neatly in the cabinet. I guess I'm so used to being around weaponry it's no big deal to me. Sophia, though, has probably never touched a knife in her life outside of the kitchen. Strange to think she's grown up that way when her birth parents were just as involved in this life as mine were. Her dad was head of the Magical Enforcement Division until he was killed.

"You should see our collection at home."

I run my hands over the textured cord and smooth leather handles of a few different sets of throwing knives before settling on the black 2.75 oz Perfect Points with a cord wrapped handle. The lighter weight will be good for her to practice with.

I demonstrate how to hold the knives, then stance and aiming techniques. The world falls away as I aim and let the knives fly. I survey my work with satisfaction. A neat line of knives crosses the center of the homemade target.

"Show off. I'm not sure you should trust me with sharp, pointy things."

I hand her the first knife, slipping my hands over hers to correct her grip before moving a few feet to the side. I have no idea where those first throws will wind up and don't really feel like pulling a blade out of my thigh. Although it wouldn't be the first time.

Lines crease her forehead as she throws the first one, which falls two feet shy of the target and thumps onto the foam matted floor.

"Try throwing a little harder."

This time she wails it, sinking the knife into the wall well above her intended destination.

"Oh my God, I'm so sorry!" She looks cute with the flush creeping up her neck. I don't want to fluster her more, so I bite my cheek to contain a laugh.

"Totally fine. This basement was designed to take some abuse. We do all of our training down here."

I correct her grip again and stand behind her with my hand over hers on the knife. A flush of heat stokes an ember that spreads like wildfire through the rest of me. It doesn't help, even when I shift back to create a bit of space. I shake off the lust fog and try to focus. I help her aim and put the right amount of force into the throw and we stick it into the edge of the target. She jumps up and down, clapping her hands.

"Ok, now same thing on your own." Who knew I had it in me to be an encouraging teacher?

We keep practicing for another hour until she's hitting the target some of the time at least. It will take a lot of practice for her to get really good, but I'm glad to be doing something.

She rolls her shoulder and groans. "I don't think my arm has ever worked this hard."

"Once you get the hang of it, I'll make you practice with your left arm, so at least you'll have a little more balance, you know. Two sore arms instead of one." I give her my evil grin.

I help her stretch it out, and we take a brief break before moving on to some magic work. This is harder because we really have no idea what abilities she possesses, so it's kind of hit or miss trying out different things. Mainly, I want her to get a feel for the source of her magic and how to direct it to her will.

After a frustrating session, we relax on the couch for a bit to binge watch a terrible show about rich kids being horrible to each other while we eat dinner.

"Great, now it's two against one." They outvoted me on the show choice.

"Yay!" Liz cheers.

The doorbell startles me out of my post dinner stupor.

I recognize Jeff's broad shoulders and shaved head immediately, but not the tall brunette beside him. I greet him with a back slap hug. "Jeff, good to see you, man. And you must be Hannah. Nice to meet you. Come on in." I'm surprised that Dad has assigned an out-of-town Mage to the protection detail. I know everyone from this area, so she must be an import.

"Hello," she says in a soft voice. Her dark brown hair is cropped in a short pixie cut, and a smattering of freckles sprinkle her nose. "I'll just wait out here and keep watch."

Jeff follows me into the living room, where I introduce him to Sophia.

"Where's Hannah from?" I ask.

"Oh, she's related to the Elwoods. Her mother is Brian's sister. They live out in Vermont. She's been with their branch of MED for a few years. She transferred to us six months ago. She's been a solid asset so far, and the Elwoods are tight with your parents."

"Gotcha. Sophia's got all her stuff together. I'll come with you guys to her house to make sure she gets there safely."

"Are you sure you're ok to walk?" I eye Sophia's ankle.

"I'm fine. It's good for me to stretch it out so it doesn't stiffen up. In case I need to run, you know." She says it playfully, but worry still twists my insides and her worry piles on mine.

We make it home uneventfully, and I'm planning on walking Sophia into her house so I can steal an unobserved kiss. Trey might be able to keep our relationship to himself, but I doubt these foot soldiers would have a problem reporting to Dad. Even with our useful bond, I have a feeling he'd pull me from guard duty if he knew how close we've gotten.

Unfortunately for me, Sophia's mom is at home when we get there. I should bail.

"Did you want to come in and meet my mom?" She spots my wary look. "You don't have to."

"Of course I would like to. Not sure how she'll feel about me, though. She thinks you've been staying with Liz."

"Right. Why didn't I think about that? Where are those two staying tonight?" She gestures at Hannah and Jeff.

"They'll make themselves invisible out here. No one will even notice them."

"They just have to stand out here all night? That sucks big time."

"It's part of their job. Don't worry about them. They'll be fine."

I cast a nervous glance at her house to make sure her mom isn't watching and pass her bag over to her, giving her hand a surreptitious squeeze. A cloud of sweetness invades my nose when I lean in, and I almost forget myself. I whisper, "I'll pick you up in the morning for a ride to school. Maybe I can lock us in the supply closet again to make up for losing our goodnight kiss. I promise it'll be way more fun than the last time."

She blushes and walks into her house with a quick glance behind before shutting the door and I turn to leave.

I grimace at the memory of our closet conversation and, even worse, how I broke the news to her about the magic world. I remember being pissed off about being sent to look after her but cannot remember why I thought that was a good excuse to be so rude to Sophia. All I can do now is try my best to make up for it. I don't know why, but she's really gotten under my skin.

Dread fills me at the sight of Dad's black Audi sedan crouched in the driveway when I get back to our place.

I swagger in and am met by a glowering father.

"Is it true?" he asks.

"Hi Dad, nice to see you. What exactly is the inquisition about?" I ladle as much sarcasm into my tone as I can.

"Don't take that tone with me. I heard you've gotten involved with the Tennant girl."

"Not sure what you're talking about. Of course I'm involved with her. You tasked me with the job of protecting her. Remember?" I'm not going to make this easy for him.

He just ignores my lip this time, which is a bad sign. He must be in the tenth stage of anger. "Are you or are you not romantically involved with her?"

"Trey is such a dick," I mutter.

"Don't speak about my guard that way, besides he wasn't the one who told me about it, if that's what you're thinking."

Desdemona. I should have known better than to trust her. My father is, after all, the one paying her bills. Of course she'd report everything to him like the dutiful little Witch she is. Probably enjoyed getting me into shit. Payback for turning her down.

"What does it even matter to you?"

"You can't properly guard someone if you're emotionally involved. You're going to end up getting her hurt, and then what's the point of all this?"

I decide to try another tactic. "Who said I was emotionally involved? What's wrong with a little fun?" Not really a conversation I want to have with him, but it has to be better than him thinking I'm in love with her and incapable of being her guardian as a result. A shiver runs through me. I think I'm actually starting to fall for her.

"She is not the kind of girl you use to satisfy your needs." Ew. Well, those are some words you should never hear out of your father's mouth. "The poor girl has been through enough. Losing her family so young and having all of this sprung on her, plus she's only seventeen."

Like my father actually cares about her emotional well-being. He's just worried I'm going to screw this up and lose him the power of the only known Archimage born within the last fifty years.

"She's only two years younger than me. That doesn't mean anything. You and Mom are four years apart."

"Yes, but she's still a minor. You're an adult."

"It's not like I've been sleeping with her or anything." Disgust and a little guilt gnaw at my resolve. Is that his opinion of me? That I'd take advantage of her? Am I? I mean, she's younger than me and innocent. Too good for me for sure.

"There it is. You admit that you're not sleeping with her, so it's not just a physical thing. I was right."

I clench my fist to keep from doing something I'll regret. I cannot believe that I've fallen into one of his traps like that. He's a master of putting you into a corner until you admit to something you didn't intend to, and I walked right into it. He's right. Not controlling my emotions is going to be my downfall.

"What are you going to do about it?" I say, not denying his claim.

"You're going to have to end it with her or I'll have to pull you and assign someone else as her Guardian."

"Is that really a good idea, what with our ever so useful bond and all? You know that's how I found her when she was kidnapped right?"

"She never should have been taken in the first place. That's on you." Like I don't know that already. Like that thought hasn't been preying on me since it happened.

"If you pull me, who are you going to assign?" I ask, knowing full well the answer to that one.

"Trey, of course."

"Fine, no big deal. I'll stop seeing her." It's not the first time I've had to lie to him, and it won't be the last. We'll just have to keep it on the quiet.

"Good, but if I catch word of anything going on between the two of you, that's it. You're done with this job effective immediately."

"Yes sir,"

"I have to be heading out. Your mother and I had dinner plans that I had to cancel to come deal with you."

"Of course you did. Say hi to Mom for me."

"Bye Lizzie." Dad's voice takes on a tender tone as he gives my sister a hug. He's never been physically affectionate with me, but my sister makes his hard facade melt away.

I don't even bother with a goodbye before I bolt for the stairs. I need some time to myself to process this.

I can't actually break up with Sophia. My hand drifts up to rub at my chest. The only other option is to keep dating but keep it as deep on the down low as we can. Maybe even secret from Liz? No, I don't think I can do that. My sister and I are a team. We don't keep secrets from each other. Plus, she's nosy as hell.

On the plus side, no one else is with us at school, so we can be totally normal there without getting caught. Outside of that building, we're surrounded by guards. The walls are closing in on us tighter and tighter. Supply closet is sounding more appealing by the minute.

I'm so screwed. I crank up the classic rock to drown my thoughts.

CHAPTER 19
Sophia

I turn my face up to soak in the sun's warmth shining through the window. Nighttime is my favorite, because I can stare up at the stars and dream of all the possibilities out there. But the sun is just a gigantic star, so I can appreciate its beauty too.

I talked to Mom about the weekend. Well, mostly I shared info about all the "studying" Liz and I did plus the movie and TV watching. I might have mentioned her older brother Logan, who's in my grade at school, in passing, but cut it off when she looked a little too interested. Logan's right. I can't just tell my mom I'm dating Liz's brother. She'll get all suspicious and not let me stay overnight there. I don't like all the secrets I've been keeping from her, but it's not like we talk about serious stuff anymore, anyway. I lost more than just my dad in that accident. My heart aches thinking about him.

I choose my outfit more carefully than usual, pairing some black leggings that hug my curves in just the right places with a bright red flowy chiffon top that slips off one shoulder. I think bare shoulder is sexy. Maybe not in your face sexy enough for males of this century. The equivalent of showing a little ankle after miniskirts came into vogue. Oh well, it's the best I can do. Nothing in my closet screams "take me now" and if there were, I probably wouldn't be comfortable wearing it.

I add some glittery gold eye shadow and bright red lipstick but swipe it off when all I can see are my lips screaming out of my face. I replace it with a more subtle red gloss. It still looks pretty kissable, though. It's like I've spent my whole life waiting to be kissed, not knowing what I was missing out on.

Am I becoming one of those boy crazy girls who acts like their boyfriend is the Sun they revolve around? I gotta cut that out immediately.

"Hi honey, don't you look nice today? Anything you want to share with me?" She raises a sculpted eyebrow at me.

"What? No."

"Are you sure there isn't a boy you want to tell me about? Or a girl. I don't care as long as you're happy."

My mom is so weird sometimes. "Welll, there's kinda someone. It's hardly a thing yet, so I don't really want to jinx it by talking about it."

"I get it. No worries. Whenever you're ready and want to share with me, I'll be happy to listen. And in the meantime, be careful and be responsible with your mind and your body."

"Got it." I need to cut this off before she can venture into more embarrassing territory. "Getting a ride with Liz. See you later."

I grab a slice of toast for the road and wait outside on the porch for Logan to pick me up. There's a good chance my mom won't even notice that I'm getting a ride from a boy and if she does, Liz will be in the car too. It's not technically a lie.

I scan the neighborhood, trying to spot my guards. They're like ghost commando good at hiding. I wonder if either Hannah or Jeff are Psyche Mages. No, there's been a shift change. It'll be Trey and the other one I haven't met yet.

Logan's car pulls up in front, and I glance back at my house nervously, trying to make sure Mom isn't watching. It's probably fine. I'm sure she's just getting ready for work like usual. Living in a constant state of fear for my life is making me paranoid. Go figure.

I slide into the front seat. "Hi, Logan." I duck behind a curtain of hair.

"Hi." A huge grin spreads across his face. He leans in and then pulls back quickly, glancing around.

He gestures to the cup holder beside me. "Picked you up a Hazelnut Latte."

"What? That's so sweet. How did you have time to make a coffee run before picking me up?"

"I'm used to waking up early. I usually get up at 5 to work out then shower. I'm actually finding myself with extra free time here since my only job is guarding you, and I'm not currently on my father's ridiculous training schedule." He says this as if it's no big deal. I find my gaze drifting to the muscles straining his blue shirt.

"Thank you nonetheless."

He's drumming his fingers on the wheel. "Look, my dad came for an unexpected visit last night." His tone and the unsettled vibe coming off him suggest the visit was unwelcome and unexpected. "He somehow found out that we've been getting involved and he came down on me really hard about it."

"That's weird. Does he have an issue with me? He hasn't even met me. How could he possibly not like me?" My stomach's full of rocks. Is he about to bail on me? Again.

"It's not about you or me specifically. He's just got all these opinions about duty and emotion. He thinks that if we get emotionally involved, I won't be able to protect you properly. He's got some deep-seated issues. He kind of found out about us and now he's totally forbidden us to date."

"So…you're breaking up with me?" My heart wrenches. We barely even started anything.

"No, no, not at all, but I told him I was. He said he'd assign another Guardian to you if we keep dating and he'll pull me from the job altogether. I can't let that happen. I NEED to be there to protect you, so I'm just asking you if it's okay if we keep it really secret. Like nobody knows."

"Nobody? Even Liz?" I ask.

"Liz is fine. She's great at secrets, especially from Dad. She's totally got him wound around her finger. He believes every word out of her mouth. Unlike me." Some bitterness creeps into his tone. Must be some serious sibling favoritism going on in their household. "No one else can know, though. Especially Trey. I don't think he's the one who told Dad in the first place, but I have no doubt that my father has now ordered him to squeal on us, and Trey won't disobey a direct order."

"What about my friends at school? I was looking forward to flaunting you a bit."

"I mean no big if your close friends know, but I don't think we should be all showy at school cause you know Trey and Roxie will hang around school grounds during the day keeping watch."

"Ok. For the record, I'm not happy about this, but I'll go along with it…for now."

"That's why we need to catch this guy." For a moment I get lost in his eyes that have darkened to the color of a storm-tossed sea. "The sooner we do that, the sooner I'm off the hook as Guardian, and I can jump right back into my role publicly as…boyfriend. If that's okay with you." I've never seen him look so unsure of himself and while I like the cocky confidence he usually wears, this side of him is nice, too.

A thrill races up my spine. "Yes, it sure is, girlfriend. Secret girlfriend for now anyway, and we'll redouble our efforts to find the bad guy because I really want to flaunt you. You are totally flauntable."

"Why thank you. I wouldn't mind showing you around town myself. You know what I like best, though?" I arch a brow at him. "Your brains."

"Uh huh. Sweet talker? Flattery will get you everywhere, I guess, including maybe a trip to the janitor's closet. I mean, if this is going to be a secret, sordid affair, we may as well enjoy the perks of that."

I laugh when the ever-composed Logan fumbles his coffee.

Tingles are running up my arm from Logan's hand brushing mine when he "passes me a pencil." Like I would ever come to class unprepared. My happy glow dims when a new student walks into our first class. Trey settles into the desk to my right.

"Hey gorgeous." He shoots me a wink.

"Are you freaking kidding me? What are you doing here?" Logan hisses at him.

"Um, learning stuff what else would I be here for?"

"Um, spying." Scorn colors his words, and his frustration floods over me.

"I'm just here to protect Sophia. Robert thought I might be better able to do that if I could be by her side in this oh so public and therefore dangerously open to attack high school."

"Of course."

The teacher launches into her lesson. The air around me crackles with the tension coming off the two boys throughout class, so I try to slip into my Zen learning state. I'm happy to find that when I'm in the calm, white space I've created in my head to deal with difficult situations, Logan's feelings don't reach me anymore. That is handy information. His irritation with Trey was distracting.

What kind of power do these Mages have that they can just flit into a school and register for whatever classes they want? This is beyond ridiculous. Logan and I won't even be able to sneak in a moment of alone time without raising Trey's suspicions. Worse, he seems to be flirting with me at every chance he gets, which is putting Logan in a foul mood.

By lunchtime I'm mentally exhausted from the secret keeping and game playing. I'm happy to settle down with my crew at our usual lunch table. So much has happened over the last few days that it feels like I haven't seen them in a year.

Charlotte asks, "Sophia, I haven't seen you all weekend! How did your date go?" I'm taken aback for a minute. I search my memory. I didn't tell my mundane friends about Logan, did I?

"Didn't go so well? Garrett not really as great as he seems? No sparks?"

Oh Garrett. It's been such an eventful weekend I completely forgot about Garrett.

"Garrett? No, that's not going to work out. He's super nice and all, but he just wasn't right for me, you know. Hopefully, we can still be friends. He seems like a great guy."

"That's too bad. And who is this other new guy? What's with all the new hot students around here? Did someone fail to mention that we've slipped through a portal to an alternate universe?" I groan, knowing full well who she's talking about.

I guess it's too much to hope that he'll find someone else to eat with. I'm sure they'd be happy to have him, but no he settles right down next to me, a little closer than is strictly polite for someone I just met yesterday.

"Pleasure to meet you. I'm Trey, and you would be?"

"I'm Charlotte. This is Xavier, Anne, and you must have class with Logan and Sophia?" She asks, giving me a not-so-subtle WTF look.

"Yes, I've just moved from Port Grand, like Logan and Liz. I knew them from my old school."

"That's weird, that you both just moved here from the same place." I can almost see the wheels turning in Charlotte's head. No way will she guess the real reason they're here, but she can tell that something's up. I don't know if I should tell her something, anything.

"Our fathers work together, job transfer thing you know," Logan gives Trey an evil look.

"Got it. That makes sense. So, have you got a girlfriend back home?" Charlotte has clearly not mastered the art of subtlety.

"I don't, why, offering?" Trey gives her a long look.

"Asking for a friend." I roll my eyes at her pointed look directed at me.

"There definitely seem to be some very nice girls here." I can hear Logan's teeth scraping together at Trey's admiring glance.

I don't think Logan can take any more of Trey's needling, so I excuse myself.

"Gotta hit the ladies, then maybe the library before next period." I book it for my locker, shooting off a quick text to Logan before heading up to the empty room Liz and I had our little powwow in the other day.

Room 226.

Logan joins me a few minutes later.

"Had to give Trey the slip. He was trying to follow me. Subtle that guy is not."

"What are we going to do now? Now that Trey is around to watch us all day at school, how are we going to get in any time together?"

He envelopes me in his arms and drops a kiss on the top of my head.

"It'll be ok. We can still hang out at my house. Trey might have his suspicions, but he can't just force his way in there. This is low even for Dad. I can't believe he sent Trey in to be his personal spy."

Being so close to him is a little too much for me. I need his lips on mine, so I grab the back of his head and pull him to me, a little surprised at my boldness. He lifts me up, setting me down on an empty desk without breaking lip contact. My hands wander down to squeeze his firm butt, and he steps into me until I can feel him pressed up against my front. I'm breathless and needy when we're interrupted by the harsh sound of the warning bell.

"I can't be late for class." I disentangle myself from him, flatten out my hair and straighten my clothes. "Am I presentable?"

"You are more than presentable. You're amazing."

"Not what I was getting at but still nice to hear. Thanks." I grab his hand for one last squeeze before opening the door a crack. The hallway is empty save for a few stragglers who are also rushing to their classes. No sign of Trey's shaved head, though. I breathe a sigh of relief before walking out into the hall and gesturing to Logan to follow me.

"He's gonna know we were together, right? When we both show up for class like this," Logan says.

"Honestly, I don't care what he thinks or your dad or anyone else. This is my life. I make my own decisions." I may not be able to control what I am, but I can certainly control who I date. "I didn't ask for these powers, or for the bond, or to have you as a Guardian. All I wanted was to live a normalish life. If I can't have that, the least I can have is you." I grab his hand defiantly and head for class.

Logan tries to shake it free before we walk into English, but I hold on tight and enter the room.

"Nice of you to show up, Mr. Armstrong, Miss Tennant. I expect better of you at least." Mr. J eyes our clasped hands disapprovingly. It's dawning on me that perhaps I could have chosen a less conspicuous moment to make a stand as the entire class gapes at us, giggling. Trey just narrows his eyes and shakes his head.

I mumble an apology to the teacher, drop Logan's hand, and sink into my seat. I glare at Trey, daring him to out us to Logan's dad.

We settle into our seats and suffer through the rest of the day stoically. Before we leave school, I track Trey down.

"Look Trey, I know we just met, and you have zero loyalty to me, but I am begging you not to tell Logan's dad about us. My life has just been turned upside down. Within the last week, I have found out about this whole magic world, been attacked, and kidnapped, and the only way I've gotten through it is having Logan and Liz at my back. I need them and if you tell his dad, they'll probably get sent away. I know you have some kind of issue with each other, but like I said, that has nothing to do with me. I've never done anything to piss you off that I am aware of, so please don't use me to try to get to Logan."

Trey's face finally softens. "I'm sorry, Sophia, I wasn't really thinking of you when I was beefing with Logan. I take my job seriously. I have zero intention of letting you get hurt under my watch. If it means that much to you, I won't tell Robert. Just please don't let on that I know and keep your PDAs to a minimum so no one else catches on. And since you seem like a nice girl, I'm going to give you a warning. Logan is bad news. He's only going to get you hurt or killed."

"Thank you, Trey. I appreciate you keeping our secret. I can handle myself, though." I give him an impulsive hug and then head back to tell Logan the good news. I'm practically bouncing at my win. Sometimes all you need are the right words.

Logan's casually leaning against my locker, waiting for me. He's oblivious to the girls checking out him out. Lucky for me, his azure eyes don't stray from me as I approach.

"So...good news," I say cheerfully. "I talked Trey into keeping our secret. We're free, or at least a little freer to stop pretending." Logan's lips press into a thin line.

"What? I thought you'd be happy?"

"I just wonder what game he's up to. He's not the type to do something nice and not expect something in return. Especially for me."

"Well, good thing he did it for me. I can be convincing when I want to. Not everything is about you, you know."

"I know that, but still I don't trust him. He's up to something."

"Whatever. Just give me a kiss." I pull him into me.

He returns the kiss before gently pushing me away. "Still have to be somewhat discreet." His breath tickles my ear.

"Sophia!!!!" Charlotte squeals, hurtling down the hall toward us.

"Oops?" She's going to kill me for not telling her about Logan.

"You've been keeping secrets from your BFF? I'm hurt?" Her full lips push out into a pout.

"This thing is new. That's why I haven't told you yet. I promise I would have. It's been a bit of a crazy weekend." Crazy, terrifying, amazing, unbelievable. It's been a roller coaster for sure.

She rounds on Logan. "And what are your intentions toward Sophia?"

"Ummm."

"Stop it Char. Put the shotgun away. I promise we can hang soon. I've just got a lot on my plate at the moment."

"Studying hard for midterms, I know. I should be too."

"Yeah midterms." Easier to let her think that than try to explain the truth.

"Kay, we gotta split. I'll talk to you soon." I lean in for a quick hug and squeeze her a little tighter than usual. I'm worried about her, my other friends, my mom.

"Bye, Soph. You better call me tonight with some juicy details."

"I will. Take care of yourself, Char."

Trey meets us at the front door and Roxie appears at his side as we exit the school. She's pretty with coffee tinted skin and long black hair pulled into a sleek ponytail.

"Any updates?" Trey's voice has gone all business. A far cry from the teasing jibes at school. Weird to see him in such a professional position, I'm pretty sure he's close in age to Logan. In the world where I grew up, he'd be away at University or College attending keggers, not working full time in a responsible position.

The two guards escort us to Logan's car.

"Did you want to come to my house for a bit? I can take you home after dinner," Logan asks.

"Let me call my mom, see if she's going to be home tonight or working late again."

I dial her up and have a quick convo. "Mom's getting home early tonight. I should head home, reassure her I haven't embraced my inner rebellious teenager."

"As you wish," he says.

CHAPTER 20
Logan

Liz is practically bouncing up and down, waiting for me to get home. I'm surprised Sophia didn't ask about her absence at school today, but it's for the best. I was trying to keep her out of the loop, so she won't try to get involved, but I don't love the thought of lying to her. I'm glad she stayed home tonight. With the guards at her place, Liz and I can get up to our investigation without fear of Red interference or putting Sophia in danger. She'll be pissed when she finds out, but I'd rather she's angry at me and safe.

"What's the word, little sis?"

"I've tracked down someone who's willing to talk. She wants to keep her identity hush hush, so we have to go meet her on her territory. On the plus side, she's willing to meet me tonight."

"That is fantastic news. Good job Lizzie."

"Don't call me that." She wrinkles her nose at me. I know it bugs her, but she'll always be my little Lizzie. It's a hard habit to break.

"We're going to have to plan ahead and be smart about this. Get ready for all angles. What do you know about your source?"

"She's a Witch who claims to have done business with Zeus. Apparently, he has a penchant for magical artifacts. That's his only weakness. The only way into his lair."

"You've been watching too many superhero movies again. Lair really?"

"Well, he's a bad guy, like a legit super villain, and it's a well-known fact that all super villains need a lair to conduct their secret business."

"Whatever. So, where are we meeting her?"

"That's the thing. I have to meet her alone." Alarms are screaming all over my head at that.

"Uh no, not part of the deal."

I might tease my little sister and we definitely bicker, but I would give my life to protect her. No way am I letting her go meet some shady Witch alone.

"First, you're not the boss of me any more than you're the boss of Sophia. She doesn't put up with that crap and neither do I. Second, she won't see me if I don't come alone and then we'll never track Zeus down."

"Actually, I kind of am the boss of you at the moment. And there's gotta be another way."

"There isn't."

My mind races, trying to come up with any option to avoid putting my sister in danger but comes up empty. Our time is running out.

"This only happens if I come with you and stay close to your meetup spot. And put a tracking app on your phone." The magical crowd doesn't always consider the fact that we might use modern technology so that could work in our favor.

"Fine stalker, but I'm taking it off immediately after." She gives me a 'whatever' look, but I know she appreciates my concern way down deep underneath all the attitude.

"Let's make a plan, then. What's the meetup time and location?"

"Eight pm in the parking lot of the Fleetwood Library." She gives me a sheepish look, knowing full well that I won't approve.

"Really Liz? I'm sure you could have picked a more secluded location if you'd really tried." The library is closed on Monday. She's really testing my patience with her 'plan.' "I'm not going to be able to get close enough. This must be some kind of trick. I can't risk you, even for Sophia's sake."

"You know I can look after myself. Hello, super speed and strength. I'm pretty much a real-life superhero. Your lack of faith is disappointing." Her overconfidence is what scares me the most. She's going to get herself into trouble. If not now, then soon.

"It's not your abilities that I doubt. Witches have all kinds of sneaky powers, and this Zeus guy has a lot of muscle on his payroll as well. Who knows who–or what–might show up."

"I'm going, and you better keep your distance. We don't want her getting skittish and calling the deal off."

I picture the area in my head. There's an elementary school a little way up the road on the edge of a small, forested area. I could park on the street in front and hang out like a creeper in the woods. Just have to hope no little kids are playing on the playground or some concerned parents will call the police on me. It's close enough that I can be back to Liz in a few minutes but hidden well enough to fool the Witch. I hope.

"Ok fine. I'll head out around six, give a quick scope of your meetup spot, see if I can get a sense of any magic traps and stick in the woods at the school. I'll keep an eye on your phone tracker. You take your car. If you see anything suspicious. If she even looks at you funny, steps one toe out of line, you get out of there as fast as your super speed can take you."

"I know the deal. I'll send the emergency text code if I'm able to."

I really don't like this plan.

After a quick dinner I get dressed in what Liz refers to as commando chic. Black track pants with a matching fitted long sleeve shirt. The satisfying swish of steel on leather comforts me as I slide my favorite Smith and Wesson throwing knives into my shoulder holster, strap on my arm sheaths with a few more daggers and jam my feet in my well-worn boots. I toss a jacket over top to conceal my weaponry from the general public.

I pull Liz in for a quick hug as the front door snicks shut behind us.

"Be careful. As much as I'm in this to protect Sophia, I am not willing to trade her life for yours, so don't take unnecessary chances."

"You should know me better than that, big bro. A risk taker I'm not."

I shake my head. Liz has never met a risk she didn't flirt with.

The air has that frosty feel it gets when the long, dark days of winter are edging closer. My car will likely have a light coating of frost tomorrow morning, but for now it's clear and growls smoothly to life as I head out to give Liz's meet up spot an inspection to minimize the possibility of an ambush.

Good thing we took separate cars. The stereo pounds out heavy rock at a decibel level that would seriously offend the enhanced ears of my sister.

I cruise slowly by the library. As expected, the parking lot is deserted, and it's surrounded on either side by empty fields until you get to the small woods at the edge of the nearby school. I don't see any obvious danger lurking about, so I pull into the school parking lot, which is also empty this late. Schools look so weird without students overrunning the concrete and brick. From there, I creep into the woods to find my best vantage point before walking back to the library parking lot to give it a thorough assessment.

I can make it over in a few minutes at a run given the first sign of trouble. The library is an older one with a gray concrete exterior and a missing 't' in its name that adds no beauty to its surroundings. I check out the small patch of fir trees bordering the back end of the parking lot. If I was seeking a hiding place, that would be it. No one is lurking there, and I can't sense any magic essence in the air. Just because no one is lying in wait doesn't mean they don't have some kind of nefarious plan in place, though.

I try to label the voice in my head that's screaming danger as the overprotective concern I have for my younger sister. Mom and Dad would definitely kill me if they knew I was letting Liz do this. They still think of her as their baby, despite her mad fighting skills and enhanced physical abilities. After a last check for hidey holes or traps, I settle in the woods to wait.

I keep a watchful eye on the place and its surroundings for the full two hours but see nothing unusual except two cars pulling in around seven. One is a beaten-up brown junker and the other a much nicer looking black sedan. Drug deal for sure. I watch the occupants pass some items to each other through their windows and then quickly depart as if they'd never been there. I scan each driver, but nothing sparks any alarm bells. Just some mundanes up to no good.

Finally, a green Taurus pulls into the parking lot at a quarter to eight. A middle-aged woman with unruly brown hair and a long multi-colored skirt falling from under her red parka steps out of the vehicle. This must be Liz's witch contact. She definitely fits the mold of many other Witches I've met. Since they often earn their living performing psychic or fake magic spells for mundanes, they tend to go with the new-agey look that's expected by the norms. Incense and peasant blouses.

I'm relieved that she's come alone, as far as I can tell, unless she has someone hiding in the trunk. It worries me that I don't know this Witch. The seed of doubt that had been festering in my gut starts to curl up and spread through the rest of my body. She glances around then at her watch before leaning against her car.

Liz shows up five minutes early and parks her car a few spots away from the unfamiliar Witch. She scans her surroundings, climbs out of her car, and cautiously approaches the other woman. My shoulders are tense in my fighting stance, ready to sprint over at any hint of trouble.

Everything seems okay. I can see them talking and gesturing to each other. Liz's posture is relaxing, and that's when the Witch reaches out and grabs Liz by the arm gently, but something's off. Liz freezes in place, and my legs propel me forward without a conscious thought. Before I can reach her, a hum of electricity spikes in the air, and a masked man appears directly behind Liz. My sister's eyes widen with shock as he grabs her around the waist, pulling her at the same time the Witch shoves her toward him. They both fall back, vanishing into the inky darkness the man came from. I lunge for her. My hands slide through the air. My aborted lunge sends me straight into the Witch where I topple her over, pinning her to the ground.

Her frightened hazel eyes meet my furious ones.

"Where is my sister?" I growl at her.

"I'm so sorry. I don't know where he took her. I had no choice." Her voice comes out weak and thready.

"There's always a choice and right now mine is whether to kill you now or later."

"I couldn't help it. I didn't have a choice. He has my Ava." Her eyes are wide, and sobs are racking her body. The tears are streaming over the smattering of freckles dusting her cheeks. She looks young and scared. I don't relax my hold. Looks can be even more deceiving than words.

"There's always a choice. You traded my sister for someone you care about. That was a bad decision. You could have tried to rescue her. Hell, if you'd come to us, we would have helped you before this. Now you've forfeited all rights of aid from the council, and you face punishment. Who took her?"

"I don't care what happens to me, but save my Ava from him. Please. I don't know where he is or how to get to him. I wish I could give you information, but he doesn't trust anyone with his location. He asked me to give you this, though." The Witch's hand trembles as she gives me a phone and an envelope with my name scrawled across it.

I drop her. She's clearly useless to me and I don't have time to take her to the council. That can wait until I rescue Liz. I ignore the Witch's flinch when I whip out one of my throwing knives. I use it to slice the envelope open. I yank out the letter out. Red blurs my vision as I scan the words.

Don't worry, your sister is safe...for now. Follow my directions precisely and she will remain that way. Deviate even slightly and I will return her to you in pieces. All I want is Sophia. She belongs to me. I'll call you on that phone with a meeting time and place. You will bring Sophia alone. If I catch wind of any company, particularly members of the council, I will divest your sister of her lovely head. Once I have Sophia, your sister will be returned to you. Looking forward to your visit.

Every curse I've ever learned erupts from my mouth in a foul jumble and I kick the Witch's car for good measure. I have no idea how to proceed, but I know I need to get back to Sophia ASAP so we can brainstorm together. How am I going to get her while her mom's home? I doubt she'll be too eager to let her teenage daughter go off with some strange guy on a school night.

I sprint back to my SUV and hit the road hard. I push the car faster than I ever have before. Luck is with me, and I make it to her house in record time.

I've gotta calm down before I get to Sophia's house. The evening watch will be there. They'll figure out something is up pretty fast if I go tearing in there like my ass is on fire. I force myself to ease up on the gas.

It takes everything in me to get out of my car and walk toward the door at a casual pace. Jeff slips out of the shadows like a ghost.

"Hey Logan, what's up?"

I force my lips into a grin. "Nothing much, man. Came by to check on Sophia. How are things going? Any sign of trouble?" I know very well nothing has happened here. I've just been a witness to all the action of the day.

"Everything is all good here. Locked down tight."

"Good, good."

I start moving when Jeff opens his mouth like he's about to say something else. I don't have time for this shit right now. My guts twist at the thought of Liz, and I've worked myself back up into a frenzy by the time I hit the front door.

CHAPTER 21
Sophia

I've been chilling with a book. My mom came home and had to turn right around and head back to work for another emergency with her project. I put it down after reading the same page five times without absorbing a single sentence.

Every muscle in my body tenses at the insistent knock on the front door. I jump up and glance around for my bag. A wave of urgency and fear that's not mine comes to me from the direction of the door. My shoulders relax. It's Logan.

I shrink from the cold fury twisting Logan's face as I let him in. I know theoretically that there's a restrained violence lurking just below the surface of his controlled façade, but I've never seen him look quite like this. It's scarier than when he was wielding his sword against my kidnappers. Then he looked cool and in control of the situation and the rage. Now he looks wild, ready to burst out of his skin.

"He took her," Logan rasps out, eyes wide with panic.

"Wha…who? What happened?"

"Liz. The Witch tricked us. She was working for Zeus. He appeared out of thin air and snatched her. I should have been faster. I should have stopped him. I knew it was a trap." His boot lashes out at an unsuspecting wooden chair, sending it crashing into the wall.

Some primal instinct is telling me to take a step back. Instead, I approach him with my hands out and place one tentatively on his shoulder. He looks up, making eye contact, and it seems to help him pull it together.

"Why did he take her?" I ask, realizing the answer before the sentence has vanished into the ether. "Me… He wants you to trade me for her."

"Not happening. I'm not trading you for her. That's off the table." I nod at him, but judging from the way he's clenching and unclenching his fists, I think we both know our choices are going to be limited.

"Tell me exactly what happened. We'll figure this out. Where were you? What Witch?" I try to keep a quiet, even tone to stop Logan from going off on my mom's furniture again. My heart is racing now too at the thought of Liz being taken.

His shoulders hunch over. "Liz arranged to meet a Witch. She said she could give us Zeus's location."

"You planned this behind my back? I thought we were in this together?" I tamp down the anger flaring up at the betrayal. I can worry about that later. After we rescue Liz.

He sighs. "Yeah, I wasn't going to put you in danger. Anyway. She arranged a solo meet up. I wouldn't let her go alone though, so I went with and hung back. I drove there, scoped it out. Nothing seemed out of the ordinary. No residual magic. The Witch arrived alone. I should have listened to my instincts." I nod and stroke his arm. "Liz showed up. They were talking. Then she made a move I didn't like, and I ran. I wasn't fast enough. The witch had used some sort of spell to freeze Liz, and a masked man appeared and whisked her off into a portal."

"A portal?" I try to wrap my head around what that means.

"Yes. There are extremely rare artifacts that can open up portals. I didn't even know there were still any around, though. I thought the few in existence were all locked down tight."

"Then she froze Liz? How?"

"I don't know. Witches can't do spells like that. Freeze a powerful Phys. Zeus has been sharing some sort of magic with her, which is completely against the rules. Not that he cares about those, obviously. I caught the Witch, but she was useless. He kidnapped someone she cared about to use her to lure Liz in. She gave me this note and a cell phone." He thrusts a crumpled piece of paper at me.

I skim it quickly before glancing back up at Logan. I'm hyper aware of his tension as fear settles over me like a blanket.

"Who knows how long we have until he calls. We need to make a plan." Planning and organizing, after all, are two of my specialties. I might not be in control of my magic yet, but I can certainly do some brainstorming. "Follow me."

Logan trails me into the kitchen, and I grab my ideas notebook from my backpack. I like to record random thoughts or ideas that come up at all times of the day. You never knew when they'll help you out later.

I push Logan into a chair and flip the notebook open to a satisfyingly blank page.

"So, where do we start? What's the game plan?" A haunted look shadows his face. I want to pull him into my arms for a hug, but there's no time for that. The best way to get rid of that look is to find his sister. We need to get on that, now.

"It's kind of hard to plan anything when we have no idea where or when we'll be going. This Zeus can obviously use the portal thing, so he could be anywhere."

"That shouldn't be a problem. For now. The artifact he used to create that portal is only good for one use, then it needs to be charged. It takes weeks. Like I said before, these are very, very rare. So rare I have no idea how he got his hands on one without anyone hearing about it. Could be a family heirloom that was hidden away."

"Or maybe whoever he stole it from didn't want to admit it?" I offer this option up.

"Good thought. Definitely possible. A powerful Mage wouldn't want to look weak." He slips into silence for a moment.

"That's positive then. He doesn't have teleporting abilities at the moment. So we need to go to him when he calls, snatch Liz, and get out of there."

"I don't want you to come. I'll go myself." I'm almost ready to growl in frustration at his stubbornness.

"That's not going to work. Do you think he's actually going to let you near him if you don't take me with you?"

"I can't...I can't just turn you over to him." The agony twisting his faces matches the feeling's he's practically shouting at me through the bond.

"It's not your decision. It's mine, and I'm going. We just have to figure out how to get in and get everyone out, while capturing this Mage so they can't harm anyone else." The thought of being able to breathe again without fear is everything. And to keep everyone I love out of further danger, there's nothing I wouldn't do.

He shoots to his feet and starts making rounds of the kitchen. "I hate this idea."

"I know you do, but we're out of options. We just need to figure out a way to do this as risk free as possible. We need to lull him into thinking he's won and then sneak up on him and take him out. What do you Mages do with criminals once you capture them? Do you tranquilize them or something to make sure they can't do magic?"

"That's an interesting thought, but no. We use dampening cuffs. They're really hard to get your hands on if you're not in retrieval. I may be able to get one on the black market. It'll have to be quick, though. He could contact us anytime." His eyes dart to the phone the Witch left him.

"What are you waiting for? Get on that!" I make a distracted shooing motion at him while gnawing on the end of my pen and consider my notes. I manage to scribble down a few more ideas before Logan hangs up his cell.

"I found someone who can hook me up. He said he couldn't meet me until tomorrow, but I used a little persuasion to convince him of the urgency. He can get them to us within the half hour. I really hope that gives us enough time."

"That doesn't sound sketchy at all. Do you know this person? Any chance he's going to turn us in to the council?" I eye Logan suspiciously. I know he's pretty much capable of anything to save his sister.

"Uh yeah, no chance of that. He'd pretty much do anything to avoid the notice of anyone in an official role. He deals in items not strictly on the legal side of things."

"I see. I thought Liz was the one with those sorts of contacts."

"It never hurts to know people outside of our circle. Sometimes you just want to get a job done without the council's knowledge. Like now? Useful right?"

"Uh huh. Loving that I just found out about this world and already I'm getting involved in illegal activities. Thanks for that." I lift an eyebrow.

"Hey, I would do anything to save my sister. Anything! And you too. Remember that." I squirm under the intense gaze that Logan levels at me and a wave of warm affection rolls through the bond.

A thought slides into my head. "Couldn't we have used one of these cuffs to hide my magic? If I couldn't do magic, then they couldn't track me down, right?"

"No way. There's a reason they're illegal. The cuffs are only meant for short-term use. If they get left on long-term, they can cause serious harm. They drain you of your magic, but also eat away at your health."

"Oh. Okay." The small bubble of hope welling up inside me bursts.

He drops a whisper of a kiss on the top of my head. I resist the urge to lean into him. We need to focus on our plan.

"How are we going to do this, then? What can I do? To Zeus. I have to be the one to surprise him. He won't see it coming. He thinks I have like zero control over my powers. That can work in our favor. I'm used to people underestimating me. I know how to work that angle. Granted, it's usually in the intellectual and academic areas, but it's a transferable skill, right?" I flip my hair and bat my eyelashes at him to emphasize the point.

"You certainly are a dangerous one, but in this case, I'd have to disagree. It's a completely different thing to fight in magical combat. You don't have control of your magic yet."

"What exactly do you suggest, then? He's not going to let you near enough to cuff him. It has to be me. And you saw me. I'm starting to get some of the magic stuff, at least."

"Please, Sophia?" Logan takes a step closer and places his hands on my shoulders. Warmth spreads through my body, leaving a tingle of his magical essence mingling with mine. I'm still not used to that. He's shielding his thoughts, though. He leans in slowly and our eyes meet right before our lips do. I slide my hands under his shirt. His lean, muscled back shivers at my touch. He backs me up against the kitchen island without breaking contact and lifts me onto the counter with ease. I'm getting lost in him as he deepens the kiss, his callused fingers edging my shirt up. My head is whirling. I'm lost in the flames his fingers leave as they glide up my sides. Something is niggling away at me. He's trying to distract me. It's almost painful to pull away, to disconnect from him, but I have to. I put my hands on his shoulders and drop my forehead to meet his, my breath coming in rapid pants.

"Stop. We can't. Not now. There's too much to do."

His lids drop closed, and he drags in a deep breath. "You're right."

As we stand there still connected, trying to regroup, a cell phone ring shatters the moment and brings us abruptly back to the reality of the current situation.

Logan swears, fumbling in his pocket for the burner phone the Witch gave him.

"Where is she?" His voice comes out like rough-hewn stone as the passion from a moment ago flips into barely contained rage.

He listens briefly. "I'm not meeting you anywhere until you let me talk to her!" This was followed quickly by, "Liz, Liz, are you ok? Where's he taken you?"

I can feel his frustration and rage as if I own it. It spreads through me, crashing over my own emotions with a strength I've never felt before, unless we're physically touching. I double over at the physical force of feeling his every urgent emotion. Either the bond is strengthening, or the remains of my magical block have just come crashing down. My entire body buzzes with the kind of magical energy I've only felt when Logan connected to me to help get in touch with it.

A faint tinny clatter as if from a distance rings in my ear and my body gets hot and sweaty. Blackness sucks me under.

An icy jolt slams my consciousness back to attention, stealing my breath. Cold liquid leaves a trail of icicles on my face. I splutter and gasp.

"Sophia, Sophia, are you ok? Are you back?"

"I've been better and also drier." I swipe my face with the back of my arm.

"I'm sorry, but I had to wake you up. What happened? You just passed out back there. Has that happened to you before?"

"I fainted? No, I'm not a fainter. I don't think it's ever happened before, actually. I could feel everything you were feeling. It all came rushing at me at once as if a dam had broken and it's like my magic came with it. I can still feel it coursing through me." My eyes are wide at the constant tingle flowing through me now. I recognize it. I've felt it before, but it's always been off and on and more muted than this.

Logan's eyes widen. "I'm guessing the last vestiges of the binding spell just collapsed, which is good but maybe not the best timing. I have to go meet Zeus. He gave me a time and location. I can't bring you in this condition."

I grab his arm. I should be shakier after passing out but my strength is returning rapidly.

"Ouch." Logan cries, jerking his arm from my grasp. I release him, staring in shock at the red marks in the shape of my fingers marring his golden forearm. "Uh, I think you may end up giving Liz a run for her money once we've got you trained and in control of that strength."

"I…was that? What just happened?"

"Pretty sure you can add super strength to your list of powers there, Archimage. See what I mean? Now that the binding spell has crumbled, all of your powers are going to start to manifest. We have no idea what they'll be or how to control them. You could end up hurting yourself or Liz and I without meaning to. It's just too unpredictable."

"You can't go without me. Zeus will kill you and Liz and then come after me. I need to go and if you end up having to knock me out at some point, so be it. As long as we save Liz that's all that matters. And like I said before, Zeus is underestimating me still. I have a little practice and a lot of new abilities that even I don't know about. This is our best chance to all make it out alive."

A reluctant sigh escapes him as he messes with his hair. "Fine, but you're following my every command to the letter. If I say run, you go. Unless…" He trails off.

The doorbell rings and Logan goes into commando mode.

Must be his shady contact. "How'd he get by Jeff and Hannah?"

"I gave them a heads up that I was having a visitor. Gave them a description. I told them not to approach, so we can keep their presence quiet unless there's a threat. Stay here. I don't want him getting a glimpse of you. He's only in it for the money. Guys like him can't be trusted to remain loyal."

I nod but sneak into the hallway and peer around the corner. I'm out of sight but able to catch a glimpse of the guy at the door. He's an average-looking guy. Sandy brown hair trimmed short and a slightly too large nose. He's wearing torn jeans and a generic black windbreaker with a pouch in the front. His quick conversation with Logan culminates in an exchange of items and then he glances up, making direct eye contact with me. I duck out of sight, but not before he gives me an appraising glance. The door slams and I creep back to the kitchen guiltily.

"Sophia, come on! He definitely saw you, and I don't want you on the radar of a guy like Brian."

I give him a shrug. I need to know all the facts of the situation, including the people we're dealing with. You never know when information like that will come in useful.

"Can I see the cuff? How does it work?"

Logan passes over a wide silver band with words etched in an elaborate script scrolling around it. There's a shiny pure black stone set into the center of the band.

"Those words on them form a spell. A powerful Witch has to etch it in by hand while performing a lengthy ritual. The black tourmaline also helps block the user from accessing their magical energy. There's only a few Witches in the world powerful enough to make these. That's why they're so rare and expensive. This is one of the few around that isn't in the hands of the council. We're screwed if we lose it, so be careful."

I trace my fingers over the unfamiliar words and find that the hard metal is warm under my touch.

"If you're going to get the cuff on him, you'll need to be quick. We should practice, but first, give me a sec."

He jogs off, leaving me marveling at the cuff. I slide it on my wrist and snap it shut with a sharp metallic click. My head spins as the magic current running through my body disappears. It's slightly uncomfortable for me, but I bet it would be almost painful for someone who's had magic all their life. Almost like a missing limb. The weirdest part is that the tingle of awareness that I recognize as the bond has vanished. A shiver runs through me at the loss of it, despite its newness. I twist my wrist around, checking out the smooth solid metal. The clasp has disappeared into the rest of the bracelet.

Logan's long legs eat up the floor as he bolts into the room. Relief smooths his face when his eyes land on me. "You disappeared there for a minute. I got worried."

I click the clasp and pull off the cuff, squinting at it. "Should this thing be coming off so easily?"

"Yes, that's part of the spell. Only the person who puts it on can remove it. They're quite flawless in design. I didn't know it would negate our Guardian bond, too." His brows pull together with concern.

"Oh, so what happens if the person who puts it on you dies?"

"That would be most unfortunate. It would take some pretty powerful spell work to break apart the magic that holds it closed. Or the creator."

"Got it. So use with caution. Ok let's get started on the practice." I wonder how this all works. I don't love that I can't analyze magic and pull it apart to figure out what makes it work.

Logan hands me a chocolate brown leather belt with lots of loops and pouches that look like they'd come in handy for carrying around weaponry or maybe test tubes and lab equipment. I'll have to keep it around.

He shows me how to use the quick release loop at the back so I can quickly access the cuff when I get Zeus into a vulnerable position. I shiver as his strong arms slide the belt in place. His hands linger at my waist after he buckles it up. He raises his fingers to brush a stray hair off my face before pulling his arms away with a slow reluctance as if they're moving through honey instead of air.

"Let's give this a practice run. I'll be Zeus. Try to cuff me. Keep your intentions quiet."

I back away and assess the situation. Logan looks slightly ridiculous with his wide stance and slightly bent knees standing on our rose printed throw rug beside my mother's white side table with the delicately carved wooden legs. I know there's no way I can beat him in a fair fight, so I run scenarios through my head to figure out an advantage. I rush him, stumbling at the last second, before swiping the rug out from under his feet.

My ploy barely affects the trained fighter. He wrenches my arms behind my back. A zing shoots down my arms and Logan flies back a foot, causing me to lose my balance for real this time, tumbling to the ground after him in a pile of tangled limbs. A giggle escapes.

"Did you mean to do that?" Logan extends a hand to pull me back to my feet.

"Umm, not exactly, but it worked right?"

"Not really. You're trying to cuff him, but if you lose control of your magic, you're going to tip him off to your abilities and lose that element of surprise. The rug swipe was a good thought, but we have to assume that he's well trained, so something small like that won't throw him off. I'll teach you a few basic defensive moves to escape from any hold he manages to get you in."

I stumble while trying to sweep Logan's leg out from underneath him. We grapple and tussle for an hour, until I'm soaked and panting. I smile triumphantly when I'm finally able to regularly break free from his grasp long enough to pull out the cuff and slap it on his wrist.

I react instinctively with a knee to the groin when he laughs and pulls me in for a celebratory embrace. He ducks out of the way and gives me a scowl.

"Sorry." Pink creeps up my neck.

"No, don't be sorry. You reacted quickly. I should have known better than to try that when we're in training mode. I certainly wouldn't have tried it on my sister, or I could have ended up on the floor, or possibly through it."

"No way she can bring you down." My gaze runs up his sculpted length, lingering on his biceps. It doesn't make logical sense that his petite sister can accomplish that feat, but then I guess magic, in general, doesn't make sense. I'm going to have to get used to that.

"For sure, she's as well trained as I am, and she usually cheats with her Phys Magic. She always says she's entitled to since I have a size advantage." His look hardens from the fond reminiscence into a steely determination. "Ok, get yourself cleaned up and we'll suit up for the meet. Should be any time now. He must just be keeping us waiting to throw us off balance. Not going to work. He's definitely messing with the wrong brother."

"One more thing? How are we going to slip my guards?"

"You're going to have to sneak out the back door while I distract them. Are you okay to climb the fence into your neighbor's yard?"

"For sure. I've been doing that since I was a kid. And then I'll meet you on the other side?" The Taylor's have the corner lot. The side of their house is on Rosedale. It's a good plan.

"Yup, and then I'll pick you up."

I nod and reach out to squeeze his callused hand before hurrying up the beige carpeted stairs to clean up and change into some not so sweaty clothes. My hand trails the smooth oak banister.

The cool facecloth feels good on my overly heated face and neck, and I visualize the coming events trying to analyze every possible aspect of a completely unfamiliar situation. That's really the problem. I like to plan and research, but I've been thrown into a situation that I'm completely ill equipped to understand. For the first time in my life, I'll need to relinquish my tight control over every detail and just wing it. I don't know what will happen, but I do know that this could end very badly for me or my new friends if I fail. As a scientist, I understand the importance of failing and learning from your mistakes. A mistake in this situation could end up with someone dead. I can't fail. It's not an option.

I throw on some workout clothes and pull my hair into two long blonde pigtails to create the cute and innocent image I'm trying to project. A swipe of light pink gloss completes the look. An integral part of our plan is for Zeus to dismiss me as weak and completely underestimate my skills. This plan will only work for so long once I really join this new magical world, but hopefully after this, I'll at least have time to hone my newfound abilities and train up.

I sigh and head downstairs to find Logan wearing a groove in the hardwood. He glances up as I approach, giving me a startled look. I twirl and give him an Olympic worthy smile and presentation.

"You like?"

"Very much, definitely working the sweet and innocent look there. Perfection." I'm pretty sure he means that in more ways than one, judging by how dark his eyes have gone. "Here's how this is going down. When we get there, I'm going to pretend like I don't care about you. It won't be real. He's less likely to use you against me if he thinks this is only a job for me."

"I get it. I pretend to be sweet and innocent, and you pretend you don't care about me. I'll even act hurt. We got this."

CHAPTER 22
Logan

My grip on the steering wheel turns my knuckles white as I grimly follow the written directions Sophia is reading out to me. I'm not sure if the drive took ten minutes or ten hours. I can't get to my sister fast enough, but the thought of putting Sophia in danger wrecks me.

Scenery passes by in a blur of colors until we reach a large empty field.

"This is number 3266? But there's nothing here? This can't be right," Sophia says, while she rustles the grocery list she scrawled the directions on.

I turn up the long gravel driveway beside the lone mailbox that appears to be the only man-made object on the property. "Oh, this is right. I can feel it. There's a huge cloak in place here. It must be masking a building or two. A lot of magic."

The heavy feeling grows stronger the farther up the driveway we get until it swallows us up. For a moment, the pressure on my lungs cuts off my breath and the world goes dark and quiet. Then, just as suddenly the world brightens, the pressure lifts, and the scenery changes rapidly.

Sophia gasps at the sudden appearance of the rambling old farmhouse and ramshackle barn.

"That's insane. How does magic like that work?"

"I honestly haven't got a clue how any magic works. It just is. I'm sure Zeus has some kind of sensor to let him know when someone passes through the cloak, so he'll be expecting us. No way we can get a jump on him. Get into character."

I swing the car into a u turn and slide over to the side of the road parking under a large maple tree. I come around to the passenger side and grab Sophia's upper arm, pulling her from the car.

"Showtime. Don't believe anything I say or do from this point on." I whisper, my lips pinched in a grim line.

It kills me to pull her along behind me as if under protest, but she obligingly drags her feet and tries to pull away.

"You're coming with me whether you like it or not." I may need to work on my acting skills if I want this to work. I may have watched too many crappy cop movies in my spare time.

Sophia does an excellent job of digging in her heels to slow our progress, which gives me time to sweep our surroundings. I don't see any goons outside, but they could be well hidden. Who knows how many he has with him in the barn.

Once I've familiarized myself with our surroundings, I give Sophia's arm a squeeze and she follows me more obediently to the large double doors that are hanging slightly off their hinges. The aging door crashes inward as I let all my frustrations loose with a powerful side kick.

Once I'm sure no one is rushing out at us, I shove Sophia through the newly created entrance.

"Well, well, well. No need for violence. As long as you brought what I've requested, I'm more than willing to be accommodating and I see you have brought her."

The man who steps forward is much too smartly dressed to be surrounded by rusting pitchforks and moldy hay. His brown hair is combed in a neat side part and he's wearing a blue and white checked button down with khaki slacks. I don't recognize him.

"Welcome, niece." Wait what? I thought Sophia's uncle was a null. "So good to see you. This could have been much easier if I had just been able to raise you after your parent's death. But they had to secret you away. I only recently became aware of your existence once your protector was sent to look after you. There's no reason to be afraid of me though child, we are family, after all."

"How am I supposed to believe you? Why wouldn't you just ask for my help rather than trying to kidnap me?" My arms are aching to pull her close to soothe the shock, confusion, and anger that are emanating from her.

Zeus, or rather Sophia's apparent uncle, steps close enough to grab her arm and pull her away from me. My jaw pops I'm clenching it so hard. It takes all my discipline not to pull her back out of his grasp. I have to trust she can handle this.

"I knew I'd never get you out of his grasp. Not without resorting to less than savory means. His sister is the only one he cares about enough to guarantee his compliance. I must say, I didn't expect it to be this easy." He narrows his eyes. "I don't really have to give him his sister back yet until he releases you to me completely. Morgan!" He calls out.

A light blinks on in the upper loft revealing Liz chained up, with a woman holding a gun to her head. I'm surprised to see Morgan. I'm not close friends with her, but she's only a couple years older than me and works for the MED.

"You've got her. Call off your henchwoman and we're out of here."

"I'm not going to make it that easy for you. Go ahead upstairs and fetch your sister. Sophia and I will head out while you do. We'll be long gone before you can get back down. Come, my dear." Zeus gently tugs Sophia toward the door.

I hesitate, glancing between Sophia and Liz. I can't let Zeus take off with Sophia, but Liz is in immediate danger with a gun to her head. It's like my heart is being ripped in two.

"As I thought, you're more attached to my niece than you let on. No worries, I'll look after her. Your sister, on the other hand. Tick Tock."

I shoot Sophia one last look, pleading with her to understand, before darting for the rickety ladder leading upstairs to the hayloft. Everything about this feels wrong.

"Go Logan, get Liz. I'll be fine," Sophia says before getting yanked out the gaping wound which used to be a barn door.

Sophia's fear compounds my own, but I push it aside as I spring up the ladder. I need to get my sister fast so we can track Sophia before they get too far. At the top, I launch myself off the last rung, landing softly on my feet and heading toward my sister and her captor.

Morgan has long, straight blond hair, blue eyes, and a petite frame. She looks more like an angel than the gun wielding demon she is. I know better than to underestimate a foe based on their looks. I hold my hands up and approach with caution. Even though every slow step is agonizing, I don't want to set her off. The gun is likely just a dramatic prop. I can feel the energy of her magic crackling in the air, waiting for a target. Just in case, I direct an intense burst of heat at the weapon as soon as I'm within range. The gun melts and Morgan swears dropping the twisted hunk of metal.

"Why'd you have to go and do that? That was my favorite gun." Her tinkling voice whines at me.

"Just a precaution. Now hand over my sister as promised."

"I would, but Zeus wanted me to stall you for a bit." She smiles sweetly before shooting toward me so fast I can't track her. It feels like I've been shot as her feet make contact with my chest. Shit, she's as fast as Liz. Luckily, I have lots of practice fighting a tiny Mage with mad physical magic. I leap back to my feet before my back can hit the ground and spin in a circle, throwing up an ice shield around my body. Morgan crashes into it and slips on some ice shards. Before she can recover, I throw down a circle of fire around her.

She raises an eyebrow at me, glancing around at the dry wood and old hay surrounding us. "That feels like a bad decision on your part," she says, before the floor gives way, and she hurtles to the ground. I imagine she'll land on her feet and be fine but don't bother to spare her a glance. At least I've bought time to free my sister.

I find her chained with enough steel to hold an elephant. That explains her inability to use her strength to escape. There are no magic blocking spells infused in the metal, so I freeze the cuffs. They snap, clattering to the floor.

"Thanks, bro." Liz tosses this over her shoulder as she leaps feet first through the growing hole in the floor that swallowed Morgan. Show off.

"Be careful!!!" I call after my sister, rolling my eyes before joining her. I slow my descent with a draft of air, but my sister, of course, has landed neatly on her feet and is already engaged in a whirlwind fight with Morgan. I can't even help for fear of accidentally hitting my sister. The two girls are mere blurs of color.

"Hurry up, we need to find Sophia!"

"This wench had the audacity to hold me hostage. She's going to get what's coming to her. I'll be fine. You go after her!" My sister calls back.

I spare one last look at my sister as I tear out of there with the winds of hell pursuing me. I have no doubt that Liz will trounce Morgan. Sophia, on the other hand, is untrained and brand new to her powers. I have a feeling she'll be terrifying with a few years of training under her belt, but I need her to live long enough to get there. This thought forces a fresh burst of speed out of me as I leap into my car. I love my elemental powers, but at times like this, it would be handy to have some of my sister's super speed.

The car protests my poor treatment with a screech as I swing it around and shoot down the driveway. The faint tug of the bond pulls me to the right, but if I don't catch up soon it will disappear altogether. At the end of the driveway, I slam back into my seat and the airbag explodes as the car hits something solid. I feel the magic barrier too late as I fade away.

CHAPTER 23
Sophia

The jolting ride shakes me awake and I pry my eyes open. I shake my head to clear the grogginess, wincing at the knives stabbing me in the side of my head. I definitely have a concussion. In the fifth grade, I fell off the monkey bars at the school playground and it felt just like this. My mom freaked out, like she probably is going to be now. I wince as the events of earlier come back to me. I went with my alleged uncle willingly, not sure why he felt the need to slam the butt end of his gun into my temple. I have to get out of here like yesterday. I'm in the back seat of a car with a thick rope binding my wrists together.

I tentatively reach inside for my powers. I could blast my way out of here, but with my hands tied by my lap, I'll probably end up frying myself. Not to mention the shady control I have over my magic. Well, I've spent my whole life without relying on magic, so I guess I'm just going to have to get out of this one the regular person way. Well, for those regular people who get kidnapped twice in one week by a long-lost magical uncle. What is my life even?

"Sophia, nice to see you're awake." The psycho's deep voice cuts into my thoughts.

"Really? You know I was coming with you willingly under the threat of you murdering my friend. Why exactly did you feel the need to give me a concussion?"

"Sorry about that. I couldn't risk you blasting me with that unstable magic of yours, could I?"

"Why? Why did you go through all of this to get me? I don't understand."

"No, you wouldn't. I need your power, my dear. I want what's rightfully mine." Confusion floods through me at his words.

"How exactly do you figure my power belongs to you?" I'm getting warier by the second. I need to get this cuff on him as soon as possible. I have no idea what he's capable of.

"I was like you once. I was born an Archimage too." He gives me a long look as that blow almost takes my breath away.

"But I thought..." They told me I was the only one. He has to be lying.

A bitter laugh escapes him. "Oh, I assure you, my dear, it's true. I was born an Archimage. They identified it when I was young, and the council stripped my powers before I could become a threat. Do you have any idea how painful that was?"

"They stripped your powers? I don't understand." Hadn't he used his powers for the portal, or... I don't know. I guess maybe he was using his hired help.

"I've been recruiting Witches, as well as some Mages. And…borrowing powers. You'd be surprised how many of our kind are discontent with the current leadership."

Borrowing powers… "You're the one who's been taking the Mages. When you say borrowing, are you planning on returning them?"

"Unfortunately not. Once I drain them, they're not much use to anyone. They're weak. That's why I need you."

My breakfast threatens to come back up at his callous dismissal. I've got to keep him talking, though, while I figure out how to get out of here and not become one of them. I'm beginning to think I'm going to have to risk using my magic. The door handle doesn't budge when I try it. It was a small hope, but I'm not surprised.

"I'm sorry, niece. I can't let you go."

"How are you planning on taking my powers? Are you going to kill me, too?"

"I would never do that. We're family, after all."

Somehow, I doubt the sincerity of his warm, fuzzy family ties. I am tied up in the backseat of his car. "So…"

"I'm going to take your powers. Don't worry, you'll hardly miss them. After all, you've spent your whole life powerless. You'll just go back to your old life. That is what you want, right?"

The thought of him stealing my powers sends a shudder through my body, and I renew my efforts to loosen the rope biting into my wrists. I thought that was what I wanted. My old life back, but when confronted with the idea of having my magic stripped away, I find I'm not so keen on the idea anymore.

"You have no idea what I want."

He just laughs.

I glance out the window at the blur of green. We're going way too fast for me to leap from the car like a heroine in an action movie. Best case scenario, I'd end up with several broken bones. I'll have to wait until he slows down.

"Why exactly did my parents not trust you with the secret of me? Other than the obvious fact that you're a psychopath. Have you always been like this?"

Red creeps up the back of his neck. Crap, I may have angered my captor.

Pain rips down my arm as I'm thrown into the side window when the car swerves to the side and screeches to a halt. I'm shocked by the sight of a huge deer blocking the road. This is my chance. I hold my hands next to the door handle and pull the magic from deep within me. Panic is riding me, and I try to temper it, go to that white room in my head. It's eluding me, though. Just out of reach. This is really going to hurt if I go overboard. I picture the light that I used to blast the Ferrebat away and send it toward the door. The door flies off with an angry metallic groan and I'm thrown back. I claw at the seat belt, blinded by the burst of bright light. After several tries, my fingers meet the seat belt release and I yank it off. I kick desperately at the hand that's grabbing me trying to pull me back. I tumble out the door after I manage to pull away.

My heart races with the adrenaline pumping through my veins as I sprint for the woods by the side of the road. Heavy steps pound behind me catching up quickly. My bound hands hamper my movements.

I stumble and fall to the ground as his hand closes on my shoulder. God, I wish I could do that jump up thing I've seen Logan do. Failing that, I kick out at his face. He takes a step back and I scrabble up. I try to remember the moves Logan taught me. If only I could get my hands free, I could get that freaking cuff on him. I knee him in the groin, doubling him over. As I'm about to take off again, a blast of light highlights two figures on the other side of the road running toward us. Logan and Liz. As they get closer, I realize it's not. Is that…Charlotte? and…Garrett?

CHAPTER 24
Logan

"Logan, Logan! Wake up!" My shoulders jerk and I blink my eyes open in a daze.

"Liz, what happened? Where's Sophia?" Shit, she's gone. She went with Zeus. I felt a flare of pain and then nothing. The steering wheel protests as I pound my hands on it. Frustration bubbles up as I feel Sophia getting further and further away.

"What happened to you?" Concern tinges my sister's voice.

"There's a shield up. Some sort of magic barrier. I was going too fast and didn't feel it until it was too late."

"Crap." Liz walks over to the end of the driveway, stopping abruptly as she hits the barrier. She walks into the grass off to the side of the driveway, running her hand along the invisible barrier. About six feet in, her hand slips through. "Got it. I figured they wouldn't maintain it for too large of a distance. Way too much power would have to go into it. Is your car still good to go?" She eyes the crunched hood doubtfully.

I can't believe I was so stupid. Of course, he had a barrier put up. I should have seen that coming and slowed down. Looks like maybe my father is right. Emotion is the enemy of reason and Sophia is going to pay the price. I crank the key in the engine. It sputters and fails on the first try. "C'mon, baby." The engine catches on the second try. "Hop in, little sister." I say, rolling along before my sister has closed the door.

I turn out onto the grass and head for the end of the wall at granny-out-for-Sunday-shopping speed. I breathe out a sigh of relief as the car eases back out onto the road and then floor it, cringing at the rattle coming from underneath.

"Hold on, Liz!" My crazy little sister just laughs as we speed down the road toward Sophia, following our connection. I stay alert to hazards this time. I can't afford another mistake.

"Thanks for the rescue, bro. I can't believe you didn't think of that barrier, though. Did Dad teach you nothing?"

"Nothing except that my sister is a pain in my ass. Seriously Liz, you don't think I feel shitty enough about this already?"

"Not my job to make you feel better. I am sorry about Sophia. It's not like I didn't make my own mistakes, trusting that Witch. I should have known."

"I mean…I did tell y…"

"Don't you dare say it!" she growls at me.

"You're right, this is my fault. Take my mind off things. Tell me about how you handed Morgan's ass to her. I can't believe she's gone over to the dark side. How many other council insiders are involved, do you think? And why?" My teeth clench, and my eyes don't budge from the road, but I need to get her talking to take my mind off the thought of Sophia in his hands.

"I have no idea, but I have serious doubts about who we can trust at this point. And my trouncing of Morgan was glorious. I took her down with a side kick to the face. I think I broke that smug little nose of hers. I left her trussed up in the very chains they had me trapped in. Lyrical justice."

"What's lyrical justice?" I raise a brow.

"Like poetic justice, only cooler. Obv."

I swerve as I'm hit by a wave of Sophia's pain and fear. My foot inches further toward the floor.

"Are you ok?" Liz asks.

"No, not really. I can feel everything Sophia is feeling, and she's not thinking about unicorns and rainbows."

Liz falls silent but gives my arm a comforting rub. I grit my teeth and will the car on faster. Sophia's dark feelings of fear are twisting me all up inside, compounded by my own rage and helplessness. Until…she's gone. Just gone. I can't feel her anymore. Panic twists my gut and my breathing speeds up.

"She's gone Liz. I can't feel her."

CHAPTER 25
Sophia

What are Garrett and Charlotte doing here? Together? They don't even know each other.

I turn to run toward them when Zeus, my uncle, whatever his real name is pulls me back again. I twist around in his grasp and a glint of silver in his hand catches my eye.

A flame sparks as I to send a panicked fireball at him. The cold snap of smooth metal closes around my wrist just below the rope binding it. My magic blinks out. The fireball hits its target, and he frantically beats at his flaming pants.

Charlotte and Garrett have finally reached us, and Garrett has a sword out. Wait, what? He's holding it with a comfortable ease, swinging it down in a smooth arc toward Zeus's shoulder. It slices through thin air as my uncle disappears in a blur, like Liz in her super speed mode.

My heart sinks to my toes, and my whole body trembles. He got away.

"C'mon, get in the car just in case he decides to make a return appearance." Charlotte pulls me with her down the road.

I stumble along after her, struggling with my hands still bound in front of me. "Can you maybe…" I wave my arms at her.

"I'm sorry." She glances back and stops, dragging me behind her. "Garrett, get your no-good butt over here and cut these ropes off."

My eyes widen at the sun reflecting off Garrett's rather intimidating looking sword. He looks different. The last time I saw him, he was all cute and soft and harmless like a puppy. Everything about him looks harder now. Maybe it's the slicked back hair or the dark denim and snug navy t-shirt hugging his chest that's replaced his preppy button up. Or it could just be the dark look in his eyes. I cringe back when he lifts the sword.

"Stay still there, Soph. I don't want to cut you by accident. Just close your eyes. I promise I won't hurt you if you don't squirm."

Charlotte gives me a nod when I look to her for reassurance. "Fine, but as soon as these are off, you're explaining everything to me. Everything." I nod at his sword.

"We will," Charlotte says.

I squinch my eyes as tight as they'll go and Garrett's fingers lock around my wrist, holding it steady. My eyes pop open when I hear a car barreling down on us at speed. Crap, we're in the middle of the road.

"Don't worry. I'll make sure they don't run us over." Charlotte throws up her hands when the car is twenty feet away and it spins out as the driver slams on the brakes.

I take in the SUV. Wait a second. I know that car.

Sure enough, Logan bursts out of his car, followed by a blur that can only be Liz.

"Get your fucking hands off her!" Logan is yelling as his long stride eats up the ground between us and Liz skids to a halt, gravel flying up in a cloud from her sudden stop.

Garrett seems to realize he's still got my arm clasped in his and he raises his up in surrender. The blade dangling from his hand somehow makes his surrender a little less convincing. "Hey man, I was just trying to help."

While I'm immensely relieved to see Logan and Liz safe, I really need someone to untie my hands. I hold them up once again. "He was just trying to help. Anyone who wants to look after this is fine by me." My skin is itching to be free of the rope. It's dragging my mind back to the helplessness I felt when I woke up in that warehouse.

"Oh shit, I'm sorry Sophia. I'm so sorry. Are you okay? You disappeared?" I sense he doesn't mean just about the tied hands, but I can't feel him. The bond is just gone, like the rest of my magic. I feel hollow inside.

He engulfs me in a shaky hug which I can't return, thanks to my arms squished between the two of us. "I thought you were gone." His voice is as shaky as the hug.

"Yeah, about that." I hold my bound wrists in front of his face. I can tell the instant he catches sight of the cuff and the knowledge crashes down on him.

"The bond too?" He rubs at his chest with an unsteady hand.

"Yes. Um, maybe Garrett should cut these off. I don't think your hands are steady enough at the moment."

He pulls away and narrows his eyes at me. "Fine, but if you hurt any part of her, you're over." He directs a steely glare at Garrett to emphasize his point.

Garrett lowers his arms and steps back toward us. "You're going to have to move, man." Logan shifts to my side and heat follows his hand as he slides his arm around my waist.

I squeeze my eyes shut again and let my head fall back against Logan's chest. I'm thankful to have him with me unharmed. A cool slide of metal slips between my wrists and the ropes drop off. A tingle of feeling rushes back into my hands, and I rub at the red indents where the rope dug in. Logan swings me around and crashes his lips down on mine in a desperate kiss. I get lost in the soft pressure and warmth heating the chill that settled in my bones.

Liz's voice cuts in. "Enough. I'm glad we're all safe, but we should really get out of here before that maniac makes a return visit."

She's right. I pull away from Logan, still clutching his hand. I'm afraid to let go.

Charlotte is eyeing me with a smug look and Garrett looks annoyed. Right, I had forgotten about that situation. "We're not leaving until you two do some explaining." I nod my head at the two of them. "What's going on?"

"Can they maybe explain in the car? I'm as curious as you, but I really think we should hit the road. I was serious. I'll feel much better once we're back in a warded house."

She's not wrong. "Fine, in the car."

"Logan, do you think your car is drivable?" Liz gives him a doubtful look, glancing at the abused vehicle.

"I'm not risking it with Sophia, and I'm not getting in a different car than her. I guess we'll all have to take his." He gives Garrett a pained look.

"Fine by me." The new Garrett lopes off toward his car.

Liz slips into the passenger seat, and I'm squeezed into the back between Logan and Charlotte. Logan's arm drops across my shoulders, and I finally start to warm up as the heat of his body sinks into mine.

I twist and give Charlotte a glare. "Spill."

Charlotte's mouth pulls up into a sheepish grin. "Well, as it turns out…. I'm a Witch."

I could catch a bird with how wide my mouth drops open. "What?!"

"I'm a Witch. My whole family is. That's why you were never allowed to come play at my house when we were kids. We're not exactly subtle about it." Confusion, betrayal, suspicion, and anger dig in. My best friend? A Witch? She's been keeping this a secret from me. So many years. I know I didn't tell her about the Archimage thing, but I just found out. She's been a Witch her whole life and never told me.

"I don't even know what to say, Charlotte. I'm going to need some time to process this. Garrett? What about you? Where do you come into all this?"

"I'm a Witch too." He states in a matter-of-fact tone.

It's like a punch in the gut. Is anyone in my life what they seem? "So…was everything that happened a lie? Have you just playing me this whole time?"

"Oh yes, he has." Charlotte answers for him.

"Explain." Charlotte opens her mouth again and I wave a hand at her. "I want to hear it from him, not you. Don't worry I'll get to you."

He cracks his neck but keeps his eyes on the road as he replies. "My magic specialty is finding things. I find and sell magical objects."

"Uh huh."

He sighs. "Someone hired me to find and get close to you."

"Are you freaking kidding me?" I ask.

Logan growls and lunges toward Garrett. Not the best idea, considering Garrett is controlling the death machine we're rolling along in.

"Logan, stop! Not the time." I pull him back into his seat. I'm shook, but crashing the car is not going to help any of us out.

"No, unfortunately not." Garrett says from the front seat. I can't stop staring at him in the rear-view mirror. He's like a different person. I think maybe he could have found a more lucrative career in Hollywood rather than becoming a thief or bounty hunter or whatever he classifies himself as. "I gave up the job though, and I was just about to bounce out of town when your Witch friend over here tracked me down. She demanded that I come rescue you. So here I am. I'm glad you're safe, but as soon as I drop you guys off, I'm out of here. I don't want any part of this fight. I'm an independent contractor."

"I'm guessing you're not a high school student either? And Emily?"

"Nah, I dropped out. I don't exactly need a diploma in my line of work. Emily is a mundane. She was just a convenient tool to get to you. Sometimes my work requires a little time and patience, but it's worth the payoff."

"Not this time," Logan says. "I'm turning you over to the council the minute we get back.

Garrett just snorts. "Whatever you believe, dude. I'm the one driving."

"It was all fake then?" I can't believe I fell for his act. I thought he'd actually liked me, not that it would have mattered once Logan entered the picture, but it still hurts that he'd just been messing with me.

"Yeah, sorry. I do like you Sophia, you're a pretty cool chick, but I don't need your kind of trouble in my life. The huge target on your back doesn't exactly mesh with my gig. Although your power could come in handy." I catch a speculative gleam in his eyes in the mirror. "To be fair, I quit the job. Once I got to know you, I couldn't stick around and spy on you or turn you over to god knows who."

"Forget you ever met her." Logan is pissed.

"Sorry, man, too late for that," Garrett says.

"Ok, cut it out, Logan. We'll deal with Garrett later." At least the guilt for leading him on is gone. Along with any trace of feeling I might have had for him. "What about you, Charlotte? How long have you known Garrett was a Witch and what's your angle in all this? Have you just been playing me too?" It hurts to think that my friendship with Charlotte might not be real. I've known her forever.

"Hey. I have nothing to do with him or his business. I'm still your girl. I recognized him as a Witch when Xavier first showed me that picture at the lunch table, but I did not know he was up to no good. I haven't seen him in a few years, but we used to run into each other in passing. I haven't seen him or his family in a few, though. I just figured they'd moved away." I catch Garrett working his jaw, his knuckles whitening from his grip on the steering wheel.

"But did you know about me?"

She throws her hands up. "I had no idea until I saw you practicing in the field the other day. I was wondering why you'd pulled a disappearing act like that. I confronted Liz, and she told me who they were. Still unclear on the details of what's going on with you, though. She was pretty cagey about it. We are going to have to have some intense girl talk." Her eyes are full of an apology that I don't think I'm ready to accept yet. Too many people in my life have been lying to me.

I turn my steel on Liz giving her my best we're-having-a-stern-conversation later look before swinging back to Char. "And how have I never known that you, one of my best friends, are a Witch?"

"Well, we're not supposed to share with the regular folks. Humans are not exactly known for their tolerance of witchcraft. As history has proven. If I knew you were one of them, I would have shared."

"I thought…" I trail off. Of course. Charlotte had claimed she couldn't have people over because her grandmother couldn't be disturbed. I always thought that was kind of fishy, but my mom was more than willing to let me have her over, so it was never really an issue. "What about Xavier? Our other friends? Are any of them Witches or Mages or…something else?"

Charlotte just laughed. "No way. Well, unless Brendan is an android, like I've always believed. But that's technology, not magic."

Nice to know Charlotte is still Charlotte despite the extra special witchiness. "I don't think I'm ready to forgive you yet, Charlotte. I still love you, but it's going to take time to trust you again." I mean, she did save my life, but friends shouldn't lie to each other like that.

I realize Garrett has pulled up in front of Liz and Logan's house, not mine.

"Wait! I have to go to my house. My mom is probably frantic by now."

"Soph, come on, it's safer here. Zeus or his people could be staking out your house," Logan says.

"Even more reason to go home. I have to see my mom and make sure she's alright. If you won't take me there, I'll go myself." I start squirming, but Logan holds tight. I haul in some deep breaths to stave off the panic that's bubbling up inside again at the thought of my mom in danger.

He sighs. "Fine, quick stop at your house. Check in with your mom and she can come with us. I think we should go to the cottage after that. What do you think, Liz?"

"Probably a smart idea. I guess you get one now and again."

My heart sinks at the big black SUV half blocking the driveway when we get to my house, as if someone was in a real hurry. My arm slips through Logan's fingers as I rush for the front door, my heart pounding. It's unlocked. My mom never forgets to lock up.

"Mom!" I yell as soon as I cross the threshold and my eyes fall on Trey's imposing figure holding my trembling mother. "Let go of her!" I raise my arm and realize my magic is locked away again, so I pull the dagger from my boot. Wish I'd been able to use that on Zeus.

Trey holds a hand up. "Relax, she's ok and boy am I glad to see you safe and sound." He lets go of my mom and she takes a hesitant step toward me.

"What happened?"

"These men came out of nowhere. I don't know. They shot flames from their hands and moved so fast I couldn't see them.

Then these other two came and there was a fight. I think I was hallucinating. It's not possible…it's just not possible." She trails off as I pull her into a hug and lead her over to the couch.

"Yeah, it must have been some of Zeus's men," Trey says. "After Roxie and I realized you'd given us the slip, we ended up here. Just in time. They must have been waiting for your mom to leave the house. They attacked her and we fought them off. They ran off before we could question them."

"Thank you, Trey, and thank Roxie too." I don't see her around. "Mom, I'm so sorry. You never should have gotten pulled into this mess. I'm so sorry." Tears are burning the back of my eyes. This is all my fault. She could have been killed.

"What are you talking about, honey? It's not your fault." I feel like I'm six years old again when she squeezes me in her comforting embrace.

"Yes, it is. They were after me."

Logan stands across from us in the living room, rocking from one leg to the other with his arms crossed. Probably not the best time to introduce him to my mother. He looks like he's just waiting for someone to give him an excuse to commit murder. Trey slumps in a chair to my right and the rest of my friends have trickled in. Notably absent is Garrett.

I go through the events of the last couple of weeks with my mom. I'm not sure if she believes me yet, but she will once she's over the shock. She's got some cuts and bruises but nothing major. Good thing for them, because I wouldn't give Logan a chance to kill them if they had seriously hurt her. I'd want the pleasure myself if that was the case.

CHAPTER 26
Logan

My muscles were itching during Sophia's explanation to her mom. Now that she's taken her upstairs, I let loose and start pacing the small living room. Liz has flopped down on the couch and Charlotte is hovering by the stairwell as if she wants to head upstairs to help her friend but is unsure of her reception. Garrett took off. The coward. I knew he was useless.

"We can't stay here. I can't leave Sophia here. She's too exposed."

"Well, big bro, I hate to be the one to burst your caveman bubble, but it's not up to you to make her choices for her. Now I'm not saying I disagree with you, but maybe try the Jeopardy thing and phrase it like a question. I don't think she'll leave her mother behind either, so we'll have to figure that out."

"I don't think the cottage is a good bet anymore, either. We should probably take her to council HQ and maybe her mom can stay at our parent's house. With that cuff on, no one will know she's an Archimage. Her mom doesn't have any magic though, so she won't be welcome there."

"Hold up. Sophia's an Archimage?" Charlotte trails into the room, her mouth hanging open. I shouldn't have said that with her here. I know how much Sophia trusts her, though, so I'm just gonna have to accept that.

"Yes, she is. That's why her magic was bound when she was a baby. Now she's got that cuff on, so until we figure out a way to get it off, we're going to need to keep her hidden."

"That is such a downer. She just got her magic back, and she's cut off from it already," Liz says.

"Well, like I always tell you, sis. You rely too much on your magic. What would happen to you if yours got drained or cut off? You have to train hard and often."

"Thanks for the lecture. I could have called Dad if I was in the market for some judgment." Liz drops her voice in a poor imitation of our father. "Precision and Purpose, Liz."

"You're hilarious."

I whip around when I spot Sophia coming down the stairs.

"How's your mom doing?"

"She's ok. She still thinks she's hallucinating. I don't think we'll be able to convince her until she's gotten some sleep."

"I think we need to talk."

I hate the wary look she sends my way.

"Why are you so bad at this, brother?" Liz gives me her patented why-are-you-such-an-idiot look.

"Right. Sorry. Come here, sit down. Please."

The wary look has not left her face, but she settles on the couch next to me. "What is it?"

"I don't think you should stay here." I reach out and rub circles on her hand. I need to be touching her.

"What do you mean?"

"It's not safe. Especially now that you can't access your powers. If you come to the council compound, you'll be safe. No one will know what you are with that bracelet on."

"I can't move. I'm in my senior year of high school. I need to keep my grades up so I can get a scholarship. I can't leave my mother either."

"I know. We can make sure you get your schoolwork. That can be arranged. And as for your mother. She can come live at our parent's house. She can't stay at the compound with you. No humans allowed, but it's really close."

"Um, she has a job, Logan. She can't just ditch her job." I don't need the bond to see the fear, frustration, and exhaustion written all over her face and it's wrecking me.

"We can make sure she gets to work safely. Port Grand is not that far away. We'll have a driver take her. She's in danger too if you stay here." I need her to be safe. If anything happens to her like it did to Ivy…well I don't even want to consider that. I don't want to scare her more, but if it's going to convince her, then I'll try anything.

Her face softens, and I know I almost have her. "Why can't I just stay at your parent's house too?"

"It'll be safer at the compound for you, plus you can get some training. Physically at least, while we figure out how to get that thing off your wrist. Trey will be there, so at least you'll know someone." I jerk my head at him. He may be annoying, but I trust his loyalties. I can't tell her the other reason she needs to be there.

"Wait, where will you be?"

"Trying to hunt down Zeus or find another way to remove your cuff, Liz can visit, though." The thought of leaving her shreds me, but no way she can come with me when she's so vulnerable, and we need to get that cuff off.

"Uh, I don't think so. You're not leaving me behind." Liz's tiny body is practically vibrating with indignation.

"Liz, you're still in high school. You know our parents will never let you skip off."

"Whatever, this is not the end of the discussion, but I'll let it go for now."

Sophia's tense body finally relaxes into me. "Fine, we can talk to my mom tomorrow. I'm not committing to anything until then."

I guess that's the best I can hope for today. The sooner I can get her to a safe place and track down Zeus, the better. Is this ever going to end, though? Or will Sophia's status mean we'll be spending the rest of our lives running from one enemy or another? She deserves so much better than living her life on the edge of a knife that could slice her open at any moment.

EPILOGUE
Logan

The sun beats down through the windshield as I slide into my space at my parent's house. The familiar gray stone is as comforting as the knowledge that we've got Sophia secured at council headquarters. My body feels loose and relaxed for the first time in days. We got her settled in and now we're back at my house for dinner. Her eyes are wide and fixed on the house. I wonder if she's nervous about meeting the rest of my family. I miss being able to gauge her emotions through the bond. We need to get that cuff off asap.

"How are you doing?" I ask.

"I'm good. I wish I could just stay here too, but I'm glad my mom's going to be safe."

A fragrant wave of garlic and tomato engulfs us as I hold the front door open for her. I lead her toward the kitchen as we pass through the front hall. I'm not thrilled about living under my dad's thumb, but the perk of my mom's cooking is a huge bonus, and it's not going to be for that long, anyway.

As I slide through the French doors, I see not one but two women working away side by side at the granite countertop. Looks like Sophia's mom is settling into our house. She gives a tentative smile at something my mom says and then they turn toward me.

"Honey. I'm so glad you're home. Hi, you must be Sophia?" My mom wipes her hand off on a dish towel before holding it out to Sophia for a shake, but she ends up pulling her into a hug instead. My heart warms at her easy acceptance of Sophia. Not that I would expect any less from my mom.

"Yes, nice to meet you, Mrs. Armstrong."

"You can call me Janet."

"Hi, Mrs. Tennant." I greet Sophia's mom.

The blonde-haired woman turns to me with a smile that spreads slowly to her eyes. Sophia's smile.

"What's for dinner?" I peer over my mom's shoulder.

"Lasagna of course. Your favorite."

"Fantastic." My mom makes the best lasagna. I'm about to swing my arm over Sophia's shoulder but pull back. We're not supposed to be dating. I almost forgot.

"Do you need any help in here?" Sophia asks.

"No, it's fine, dear. You two can go watch TV or something in the den." My mom waves us off.

"Great." I scan the house. Where can I sequester Sophia for some alone time?

I'm about to take her upstairs when the doorbell sounds.

"I'll grab it!" I call to my mom.

Sophia trails me to the door.

I swing it open, and all the air is knocked out of my chest. I'm speechless. My arms go numb. My entire being rocked.

"Hi, Logan." The soft voice does nothing to soothe my shock.

"Ivy??

THANK YOU TO READERS

Thank you so much for taking the time to read my novel. Reviews mean everything to indie authors, so I would appreciate it so much if you leave a review on Amazon, Goodreads, or wherever you purchased my book.

If you'd like to keep up with the latest news on the Archimage series, please sign up for my monthly newsletter. You can check out my website for sign up links and other information **www.nicoleaoliverauthor.com**

Or follow me on Twitter (@nicoleaoliver), Facebook (facebook.com/nicoleaoliverauthor), Instagram (@nicoleaoliverwriter) and TikTok (@nicoleaoliverwriter).

Never stop turning those pages.

ACKNOWLEDGEMENTS

And now for the long-winded acceptance speech. Publishing a novel has been a dream come true, but you're never alone on your author journey.

I couldn't have published this book without my amazing husband who puts up with all my crazy ideas. You're always there to manage the small people when I need to lose myself to my muse. I love you always. Olivia and Ian, my wonderful twins. You are my inspiration to live my best life.

Steph, thanks for being my number one fan. See you at the end of days. To the HAFAs: you helped shaped me into the person I am today. I don't know what my life would be like if I had never moved into 2D.

I definitely could not have done it without the help of my Beta Readers, Editors, and ARC Reviewers. Thanks so much to my cover designer Emily Wittig. I still have no idea how you turned my random jumble of ideas into the perfect cover.

I have also learned so much from the amazing achievements and advice of the supportive social media writing community. Thanks for being awesome.

ABOUT THE AUTHOR

Nicole A Oliver is a Fantasy author from Hamilton, Ontario, Canada. A voracious reader, Nicole has always loved becoming lost in magical realms. She loves to travel, but she believes there is no better substitute than getting lost in a book world when that's not possible. Her passion for the genre and the power of words led Nicole to aspirations of becoming an author early in her life.

Nicole, her husband, and her two biggest fans, her twin son and daughter, love to hike and always have their eyes open for magical creatures when they do. During the day, Nicole indulges her love of coffee and fuels her writing by slinging mugs of java. Her family enjoys putting their heads together over jigsaw puzzles, spending time outside, and trying out the fares of local restaurants. Nicole is a horse lover and will admit to imagining herself as a fierce warrior heading into battle whenever she is lucky enough to get to the barn.

Logical Magic is Nicole's debut novel and the first in a planned trilogy.

www.ingramcontent.com/pod-product-compliance
Lightning Source LLC
Chambersburg PA
CBHW030802210726
48290CB00002B/378